Alien Abduction

Every day around the world hundreds of people go missing without a trace. Year after year they add up to millions of lost souls who are never to be seen again, and their numbers keep climbing

...this is where many of them went.

Table of Contents

Titles by Michel Savage

Faerylands Series
The Grey Forest
Soulstorm Keep
Sorrowblade
Ivory

Shadoworld Series
Shadow of the Sun
Veil of Shadows
Shadows Gate

Outlaws of Europa
Rebels of Alpha Prime

Hellbot • Battle Planet

A Couple of Zeros

Forgotten Future

Broken Mirror

Project EVE

Witchwood

7

ะฤับ

WITCHWOOD

THE HARVESTING

MICHEL SAVAGE

Enter the Grey Forest

www.GreyForest.com

Witchwood – The Harvesting

Copyright © 1986 by Michel Savage

The Grey Forest
P.O. Box 71494
Springfield, OR 97475

www.GreyForest.com

Cover art by Michel Savage

ISBN: 978-09719168-4-5

First Edition: Oct 2017

Printed in the United States of America

0 9 8 7 6 5 4 3 2 1

Living on the Fringe

It was just another average boring day in late July, driving the long journey home from work where I slaved away at a restaurant for little pay and even less respect from the owners. It was a rather pleasant ride back to my little shack in the boonies, which was just thirty minutes outside of town. The sun was reaching for the horizon, washing the encroaching clouds with bright golden hues. A summer storm was long overdue for our area and I was looking forward to getting my rain barrel refilled, so I could tend to my garden which had started to turn a little parched and wilted.

My outdoor water hose had broken weeks before, but for the life of me I could never seem to remember to buy a new one whenever I dropped by the hardware store. I just shrugged and realized I was getting older in my years and had to learn to get used to the noticeable memory loss.

"Oh, crap; I forgot to grab that damn hose again! Oh well; you're losing your crackers, Tyler," I admitted with a touch of feigned distress. I also kept several dozen indoor house plants which I tended to almost every day; which was my emotional replacement for having to care for something other than myself in lieu of having a wife or girlfriend. I certainly had my own character flaws, and if anyone doubted that, I've had my share of failed relationships to prove it. I found gardening to be a positive distraction; even to the point of forging one-way conversations with my collection of houseplants in an effort to overcome the crushing loneliness.

I had been living alone for more than a decade now and gave up on meeting anyone worth my time; because it never failed to end up in heartbreak. Well, scratch that – I deeply believed that nobody should ever act like they owned someone; so I usually let my significant others do as they pleased. Sometimes though I would wonder at how devious women could be, and if perhaps that very first fight or break-up they skillfully initiated was some sort of sly test to analyze my impassioned response ...or lack thereof. If so, I always thwarted their expectations to display emotional loss; due to my simple outlook that people come and go in your life. Unfortunately, I was attached to my flaws and I had found close interpersonal relationships to be emotionally draining; thus, I lived like a hermit out in the woods. It was a lifestyle I had grown into, which I later found far too difficult to discard.

Outside the car, the dark clouds were starting to roll in quickly above the surrounding mountains, as the waning sunset faded while taps of rain began to speckle the windshield. I didn't mind the storm because I was fond of the sound of rain; besides I was looking forward to getting home, taking a shower, and catching up on the daily news. The power out here was a little sketchy at times, but I wasn't concerned since I had taken the time to stock a morbid amount of supplies and prep everything I would possibly need for any long term outages. I pulled up the winding driveway to my abode just as waves of heavy rain began to blast the side of my truck.

"Well, at least I'm getting a free car wash," I babbled to myself, trying to find the positive outlook in anything. It was a little technique I had learned in many a therapy session back in the day. When most people dropped something, like say a cup of coffee for instance, or anything which made a mess, I noticed they would react in explicit anger which gave a window of insight to their true personality. They would scream out loud with a slew of ugly and colorful obscenities; while I, on the other hand, would blame it on 'gravity' in mere jest. It was an easy way to brush the blame off of myself; which I humbly admit, I had a talent for.

I always parked out along the fence of my property so as not to squash the grass or dig ruts into my dirt driveway when it was wet, and tried my best to avoid making my place look like some unkempt hillbilly lived there. Luckily my neighbors out here were far and few between; though unfortunately, not far enough away to keep from hearing their yapping dog from time to time at all hours of the evening. Tonight though, their obnoxious mutt seemed unusually quiet for some reason. I noticed the falling rain felt remarkably warm as I stepped out of the vehicle and slammed the car door shut behind me. I nearly jumped as a flash of lightning, followed by a sharp crack of thunder, began to roll in seconds behind it. I grumbled to myself as I expected it might be one of those nights I'll have to break out the emergency candles and be forced to entertain myself with reorganizing the pantry by lamplight in case the power went out again.

Halfway to the front door, I was bombarded with another angry roll of thunder, but was perplexed when the torrent pelting upon my shoulders abruptly came to a sudden halt. There was another bright flash that lit up the sky, and I was suddenly startled by what I took was a lightning strike which whitewashed the clearing around me with a blinding light; and a spark of worry entered my mind that a bolt might have hit a nearby tree. It was an odd sensation to feel the electricity in the air as my fingers began to turn numb. A brassy stench of ozone wafted over me like an impenetrable wall, leaving me in a haze as I turned my eyes upward towards its source.

I felt a deep fear began to churn within me, of a deeply troubled time in my life which I had nearly forgotten. My vision was met with a bright orb above, which pinned itself to the ground around me in a ring of hard and unforgiving light. The lingering aroma that filled the air began to awaken old and unpleasant memories as they emerged from their deep hibernation from the chambers of my mind. Unable to resist the charged energy which now entrapped me, I felt my body go suddenly limp as I lost control of my extremities. A twinge of panic rose up my spine, and I slipped into unconsciousness just as I felt my feet begin to lift from the ground and my body began to rise. After all these long and tiresome years, the visitors had finally come back for me.

Beyond the Veil

I felt a tapping on my face which caused me to wrench my eyes open as I jerked upright and suddenly felt the urge to vomit. I turned to my side and let forth a slosh of white foam across a darkened floor; the film from it still dripping from my chin. I rarely ever drank milk and had no idea what the hell it was I had just expelled from my gut. While my blurred vision began to focus, I could see there were tiny pea-sized black spheres mixed in with the cold creamy soup. Just when I thought I was done, I choked up another slurry; making even more of a mess.

"Whoa there son, take it easy," a tall black man said who stood beside me, though he had taken the precaution to jump back when I hurled up the gooey liquid now sloshing near his feet. I looked around for a moment, still in a daze as I tried to stand up. The man who addressed me placed his hand upon my shoulder to support me from falling over, and with little effort, he swayed me to sit back down. Honestly though, it was my legs which had gone all wobbly with weakness that prompted my compliance.

"*Whew*, well, you're a lucky one. We thought you might have gone squishy on us," a female voice beamed from behind him. It was rather dark in the room we were in and I began to notice that the floor resembled something like hardened plastic as I tried to prop myself up on my trembling hands.

"*Wha-ga hehg...?*" Was all I could manage to choke out until I wiped the sticky goo from my lips. It was mixed in with an odd slippery film that I could feel down the entire length of my throat. All I wanted was to get it out.

"Candice, hand it over," the dark-skinned man demanded to the girl standing in the shadows.

"No way, he'll waste it!" she spouted back in defiance.

"Don't make me take it from you," he barked back as I heaved again, feeling as if I was coughing up a lung. I didn't know what they were arguing about, and then suddenly became aware that I was laying there entirely naked before these two strangers. I guess the girl was getting an eyeful and didn't like what she saw. Behind me, the large black fellow swiped something from her grasp and handed it to me.

"Here, use this to wash out your mouth and spit it out ...but whatever you do, do not swallow it!" he instructed.

The canteen he handed me was made of bare metal. The liquid within it smelled a little off, but I was in a desperate state to wash out this gunk plastered within my throat. I took a gulp and swished it around and I could feel the film of the thick substance start to become taut. I grabbed onto a length of the coating coming off of my teeth as I spat out the juice while he took the canister from my trembling hands.

"That's it, just pull it out slowly ...slowly, now. It might feel a little weird, but it shouldn't hurt you," the strange man advised.

"Humph," the girl grunted as she stepped forward into the dim light to recover her canteen. I was too busy feeling like a sick dog to argue as I began to pull several feet of a flimsy tube from my stomach. It slipped and snapped as it went up my throat, and I started to become anxious when I noticed that after an agonizing minute that the coil of it accumulating in my lap had already produced nearly a dozen feet or more. With a final tug, the last of it snapped out of my mouth and I could feel like I could breathe again without obstruction. At the moment, it felt as if my stomach was churning, but after several more minutes of convulsive dry heaving, I realized the worst of it was over.

"You should lie down. That headache you feel coming on will pass in about a half-hour ...Earth time," the man acknowledged.

I didn't understand what he meant by that little connotation about '*earth time*' but I did start to feel a pressing migraine begin to swell, as if someone had placed lead weights directly upon my brain. I sprawled across the hard floor and tried to suffer through it as I gritted my teeth while the tension worsened. Apparently this guy knew what he was talking about. I could overhear their conversation as I laid there in agony.

"So what are you going to do with this little rescue, Aaron? If you treat him like a lost puppy, he'll only end up like the last one," the girl demanded towards the older black man.

She was young, maybe late twenties or early thirties; with a mess of dirty blonde hair tied up into a ponytail. She had a gleam in her eyes and a tone in her voice that belonged to someone whose character had been deeply etched from seeing too much pain in their life. Living with that type of anguish will twist anyone the wrong way. She had an aura of stout hopelessness; which didn't do much to help my mood at the moment.

"Let's get him on his feet and get someplace safe. At least we can find out who he is and any news about home," Aaron sniped back towards her. He began to pace back and forth in the Y-shaped corridor where I had awoken. Noticing the trail of slime down the hall behind me, it was starting to become obvious that I had been dragged here from somewhere else.

It took a while for the debilitating headache to subside, and that's when I started smelling a strange odor emanating from my skin. Giving several passes at my hands and forearms with my nose, the reek started to become ever worse.

"What the hell happened to me ...where are we?" I blurted after regaining my sense of equilibrium while my migraine cleared. Noticing I had regained my senses, Aaron pounced over and took my arm, appearing quite eager to get me up and moving.

"Look, we'll explain everything to you when we get the chance, but right now we have to get out of this section, pronto!" He declared with measured urgency, "We've already spent too much time here."

"Are you really taking him back to the cube in that condition?" The girl inquired with a skeptical tone.

"What is this *cube*?" I chimed back while not trying to be self-conscious about being bare-ass naked in front of the girl. I had been to several nudist camps in my past, so I really wasn't bothered by anyone seeing my junk hanging out in the open. To me, nudity was only natural; it was actually the edict of our modern culture which had groomed us to view it as taboo. I did, however, notice that they were both clothed in what looked to be some sort of dark ragged jumpsuits that looked as though they had been made from a patchwork of different sized dancing tights which had been sewn together haphazardly. I felt like a third wheel standing there among them, entirely exposed as I was while they argued.

"It's a sanctuary, you'll be safe there," Aaron answered as Candice turned back down the dark corridor.

"I think this is a misstaakke..." she trailed off as her patronizing words echoed down the curved hall. My toes and fingers still felt a bit numb, but I was able to walk. Aaron though, was kind enough to assist me.

"She can be a bitch sometimes, but don't worry about her; she's really a decent girl," Aaron mentioned while he helped me up, and motioned that I should follow her lead.

"It's starting to get a little cold," I stated with a jitter of my teeth as the temperature dropped dramatically the farther we progressed into the strange labyrinth ahead.

"And it's going to get colder before we get to our destination. Sorry about that, but you'll just have to endure it," Aaron offered with a note of sympathy.

The biting cold was made worse by the residual slime that still covered my body, which began to smell like it was starting to rot. The stench was so bad, it was starting to get to a point where I couldn't take it anymore.

"Aw, uck!" I gasped in disgust, and the air was becoming frigid to the point I could see the cold mist of my own breath in front of me. Barefoot as I was, the feeling in my toes were starting to come back as I tried to catch up with the girl who had weaved us through the dark and winding corridors, "What the hell is this crap? It - it smells like..." I grimaced as my mind failed in its attempt to identify the rancid fragrance.

"Like a bloody vaginal fart," Candice smacked back rudely. Unfortunately, her distasteful remark was more comparable than naught, "that sticky crap that's covering you is the remnant of an artificial womb, which quickly decays when it's separated from its embryonic fluid and exposed to the air," she professed bluntly.

"And that film I pulled out of my throat?" I inquired while she seemed open to offering some overdue answers.

"That was a type of arterial feeding tube, which kept your sorry ass alive while you were in stasis," Candice replied over her shoulder just before she came to a stop and cautiously peeked around into a shadowy corridor before continuing onward.

I was righteously confused, and even had the inclination to go back to view this 'artificial womb' device with my own eyes so I could verify the cause of my trauma. Evacuating that slimy tube from my guts was unpleasant, and I didn't want to think about how it got there.

"Hush, we're almost there, but you have to stay quiet," Aaron whispered in a low voice, so I conceded to his note of caution.

The rotting liquid began to trickle to my feet, causing me to frequently lose my footing and I slipped off balance several times while we crossed the smooth floor. It didn't help that I was shivering uncontrollably at this point and that my body weight felt somehow off; which played some serious tricks on my dexterity. Jumping past an opening into a dark chamber, Candice turned back to put a single finger to her lips, ushering me to be silent. I quickly followed behind her, noting a creepy shadow casting a single strange silhouette in the room as we slinked past.

Farther along, there was a gap with several glowing red orbs spinning around the circumference of the room beneath the transparent flooring. At the base of the circular room was a vent covered with a thick brackish film. Candice grabbed the upper rim of the oval vent, and like a gymnast, she kicked up her legs and pressed them into the membrane, feet first. The seal split open in equal sections upon the force of her body and she disappeared behind the rubbery sheet as it promptly resealed behind her. Aaron came up behind me and motioned for me to do the same.

"Just push your way through it. You can choose to go head first if you prefer, but I would recommend the other way around," he suggested.

"Why does it matter?" I felt it necessary to ask.

"Look, you can take my advice or not; but you're going to find out one way or another," Aaron granted as if my question was moot. He looked tired and physically worn; like someone who had rescued some stranger from a biological stasis womb and carried their heavy limp body a little too far for his own good. I guess he had saved my life, so I wasn't going to argue with him. I was still feeling far too numb from the recent cold to make any nimble ninja acrobatics, so I went in headfirst since it was easier. Oh boy, was that a mistake.

The slant of the tube beyond the seal wasn't too bad for the first ten feet, but then its angle altered abruptly and I was sent careening down the vent like a greased pig on a slide. The walls were slightly ribbed, and it was only the rotting slick still covering my skin that made the ride even remotely endurable as I slipped down to the bottom of the shaft. At its end, I tumbled out onto the hard floor into what was nothing more than a large bowl. I sat up and tried to regain my sense of dignity in front of Candice, who stood there watching me with an evil smirk of amusement carved upon her lips.

"Aaron should have told you to take that ride feet first," she declared as a slight towards him. I stood up, only to quickly jump out of the way as Aaron shot out of the vent. He caught his balance at the end of the chute with ease, which made me realize they were both quite familiar with this route. I took a look at my forearms which I had bruised badly upon the rim of the bowl in my clumsy attempt to protect my face from the impact. Candice noticed me inspecting my wounds, which looked far worse than they actually felt.

"Don't worry about those scrapes, you'll heal up quickly for the next few days until that embryonic fluid passes out of your system," she mentioned halfheartedly as she glanced my way. Turning back to the enormous chamber where we had deposited ourselves, I saw a giant metal box looming above, standing upright upon its tip, suspended by the various tubes and vents that snaked around it. An educated guess told me this was our destination, which they had mentioned earlier.

"This is the..." Aaron began until I interrupted him.

"The cube, yeah ...I get it." I trailed off in thought while I stared up at the strange silver block in wonder. It was remarkable enough trying to soak in the immensity of the chamber itself. This was obviously some sort of advanced technology beyond anything I had ever seen before, yet the construction held a distinct fluidity to its overall design. Large areas of the containing walls were composed of the same mixture of contrasting dull and polished black materials of different shades, but the cube itself was constructed of shiny pewter, it's structure encased by lights which illuminated it from below.

Leading us to an enclosed area directly beneath the hanging monolith, Candice strutted off ahead while leaving us behind as I stood gawking at my surroundings.

"It's better if we talk within the enclosure," the dark-skinned man suggested as he helped me keep steady on the slick floor, "we'll get you cleaned up and fill you in on the details. I bet you've got a million questions," he added with a brief smile.

Oh, I sure as hell did; but what I was feeling at the moment was the paralysis of delayed shock. Waking up on a cold floor covered in slime, followed by choking up a puddle of goo, took a back seat to the encroaching awareness of where we actually were. We stumbled into the central chamber directly below the massive cube hanging overhead, which was surrounded by thin walls comprised of several curved panels. Sitting there in the middle of the small cell was a brown-skinned fellow who appeared at first oddly pale for his racial origin; a closer look revealed his face had a weird silver sheen to it. Across the deck, Candice was rummaging through some stacked bins and make-shift containers as another bald stranger was helping her find something in the disheveled mess. The guy with the glitter on his face looked up at me in surprise, then his eyes dropped towards my groin to notice that I was naked, and his expression slowly turned to one of disgust.

"Ahh, he smells horrible," he jumped out of his seat to take a step back, "you can't bring him in here like that!" he whined without a care or concern for my condition.

"Renzo, shut the fuck up and help me," Aaron barked back at him; but Renzo didn't seem as if he was going to comply as my guide sat me in his place, "Candice, did you find one?" Aaron yelled back across the room towards her. He motioned me to stay seated where I was and walked off to help the girl and the bald man rummage through their scavenged supplies.

Renzo took a defensive stance and backed away, curling his nose and choking with fake coughs like a whiny bastard. I would imagine it smelled far worse to everyone else besides me who got within range of the foul stench. Aaron handed a large tube to the bald man, who promptly made his way over to me. I was a little stunned by his odd appearance, but I wasn't in the position to complain about his assistance.

He looked like a classic clone, one might see in any science fiction film. No hair nor eyebrows, whatsoever, with smoothly glazed features and eyes twice the size of anyone ...well, anyone normal that is. He held a slightly-bowed staff made of the same shiny black material used in the architecture, and he shook it several times in front of me as a grimace grew upon his thin lips. Apparently, whatever the device was he was holding, wasn't working correctly.

"Candy, this doesn't have a Node," the slim man relayed back to the girl after inspecting the bottom part of the apparatus.

"One power node coming up," Aaron announced as he reached into a bin, and playfully tossed a small golf-ball sized sphere to Candice, who strode over in a huff to hand it to her bald companion.

"It's *Candice*, got it? Don't call me your pet names like that in front of new recruits," she beamed at him with a glare. He took the brass colored orb from her and promptly pushed it into a depressed socket on the backside of the device, and the thing lit up like a Christmas tree.

"Hold still ...and uh, cover your eyes," he advised a little late as I had already held up my hands in front of my face to protect me from the blinding light emanating from it.

"You might hear a little sizzle," Aaron chuckled as he came up beside him while I was getting my tanning session, "but don't worry, it's only baking the film away," he stated while prompting me to stand and slowly turn so that they could get all sides of me as I stood there in my birthday suit. It took several embarrassing minutes to cook it all off while running my fingers through my hair, and even down to spread my ass cheeks, and even to the bottom of my feet. The strange man made sure to be quite thorough.

All four of them were wearing the same mish-mash of black skin-tight material adorned with a patchwork of ragged edges. I assumed they weren't originally designed that way, as they appeared to have been pieced together from bits of scraps.

"Eh, that's good enough Mark-1; find him some clothes from the pile," Aaron ordered. Without offering a hand whatsoever to help me through the entire episode, Renzo finally took a moment to step forward and blocked the path of the bald guy named Mark, though I had no clue why they assigned him a number.

"Oh nooo, you clean off that seat too; that's my favorite chair!" Renzo snapped with an accusing finger towards the bundle of boxes they had bunched together to form the framework of a bench. Mark-1 complied without question under the glare of Renzo's beady eyes. The lingering nausea I had felt earlier began to dissipate with the biological perfume. I assumed the glowing rod that he used was some sort of UV light, but I was too busy picking out flecks of the crusted stuff from unnamed cracks to bother my hosts with petty questions. Candice finally came over with what looked like a pair of cotton jogging shorts and a torn blue sweater.

"Here, leftovers; knock yourself out," she announces as she tossed them unceremoniously into my face. I caught them in a bundle, and wondered what her personal issue was with me as Candice stormed off to the other side of the room. I saw her take the jug from her hip and take several swigs of it, herself.

"I thought you said not to swallow that stuff," I asked Aaron as I nodded over to Candice while I tossed the musty sweater over my head. Aaron gave a quick glance towards me and put the pieces of my question together in short order.

"Ah, well, that's what we use in place of real water around here, but it has a severe chemical reaction with the feeding membrane you had lodged down your throat. If you had swallowed it, the film would have crinkled up and cemented itself in your guts with no way of passing it out. It's not a pleasant way to die ...believe me," he added as if he himself had witnessed someone experience such a horrid fate.

"Well, I appreciate the help," I thanked him humbly, though I could hear my stomach rumble in defiance. The noise it made was mildly disturbing if not downright unnatural.

"Come, you should get some rest and try to recoup from your extraction; straining yourself now could lead to complications," the bald man offered as he took my arm to test its integrity, while performing several slight twists and pinching the muscle, "Ah, good, he hasn't gone squishy; you must have been a recent addition to the stockpile," Mark-1 declared with what looked like a strained smile on his mannequin-like face.

"...Squishy?" was all I could manage to spout, trying to make sense of his odd examination.

"We are sitting in the belly of an intergalactic harvester, and biological beings, such as yourself, who are taken, are usually placed in suspension, which was that fluid sack that we had just removed from your skin," Aaron filled me in as they led me to the ruffled makings of a bed placed upon the floor so I could rest, "unfortunately, the process has a habit of liquefying the human skeletal structure, which tends to dissolve away over long stages. People who spend too much time in stasis will never recover, as their calcium liquefies and they become..."

"Squishy! Like he said," Renzo commented as he cut into the conversation while eavesdropping on the three of us.

I was sure glad I wasn't in that soup for too long, and it was a long discussion that followed between us before the sheer exhaustion of it all finally overwhelmed me. I woke up for what I assumed was the next morning, just to be advised that they only still used days and hours to count earth-time; which only made sense when Mark-1 finally announced that we were in space. I had to absorb the fact I wasn't on Earth anymore, which partially explained why I felt curiously lighter than usual on my feet.

"So, do you think he's a veteran?" I heard Renzo whisper to Candice behind my back. For lack of any heavy machinery noise from the tubes and vents attached to the giant cube hovering above us, it seemed fairly peaceful in this small refuge they had made. That all changed when a pumping sound began to reverberate through the chamber above, and I jolted upright in alarm from my makeshift cot.

"Take it easy," the odd-looking man offered as he handed me a plate of what I would describe as a pile of glop. It was slightly stretchy with a moldy green hue and literally looked like a giant booger. I just curled my nose and looked up at him while taking the plate.

"*What the fuck...?*" I chattered to myself, wondering if he was expecting me to eat this thing, which appeared like pea soup mixed with rubber cement. Carefully lifting it between my pinched fingers, I let it bounced back down on the plate where it wiggled like jelly.

"I know it looks like snot; but *it's-not*," he chimed with a strange laugh at his own raw sense of humor. I just put down the plate but not for my loss of appetite, for I didn't have one at the moment. My intestines where still saturated with that milky stew which had been pumped down my throat. True to her word as to what Candice had mentioned prior, I began to notice that the cuts and bruises I had suffered earlier had nearly disappeared.

"You can eat it now or later, son; but that's close to our only source of nourishment and hydration down here. You'll get used to it," Aaron mentioned with a note of seriousness as he grabbed a handful of the goo himself from the container. Taking a bite of the green mush and slurping it down, I could tell by the look that washed across his face that he was trying to conceal a cringe.

"No, you actually don't ever get used to it," Mark-1 confirmed with his tight smile, while also noticing Aaron's reaction. Renzo and Candice strode over to join our bizarre little picnic; though in their company, I certainly felt like an unwelcome guest.

"So ...is he?" Renzo demanded, calling to Aaron's attention. The black man just gave me a quick visual survey up and down, and shrugged his shoulders.

"Why don't you ask him yourself," he stated.

"You were asking if I was a Veteran," I inquired, while my question surprised Renzo with how quick I was to catch on, having overheard him moments before, "Nope, I've never been in the military, pal," I shrugged back, thinking it would be to his disappointment; but discovered I was far removed from the actual subject of their conversation.

"He didn't mean if you were a soldier in the armed forces," Mark-1 revealed as he nodded towards Renzo and his silver-smeared face.

"He was trying to inquire if you've ever been taken before?" Aaron responded with a sober expression. He looked me sternly in the eye as my gaze moved around to see the same question lingering in each of their faces. My voice caught in my throat as I tried to respond, and it almost felt as if I had swallowed an entire roll of plastic-wrap soaked in vegetable oil and tried to pull it out an inch at a time; which was exactly what that vile experience with extracting that feeding tube felt like, and now here I was repeating the act by choking on my own words. With a sigh of admission, all I could do was solemnly nod my head in agreement.

"Don't feel so ashamed about it, all of us here have been abducted before..." he added to my surprise.

"Technically," Mark-1 butted in as a correction, though I was unsure what he meant by that comment. Aaron seemed to be lingering on the thought but slapped his knee to break the awkward silence which had settled in the room.

"You know what, we haven't even gotten your name, son," he professed with a look of anticipation.

"It's Tyler ...my friends call me Tyler," I blubbered on, still feeling the emotion of the moment.

With jolting flashbacks it was just sinking in, that I had been snatched by a UFO in that beam of light which had hit me in the driveway to my home during that violent storm. Ever since I had revived, my subconscious mind was trying to convince me this was all some sort of weird black budget government facility; but I was staving off the approaching panic attack growing inside me by desperately washing it away with buckets of denial.

With impatience, Renzo drilled me on my past arrivals by extraterrestrials so he could determine what type of encounters I had, compared to the rest of their group. They appeared particularly interested in my story, but displayed a note of confusion when I admitted that I had actually went unmolested by alien visitations for the past several decades, and for some mysterious reason, they had chosen to return and scoop me up after all that time.

"Eh, well I did a thesis in college once where they calculated that time runs much slower in deep space; which had some bullshit to do with gravity wells and other such anomalies surrounding large planets. So for you, it might have seemed like decades had passed, but it might well have been only a drunken weekend for them ...who knows," Aaron added with a shrug.

Candice revealed she had similar visitations, but she had been harvested within a few months after her first encounter. Apparently Renzo had been on some aliens' shit list for some time, since he had nearly half a dozen traumatic encounters before he was swept away on this permanent intergalactic pleasure cruise. Aaron soberly admitted his own life had gone to hell in a hand-basket after his first abduction; and that he had suffered through a consecutive series of mental breakdowns. Within a single year he had lost his job, his wife and kids, and became overwhelmed by depression and bouts of paranoia. He mentioned that he faced the full wrath of skepticism, and even his own parents had thought he had lost his mind. It was the stigma of his abduction experience which had piled upon him; destroying everything he thought he had known.

He had even made calls to the military, which turned out to be a tragic mistake by getting himself flagged on their radar. He had also written letters to news stations, which apparently, had gone entirely ignored. Whenever he made new friends and revealed his bizarre story to them in trust, they rolled their eyes as if he had gone full fruitcake. In hindsight, the treatment he received from his own kind turned out to be far more distressing than the actual abduction he had suffered. In the end, Aaron realized he had to make sense of it all on his own.

"I was never the same man after that," Aaron admitted with a sigh. Looking around, I could tell by the silent response from the rest of the group that they had also felt that same jagged wound scar their lives, at one point or another.

"When did they take you?" I had to know, while stringing the puzzle of our dilemma as best I could.

"A while ago, but we've been here long enough to know that our time is short," Candice answered bluntly with crossed arms. Even Renzo himself didn't have a quip for that somber statement. It was then that I recognized that their bitter anger was not directed towards me, but from a blemish that revealed an overwhelming sense of hopelessness they carried with them.

They had been stuck here struggling to survive against a foe that couldn't even comprehend how or what they felt. I was about to be brought up to speed on the situation at hand.

The bald guy's story was the hardest to swallow, since everyone accepted that he was the result of a cross-species cloning program. When I asked as to why they called him Mark-1, he replied that I should direct that question to Mark-2, whenever he arrived back from his foray out hunting for essential supplies. Apparently, Mark had several duplicates, and there were many other such hybrids of various flavors which their alien hosts had conceived. Mark-1 and the others of his gene pool were a crossbreed of human and alien DNA; which were utilized as a test phase to acclimatize their kind into Earth's atmosphere and gravity.

I was a little lost when Mark made a statement about '*their kind*' since he was clearly just as much a rogue element as the rest of us. He just laughed in his weirdly forced way, as if he was learning how to react as a regular human might to my comment. Aaron had rescued both Mark-1 and 2 from what might be considered a lab disposal, and they both wouldn't be alive today if it hadn't been for his assistance. Aaron made a point that even human scientists had conducted genetic experimentation on animals and would harvest stem cells from human embryos; however, our paltry genetic programs were considered as mere amateur-hour compared to their advanced level of technology. Looking around the chamber, I could see for myself that our alien hosts clearly had the means to mesh both mechanical and biological devices.

"You called this a harvest ship, what exactly does that mean?" I stammered aloud, while subtly hoping I wasn't coming across as rude for my continuous staring at Mark-1, and his unusually symmetrical face.

"It's a bit complicated to explain," Aaron admitted, and he elaborated with the other clone's assistance to help fill in the gaps. It turned out that there had several survivors before them, who had either escaped some lab table or faulty stasis pouch and scurried off to hide within the crevices of the ship; eventually finding this unlikely sanctuary. He admitted that there were some escapees who had come to a very bad end. Actually, their numbers were now halved from what they were several weeks ago when a number of their comrades had been cornered and caught while scavenging the decks for food and supplies.

"I still don't understand. Why did they place me in stasis like that if my bones were only going to dissolve?" I asked, not really wanting to hear the answer.

"From what Mark-1 mentioned, we believe they use organic proteins for their ship, and the leftovers are processed into nourishment packets," Renzo answered for them over Aaron's shoulder. Renzo made sure that I followed his eyes down onto the plate of putrid green goo jiggling there like jello. He had a cruel look on his face that was hard to read; so I didn't know if he just got off acting like a dick, or if his humanity had been slowly whittled away over the time he had been trapped here. The reality was, this was a heavy burden that most people wouldn't be able to handle on a mental level; unless they already had experiences that prepared them for this kind of scenario.

"Ah, don't let him get you riled up," Aaron protested, "the food supplements aren't *all* human, there are several other additives mixed into it; and frankly, we don't have much of a choice. It's this crap or nothing," Aaron admitted with a scowl. Deep in the jungles of old Earth, our species had several such tribes both large and small which had been equally cannibalistic. In all honesty, I was just glad that I wasn't hungry at the moment.

"So, they planned on eating me?" I inquired with my mouth agape like an idiot.

"They actually place several species of animals in stock. Think of it as a handy pantry whenever they want to do some biological tests. I've personally seen them conduct such grisly experiments once before on a subject, and truth be told, I was pretty god-damn lucky that I managed to escape myself," Aaron shivered at the memory of it.

"It's far too easy for them to capture us, so we always have to stay out of their line of sight," Candice warned.

"Why is that?" I inquired, until I heard her answer and old memories of my encounters decades ago came flooding in to remind me of what I already knew.

"Those fuckers can read your mind!" Renzo replied, "If they see you, then they can put you to sleep or make you go all loopy so that you're nothing more than a helpless zombie under their control. It's some sort of biologically induced hypnosis where they can press their will upon your mind and bodily functions to a certain extent. It's kind of like turning a knob on your brain to dumb it down."

When I inquired how everyone here had escaped capture for so long if they couldn't see these creatures, and why they chose to hole up here, Mark-1 was able to clarify the details in one fluid response. This chamber we sat in acted like a spill container from the energy core which powered the ship. If there was ever an emergency or damage to the vessel, then this alcove would flood with plasma or anti-matter, or whatever the fuck they used as their energy source. Frankly, nobody quite knew what they used for fuel.

That meant the alien beings merely considered this place a dangerous flood chamber and had apparently never thought to search here. As it turned out, the real trick to survival on this ship was to remain invisible and unseen. Aaron believed that there were actually only a handful of alien crewmembers onboard this colossal ship, since he had never gotten a glance of more than two or three of them at a time. As for Aaron, Candice, and Renzo; they conceded that they had all displayed a certain mental resistance to their alien hosts.

"It's not like they shoot you with a dart or anything, and I've never seen them use a device or contraption to control a subject," Candice revealed as Renzo nodded in agreement beside her, "it's almost as if it depends on the mental strength of the creature they are attempting to control."

"So you're all immune to whatever you would call it ...their power of suggestion?" I asked with skepticism, even though I had more than a few similar occurrences myself with these visitors during my encounters all those years ago in my youth.

"I wouldn't say we were impervious to it," Aaron chimed in to clarify, "though, apparently, certain subjects can build up a resistance over multiple encounters; and Mark-1 here has a natural defense to it, which is likely a genetic trait for most of the clones. It's more like being mentally overwhelmed, but you can struggle against it like a wrestling match in your head. Hell, I know it's a shitty analogy, but that's the way I felt when they did their *zappity-zap* paralyzing act on me and spoke into my mind," he spouted.

Honestly though, I was already familiar with such an unusual experience, as these beings could communicate without uttering an audible sound by speaking directly into your thoughts. It could be compared to listing to someone talk through a microphone while you had earphones on, and their voice sounds like it's coming from the center of your head. Oddly enough, their speech was similar to sounding like your own voice. When it happened to me all those years back, I thought I was going nuts, and it put me in a state of withdrawal from my friends and family for a long while.

Mark-1 admitted that he and most of the other hybrids had the ability to communicate with one another by the same means; although their skill at telepathy lacked the level of finesse compared to our alien hosts. When I asked him to try it on me to prove it, he advised that the giant cube above us emanated a cascade of mental white noise; which was why this spot was the perfect place to hide, as it effectively camouflaged them from such cerebral trespassing. The harvest vessel we occupied was immense, larger than a stadium by Aaron's estimates and fashioned in the shape of a long tube. It was the typical cigar type craft I had seen in many blurred photographs, from my years of exhausting research on UFO's in the past;

the very same evidence which had always been labeled as fake or debunked by our distinguished authorities in the military complex, along with their equally flimsy excuses.

Adapt or Die

I was perplexed as to why such an advanced species would bother to go through the effort of abducting human specimens when they could apparently grow their own in a test tube. Mark-1, on the other hand, was intent on clarifying my mistaken method of thinking. Apparently, there was scientific support that DNA degenerates quickly throughout second and third-generation interbreeding by such artificial means. Thus, fertilization in living beings was something that could not be reproduced in some cold lab, which produced the beneficial results they were seeking. He touted it as 'the miracle of life' which made Earth of such special interest because of the incredibly vast diversity of life forms on our little blue planet.

"I hope I was able to dictate that explanation properly," the bald man offered, "and illustrate that reproductions derived from a first-generation clone to a second tends to filter out many desired characteristics, and are further diluted by their successive third generation, and so on," Mark-1 finished.

His analogy made perfect sense, but I was still stuck on trying to grasp the mechanics of it. With aid from Aaron, they both rationalized the complexity of what turned out to be my complete misinterpretation; likely from having watched far too many sci-fi flicks. Mark-1 was a result of genetic manipulation and incubated for up to one or two trimesters in a human female, then extracted and placed within an encapsulated artificial womb that was far more advanced than the variety of stasis vessels, such as the type I had been contained in before being rescued by Aaron. Mark-1 and 2 were only considered clones by definition, as they were in fact created from different parental donors; but had utilized the same laboratory womb for a portion of their life before their birth.

"Well, it's really considered an *extraction*; not a birth, per se," Aaron advised as Mark-1 nodded in agreement. He tried his best to clarify by the end of our lengthy conversation that the hybrids where actually born and raised over a wide span of time; and were not the spontaneous pod-people replicas one might think them to be; with the exception of their Overlords. The mention of that particular name threw me off.

"By calling them overlords; are you referring to the alien pilots of this ship?" I inquired with wide eyes. Aaron attempted to respond as he searched for the right words just before Renzo beat him to the chase.

"In truth, there are several different alien races; we merely call the ones who seem to be in control of the Harvesters by that pompous title," Renzo blurted with his arms folded and an arrogant smirk painted upon this face, "but sometimes the crew, and even the pilots, are merely subservient minions. We're still trying to figure out their hierarchy, which is likely far beyond our small-minded human terms."

Mark-1 merely sighed in agreement, as it was a subject that was based on raw speculation at this point. Aaron noted that there were several other clones like Mark in different stages of development aboard the vessel, but he had only been to that section of the ship twice before it became too dangerous to return. Just then another bald man clambered into the room and plopped down a net full of oddly assorted containers. He appeared similar to Mark-1, as though the two were twins.

"Oh, a new visitor I see," he smiled while approaching where we were situated, while Candice marched over to rummage through what he had obtained on his scavenging run.

"This is Mark-2," Aaron smiled toward me and motioned over to the bald clone, "Mark-2, this is Tyler," he offered as an introduction.

"Uh, why are they named 'Mark', is that some sort of special term?" I inquired towards Aaron as the hybrid approached.

"Eh, well he looks like a 'Mark' to me," Renzo answered in a cocky tone over his shoulder, "we could have called him Bob or Carl or whatnot, but Mark stuck," he admitted as he turned to help Candice go through the goods they had collected.

I held out my hand to shake his, but Mark-2 merely stood there in front of me with a quizzical look plastered upon his face at my cordial gesture. Feeling like an idiot, I lowered my hand back into my lap; being unsure if he was socially inept to the cultural practices of our kind, or was just being rude to me. Regardless, I didn't take it personally. Aaron noticed my confusion and gave a little snort of laughter.

"Human gestures are for humans, Tyler," he chortled, "but you'll get used to it," Aaron stated with a hand to my shoulder.

"Was that a salutation?" Mark-2 spat out in mild confusion as he turned to Aaron; but the black man just shook his head at the comedy of it.

"Don't worry about it," he patted the second clone on the back, and made his way over to Renzo and Candice as they rifled through the bag of goodies recently brought in.

"Weren't you given a name when you were born ...I mean extracted?" I asked Mark-1 who sat beside me. He stared at me for a moment then shook his head side to side as a 'no', almost as if he had to remember to make a visual answer instead of one by telepathy.

"We have no need for names in an open consciousness which functions as a collective," he noted in his response. Mark-2, who stood above me, finished his sentence for him.

"When you can communicate telepathically, there is no real need for singular names; for each sentient being is identified on a subconscious level," Mark-2 allotted.

"To your disadvantage, we have noticed that your species furiously defends their individuality, which is viewed to us as your most instinctive flaw," Mark-1 continued as I turned my attention towards him.

"Whatever it is we are actively doing, is our task and identity. However, your species seems to be oddly stuck on erroneous titles that define you; and even though that places the majority of your kind in unbefitting categories, your people still appear to wear them as if they were badges of status and superiority. Fundamentally, your cultures' system of stature and position is quite strange and wholly irrelevant in most every aspect," Mark-2 finished his twin companion's thought.

It took me a moment to embrace the concept of what they were trying to say. Considering I had spent a lifetime groomed to the human existence of title and position; it had obviously never occurred to me that our human forms of communication were actually what defined us, rather than our actions. On a deeper thought, it made perfect sense that miscommunications between our own kind were truly an enormous defect which crippled the progress of our civilization. Mankind's own weakness was our inability to collaborate points of view towards a common goal, and we tend to misinterpret our fellow man, which continuously led to hostilities between our neighbors and nations.

If we had the ability to all speak one transparent language without the capacity to lie or misread one another's true intentions, there would be little room for fault. Basically, by adhering to our own 'Human Nature' it could be interpreted that our species was solely proficient in creating needless drama for ourselves. In reality, their position didn't seem so haughty after I stood back and got a glimpse of their perspective. Our own human individuality and privacy were fueled by an inherent need to conceal our thoughts in the process. Taking a view from their eyes, I could see how our entire species would be regarded as highly paranoid by any outsiders.

With a moment of reflection, I could imagine that if the entire human race was unable to lie to one another for merely one day, our civilization would likely burn itself to the ground before the next sunrise in the chaotic aftermath that followed. Honestly, even I wasn't keen to the idea of having my every thought being read by another. The hairless twins were quick to relate that it doesn't actually work for them that way; for they were raised with a different set of ideology regarding what humans considered as 'ethics' to the way they view life in general. However, from the way they interpreted their shared perspective, I could see that practically every human on earth would fight tooth and nail against such alien principles if they were coerced to comply.

I was also surprised to learn that they apparently didn't possess an intrinsic fear of death, in the way we thought of it. There were no ambiguous religions or morals to cloud their judgments or to brush aside logical thought. The hybrids like Mark and his twin, possessed a sense of empathy and mercy where these extraterrestrial Overlords did not. There were, however, many different races among them that leaned one way or another along that fine line of varying temperaments. It was worth noting that they didn't view their conduct as good or evil by any such frail human standards; for their inherent racial dispositions molded their own social perspective.

Humans were seen as wildly over-reactive and unstable. On that point, I had to agree with them entirely. However, it did make me wonder that if these Overlords could influence the very essence of social awareness and education; then why not just teach human children their philosophy and the following generations could ascend to a better existence. Mark-1 was eager to answer that line of thought.

"Oh, you must mean to have the entire human race engage in a more positive direction through tutoring and guidance ...ah, I believe your phrase for it is called *attaining enlightenment*," he suggested while searching for the right words.

"Well yes, that certainly would have saved a great deal of grief for people like me and many others," I responded with a wave towards Aaron, Candice, and Renzo. Both Mark-1 and 2 took little time for reflection before conveying their response. Aaron had overheard this exchanged of philosophy and intervened in an attempt to help me get my head out of the clouds and fully absorb the reality we were in.

"That's amazing, you really think that an alien species would just come down out of the stars and help the human race to save us from ourselves?" he offered with a condescending chuckle, "And while they're at it, maybe they should hold our hands and waltz us into the Age of Aquarius, with a shower of glitter and dancing unicorns and all that jazz..."

"He has a point, ya'know," Candice shot back towards me with a hard glare while the patronizing resistance they slapped back with made me start to feel like an idiot for asking such an innocent question.

"Of all things," Mark-2 allowed himself to butt in, "the Overlords have a sacred doctrine they retain above all else," he explained, "that in their journeys across the cosmos, whenever they find a species displaying such a limited mental capacity that lends itself towards social self-destruction, that there is little anyone can do to sway them from such a dark path."

"So ...you're saying the human race is fucked?" I shot back, but with a lack of energy that held any true conviction in its tone; which made it sound more like a statement than a question. Mark-2 just gave a confused look towards Aaron, who bid him not to bother trying to understand my blunt, if not crass response. The clone obviously didn't understand the meaning of my use of obscenity in that context.

"Tyler, we have to agree that the human race is a violent species," Aaron placed his hands on my shoulder, seeing that I was moved by the sudden and overwhelming depression which my slumped posture began to reveal, "and the only way to save ourselves at this point would be to withdraw our entire society, worldwide, back into the pre-industrial age; and we both know that isn't going to happen. Mankind is a curious animal, my friend, and we love to tinker and forge new inventions. However, when we produced fission bombs, that drew some seriously negative attention from across the cosmos," he tried to relate, "and I think you can understand, that any species which chooses to possess the ability to destroy all life on their own planet, might be considered a menace to everyone."

"These Overlords, as we call them, are trying to protect the life of the planet that you evolved on. There are many millions of species that exist on your planet; and the human races is but a single one, and your race tends to forget that your world would get by just fine without you," Mark-1 shrugged while looking at me with his large dark eyes, "and in this current stage, they would venture to say that the Earth would be better off without your caste polluting the ecosystem and the serious danger your weapons pose to all forms of life within it."

He had a point, one so sharp it struck like a hammered nail into my skull. The alien agenda wasn't to protect mankind from itself, but to keep us from obliterating the planet we lived on. That methodology did not bode well for our race. These extraterrestrial species were practicing eugenics to breed the hatred and violence out of our lineage in an effort to wean out our most savage and unsavory flaws.

I had heard several theories which proclaimed that it was either aliens, or our own governments, who planned on wiping out a great deal of the world population to regain control over the masses; with conspiracy theorists busily running around screaming '*they're going to kill us all*'; as if it was some planned massacre knocking at our doorstep. The same result could be applied in a way that was far more mundane by implementation; which would be by sterilizing our species with a wide-spread contagion, but one that would allow mankind to live out their natural lives; only without any offspring to replace them. Introduce a simple genetic virus and *poof*, the human race is gone, replaced by a close cousin that could utilize the same infrastructure we had created, and effectively improve upon it.

"In their recorded history, there have been millions of worlds with sentient beings who had destroyed themselves by their own hand, and humanity is but one of many to fall victim to the outcome of their own folly," Mark-2 chimed in.

"So, you're saying they're actively replacing the human race with hybrids, like yourselves?" I tried to choke out as I felt a sudden lump in my throat. It then dawned on me that that type of infiltration was the perfect tactic. It would be the most effective way to assume control with minimal loss of resources, all while the native population dies off. Their tactic was the ebb of a slow tide, to phase out one species for another. The question was if that was really a bad thing?

"That is the point we are trying to get you to consider here, Tyler," Mark-1 seemed to be getting flustered as he attempted to widen my point of view, "you're closed-minded cultures have evolved into a masquerade, where they try to claim that each person possesses an individual energy, or a soul, as you humans put it," the hybrid tried to vocalize, "and readily claim that all other life is inferior to yours based on that single, and entirely unsupported, allegation."

"You mean that cats, and dogs, and bunnies, and squirrels, and everything in between, also retain what we call a spirit?" I blurted back, though without conviction to how ludicrous my question sounded. Mark-2 sat down beside his twin and answered for his genetic brother.

"No, what he was trying to get you to consider was ...if there was no such thing," he gave a slight shrug, "and if an alien race could prove that concept to your world's population; how do you think your esteemed religious institutions might react?" Mark-2 inquired as food for thought.

Holy shit, he was right. If perchance an advanced species plopped down one fateful day on Earth and told us; "*Hey, aliens are real; and by the way, there really is no such thing as a soul, nor a god, so you really should make the best of your lives today,*" then every religious order around the world would rebel in the most fanatical way. There just weren't enough hippy flower-power new age freaks to counter such an uprising of single-minded drones who had been guaranteed their real estate in heaven, or paradise with wings and a harp, or six dozen virgins, or whatever wet dream they had been promised was awaiting them in the afterlife. The entire episode would likely turn violent in the worst possible way. Human history had proven that religious wars were always the bloodiest.

"So, you predict there would be a theological rebellion, and that all the factions among our various religious sects or groups would declare the alien visitors as demonic enemies to their system of belief?" I responded.

"I could imagine a worse scenario, where confused devotees might instead turn to worship the alien Overlords as a higher power, above all else," the hybrid answered, "which frankly, is a title they have no interest whatsoever in fulfilling."

I had to admit, that I was having a hard time swallowing this existentially wide-sweeping narration. However, their argument had a ring of logic to it. Human history was filled with countless examples of people displaying irrationally strong devotions to icons and deities they had never actually seen nor met, nor even proven to be real for that matter. Even in our modern era, there were untold millions of fanatics that would lash out in violence in defense of their given doctrines. If they were suddenly presented with a verifiable entity that appeared to possess mystical powers such as telepathy and anti-gravitational flight; then such extremists might very well use them as a symbol to continue to enact their own psychosis.

"Well, you do have a valid point I suppose," I admitted with humble submission, "if even a small number of the population declared a religious war against their standing governments, it would not come to a pretty end," I concluded with the realization that any alien race would be seen as a higher power of authority. Maybe that was why our entities of government always stonewalled every bid for public disclosure about the existence of alien life; because they were justifiably afraid of the outcome.

"It would be a righteous clusterfuck if they admitted the truth," Renzo declared, "the very small percentage of the public who could handle such an idea with an open mind would be at the mercy of those masses and nut jobs that couldn't," he professed as Aaron shrugged in agreement to his analogy.

"Now that you're filled in with the challenges of this situation, there is another matter at hand that we need to consider," Aaron related in a gentler tone, "and I assume you've begun to wonder where we go from here?" he granted.

I had mistakenly assumed they were all trying to find a way back home. I played with the possibility of hijacking a flying saucer or escape pod and zip back to Earth. Then again, the simplicity of my thinking was due to watching too many goddamn movies where the hero always wins the day. Unfortunately, this predicament was all too real. The hybrids advised that the vessel we currently occupied were enormous by any standards, and the transit vehicles the Overlords used were of a technology we simply couldn't even begin to understand how to operate. I was left speechless when they conceded that there were several thousand preservation tanks which contained everything from humans, to wild animals, to aquatic fish that were held in stasis onboard the harvest ship.

From what Aaron had explained it was an entire god-damn zoo they had collected, but that it contained mostly larger animals of a certain range of size. Mark-1 and 2 admitted that the purpose of their capture was to be able to study and test the organic specimens at leisure. Of course, the living samples that were held too long would usually go 'squishy' as they so colorfully put it, to a point beyond any revival stage, and their living remains would be absorbed into the recycling system as a source of nutrition for both the occupants and the ship itself to use as a part of its functioning systems.

It made sense; for the reality was that in most countries people waltzed into their grocery stores to buy animal products all neatly packaged in convenient little containers, with nary a clue as to the truly horrific conditions of how those animals were grown, treated, or methods used to kill and processed their remains. Animal fats and their oils were used in everything from our machines to makeup. Basically, we were doing the same thing on Earth as what was going on here in the bowels of this alien ship; only their method of process was far more efficient.

That's when Aaron hit me with the choice I had to make. There were rare occasions when test specimens in stasis were returned to their native environment, but by his opinion, that was a pretty low percentage.

"You may have heard of the rare abductions where the victims were held for several days instead of just a few hours for examination," Candice offered with a cold glare in my direction, "in nearly all such cases they infuse a marker or tracking device within the subject."

"Yeah, and that shit doesn't always show up on X-rays either," Renzo shot back.

Come to think of it, I did have several MRI's later in life, and had always feared something odd might turn up in the images; but they hadn't. Of course, those scans are outrageously expensive, and I actually didn't have my whole body done; so there was the chance it was easily missed. It still irked me that these creatures had somehow still found me after all those decades had passed, just when the pain of those unpleasant memories began to fade. Now here I was, pumped full of embryonic fluid and held like a caged animal while cruising somewhere out in the galaxy, with no apparent way home. I suddenly felt like I was going to have a nervous breakdown, but I was too worn out to become unglued at the moment.

"The thing is, Tyler, you can either go back into the stasis pouch where you were extracted, if you wish to take the chance that you'll be returned home," Aaron advised, "but the process might not take again, and you would eventually go all..."

"Squishy... yeah, I get it." I sighed as an afterthought, knowing that it wasn't even a choice, "or, what is the second option you were getting at?"

"Or, we sneak you into the recruitment chamber for induction into the frontier groups," he stated to my utter confusion as to what he was talking about.

"Frontier groups? What the hell is that?" I queried with a furrowed brow, "You said it was safe *here*," I referred to the cloister under the cube, "why don't we just hole up here until we can find a way to escape?"

Upon that exchange of words, the pair of hybrids glanced at one another as if something was left unsaid; which made me even more uncomfortable than when I was choking up that brackish fluid from my stint in stasis. As it turned out, I had not even contemplated that there was a bigger picture to consider, showing just how deep in this shit we actually were. A harvest ship was not something someone escapes from; you had to either learn to adapt, or die. The frontier crew members were an assembly of humans and other hybrids utilized by our alien hosts as shock troops against adversarial races.

"Wha ...what?" was all that fell from my stuttering lips as I shook in disbelief, and feeling myself starting to get lightheaded as if I was going to faint. Both Aaron and the hybrids tried to gently explain that the dual purpose of a Harvester Ship was to collect species for genetic testing, and to recruit viable pioneers and combatants for skirmishes on hostile worlds. A part of me wanted to laugh at how ridiculous that sounded, but the stern look in their eyes kept my racing emotions in check. The only way to survive this situation was to take orders from our captors as their new recruits. It was either that, or end up dozing off the rest of your short life while your cells were being liquefied into the equivalent of motor oil and soylent green.

Personally, I would rather stand on my own two feet and face the challenge of confronting our alien hosts. I had never imagined that they were warlords or would stoop to kidnapping sentient beings for such an arcane purpose. The point was, whether they were benevolent or not, they merely saw us as a useful resource; which in perspective, was actually a pretty darn human trait when I stopped to think about it.

As it turned out, our little refuge in the overflow chamber was merely a temporary sanctuary between such missions, from where the rest of the abductees were kept corralled. Aaron and his crew had built up a resistance to the mental sedation, which was utilized to control the terrestrial subjects while they waited between assignments. Akin to prisoners of war who would collectively conspire in rebellion against their captors, leaders like Aaron and his friends would try to rescue other abductees where and when they could. Unfortunately, not all attempts were successful.

"Revived human captives recently removed from stasis are put through a battery of tests, and usually implanted with a type of tracker, which can also influence and control their behavior to a certain degree," Mark-1 informed me, "those individuals we remove ourselves and insert into the active groups before induction to the medical phase can be performed, have a much better chance of retaining their individual will," he noted.

"But there are only five of you..." I replied while trying to comprehend the odds we were facing.

"Not so few, actually," he replied, "There are several more individuals who have escaped the implant process in several other sections of this vessel. Unfortunately, there were many more who had been caught and reprocessed."

"Reprocessed?" I blurted while offering my hybrid friend a worried glance.

"Yes, they were either cycled through the medical phase to be 'chipped' as Aaron likes to call it, with a viable implant; or if the Overlord crew believes the patient to be too troublesome and resistant to mental commands, then they are reinserted into permanent stasis or parted for medical experimentation."

I was leery of the words he used and didn't like the idea of being captured and dissected. The alien crew had the means to read peoples minds, but it was most usually only effective in close proximity or direct line of sight; which was how Mark-1 and 2 were able to communicate when they were beyond the mental white noise radiating from the giant cube looming above. They claimed that even though their alien hosts had a much higher efficiency at telepathy; there seemed to be a technical lapse in their ability to pinpoint individual implant markers within sizable crowds. It was a security flaw they had learned to exploit, one which allowed them to slip away into the bowels of the ship unnoticed.

Their numbers were always in flux, but they supported the resistance and strove to recruit new members into their folds at every chance. The trick was to not get caught. This reminded me of several old black & white Nazi prison camp flicks I had watched as a child. One had to avoid falling under scrutiny, or your goose was cooked. The hybrids were further pleased to hear that I had also experienced a degree of mental resistance during my previous encounters with our alien hosts.

I was fascinated to hear that the Alien crew pooled and sifted the thoughts of any given person they tried to communicate with, by using words they already knew. This was how they were able to speak to anyone across the globe, no matter what language they spoke. Their thoughts were translated into the equivalent context buried within the subject's own mind; and voila, you have an instant psychic-to-organic linguist interface.

It had limitations of course. For example, aliens could speak with a human child via telepathy, who might only know what the color 'Blue' is in their unschooled mind; but had not yet learned additional descriptive words such as: azure, or aqua, cobalt, or sapphire, which might help express additional details to their subject; or in this case, the tone of color they were trying to get across, but can only adapt to the conversation with limited words that are already held within the subjects mind. It was a unique type of cerebral interpretation, though sometimes the intended context might be lost in translation.

"So you're saying it's like sending a file document from one computer to another, but if it's written in, let's say, a particular typeface the second computer doesn't retain on its drive, then the message comes out all wonky," I surmised.

"That's a pretty close comparison," Aaron smiled, as he started to figure I was slightly more astute than the average bear, "and we suspect that the more they press their mental commands onto a subject who isn't implanted, the more resilient that person becomes to their mental pressure. Since you remember your previous encounters with these beings, that tells me that it happened more than once, and their ability to blot away your memory began to weaken," he finished as he reached out to shake my hand, "We are glad to have you aboard, Tyler."

Overlords

What passed here for consumable food and water was hard to come by outside of the holding chambers for the abductees who were kept alive and active. Regretfully, I would have to be slipped into their midst where they administered the implantation devices. This was the only way I could get the proper set of protective clothing after waiting it out in one of their many holding cells. Renzo approached me with a small black tube which opened by a hidden hinge along one side. The interior was filled with an aluminum colored substance, and he instructed me to smear this onto every square inch of my skin down to every nasty crack and crevice.

"And what exactly is this?" I asked while taking a few fingers full and started smearing my arms and legs. It felt slightly oily but noticed that it almost instantly absorbed into my skin, leaving it with a silvery sheen similar to what Renzo had on his face this entire time.

"This shit is great," he offered with a sarcastic smile, "the recruits are given this to protect them from various forms of radiation when on assignment outside of the ship. Without it, you would start to feel the effects of radiation poisoning once that milky crap in you begins to flush from your system," he added, noting that the symptoms to watch out for were debilitating headaches and continuous dry heaving; and once you start coughing up blood, you can pretty much consider your ticket punched, "We found it also has a useful collateral effect of mildly reflecting overpowering mental control. This cream is only given to recruits who already have implants, which is what they seem to rely upon for effective mental restraint," Renzo added.

"Well, that's convenient," I added while smearing it onto my private parts while Mark-2 helped me get a layer onto the unreachable section in the middle of my back, "does this stuff also protect from solar and cosmic emissions?"

"Absolutely, and it will help to keep your internal liquids from being lost through your pores and becoming overly dehydrated," the hybrid informed. He finished by taking my clothes, leaving me standing there stark naked as I glimmered like a pewter statue.

"Well, you won't be needing these where you're going," Renzo advised as he tossed the garments aside, "once you are directed to leave the holding chamber, you will be given your own permanent set of threads," he related while referring to his own ragged jumpsuit. Mark-2 was kind enough to help educate me that the black suits allowed the skin to breathe and also regulated body temperature; which would be invaluable equipment to have on many parts of the ship. I was a little embarrassed to inquire, but was wondering what they did when mother nature called, since the suits didn't seem to have a fly to open to urinate or an obvious way to pull it off to use the toilet. I didn't like the way Renzo smiled at me, as if he knew I wasn't going to like the answer.

"About that," he grinned, "...you'll cross that bridge when you get to it," he noted with a huffed giggled, while thoroughly relishing in his twisted sense of humor. Whatever genealogy Renzo might possess that was of interest to the alien entities, I was guessing that being an arrogant asshole was somehow infused into his DNA.

The three of them had been trapped here for a questionable amount of time, all they could go by was the month and year they were taken aboard, but there was no way of knowing how long they had been held in stasis before being revived. With no watches, or calendars, or day and night cycles, the human body can revert to its internal clock and go wildly off-kilter from its normal rhythm. The artificial gravity certainly didn't help either, it made me feel as if I was going to gurgle up something from my stomach if I stood up too fast.

The plan from this point was simple enough; which was to sneak me into one of the holding cells where I would wait until our unit was assigned for duty. I was still a little muddy about what that meant, but Renzo assured me it would be a real treat. In the meantime, Aaron advised that I get as much rest as possible and keep myself well fed and hydrated during my stint inside the holding cell. What they provided there were the healthiest nutrients available on the ship for our particular species. He told me to keep an eye out for strange plants there which grew edible fruits.

"You mean I won't have to eat that puke-green jello crap you were serving up before?" I was glad to hear.

"Look Tyler, there is really nothing I can say that will prepare you for what you are going to encounter once you're in there; so just suck it up and deal with it," Aaron instructed with a serious tone that was out of character for him, but I was guessing that he was gravely concerned for my safety, "most Rescues like you break at this stage and end up getting their asses recycled; and I would hate to see that happen to you, son," he offered with a grim smile which quickly faded. It would have been an emotional heartfelt moment, except for the fact that I was standing there holding my nuts in my cupped hands out of embarrassment, in addition to the ambient chill.

A short while later a strange tone began to pipe through the ship. It was a low reverberating rhythm that echoed gently, resonating as if it was coming from an underwater speaker. Aaron and Candice rushed to get the silver cream onto their faces and scalp, while both Mark-1 and 2 departed the sanctuary of the cube back towards the hybrid chambers.

"Follow me, kid," Aaron ordered as we made our way back to the outer edge of the hollow, "and once you get into the chamber it would be best to keep your thoughts as blank as you can. If they enter your head to give you orders, just repeat whatever they say to yourself over and over and try not to draw any attention; got it?" he advised.

I nodded my head in agreement, but started to feel more than a little nervous about exposing myself to the mental range of these beings. Old fearful memories began to drift into my head once again, and I had to remind myself not to let it overwhelm me and fuck-up as others had done before. I really didn't want to end up as a Squishy.

We had to free climb a pair of rails to an exit spout and make our way through another maze of oval vents. The strange alarm was significantly louder in this section of the ship, and Aaron advised me not to talk out loud if I could avoid it. He also pressed their 'line of sight' rule they had for the telepathic detection, and to try and avoid getting nervous at all costs. Candice described their transmission as some sort of radio wave which affected the implanted subjects; causing them to become sedated and would respond as though in a trance.

We neared the end of the vent which fanned out into a chamber littered with scraps of clothing and other discarded garbage one might find in any abandoned house. It took me a moment to realize that these items were the property of other abductees who had been stripped of their possessions. Hell, I might even find my own work clothes and car keys in this mess if I had the time to search. That thought would have to wait as Candice crept ahead and flagged us to approach her position with caution. At the edge of the chamber in a dimly lit alcove, stood over a dozen people of various races and gender; every one of them naked as the day they were born.

Long tall shadows of the aliens were cast upon the far wall as they operated on a victim just out of sight. I became still as a post when a little creature with dull skin quietly pushed through the crowd, dragging behind an older woman who was shuffling along in a daze. The being was merely the size of a child, although it possessed a noticeably larger cranium. The creature looked somewhat frail and roughly ghoulish; which only added to the fright of it.

Then it hit me, and I staggered as a waft of foul air like the smell of burning tires which lingered around this alien being. The stench of it was horrible, but the pacified victims never reacted to the nose-curling reek that hung in the air like a polluted haze. Again, I had to remind myself to not react; and started to gain a real appreciation for the mental discipline my comrades displayed.

The horrid vapor brought back disturbing memories of my encounters all those decades ago; whenever I woke up from a visitation to cross that same lingering odor which smelled like scorched plastic contained to small areas in the middle of a room or hallway. The stench left behind was their calling card that the aliens had recently arrived. They could entirely wipe away or dull the memory of their visitation, but they left other markers in their wake. It was a horrible smell you would never forget, one that was forever burned into my memory.

In deathly silence, the small being left the woman there and returned back to the center of the alcove to await the next patient. That was my cue to slip from the shadows and into the crowd. Aaron motioned me to be silent and mimic the actions of the others in the group. He had assured me earlier that they would try to find me later when it was safe.

I tiptoed my way over to the back of the assembly and slowly nudged my way into the thick of them, while my comrades slipped away into the darkness of the vents. I ended up standing there for what seemed like hours as the procedures continued to no end. Standing still for that length of time was a real test of willpower, as you try not to squirm while your body gets achy and your legs go to sleep from lack of movement.

Tried as I might, there were too many heads crowding my view to see clearly into the operating chamber. The scant glimpses I caught were of tall slender beings pulling tubes or handling mysterious metallic devices; the creature's slow and graceful movements only terrified me into keeping myself silent and poised. Around me, a few mind-drugged victims would release flatulence without any reaction; they just stood there staring straight ahead behind glazed eyes, unflinching while muffled cries could be heard escaping every so often from the operating table they faced.

I was becoming increasingly antsy as I waited, because I had been suppressing the welling urge to take a wicked piss. I feared what might happen if I got caught trying to sneak off into a dark corner to relieve myself; or if I would draw unwanted attention if I just released my bladder onto the floor around me. Just trying to hold it in made me nervous enough to worry if I would spike some mental alarm in these extraterrestrial creatures; only to get caught and end up with my sorry ass on the table pissing myself like a little girl as they injected an implant into me while I struggled helplessly.

Right when I was on the verge of executing a poor decision to my current dilemma, the entire crowd turned and started shuffling down the curved hallway to our immediate right. I followed along in my act with the rest of the herd. At least the movement helped to alleviate the stiffness in my back and hold in my urge to pee for the time being. What I hadn't expected, was that the place we were being led too seemed like it was a freaking mile away; while we shuffled along at what I would consider a snails pace.

It was certainly a test of patience and self-control; but all I kept imagining was being slowly liquefied in an embryonic sack, along with those haunting muffled cries from the operating table while everyone stared on in dreadful silence. It was enough to send chills up my spine. Though I was already freaked out as it was, the mortal consequences of breaking character scared me even more. So I marched on in a daze like the rest of the naked mob until we were finally deposited into a brightly lit room. What was so weird about it, was that the illumination appeared to come from the walls themselves which were designed with a sloping ceiling and floor that lacked any architectural corners whatsoever.

The chamber was all one smooth surface of a frosted white which really fucked with my depth perception, conjuring a sudden sense of dizziness. This growing feeling was similar to the way you feel when you spin in place for several moments and come to a sudden stop. The walls and floor seemed to pulse brighter and brighter, but I couldn't tell if it was the illumination, or if my iris was contracting out of focus with uncontrolled spasms. I started to feel ill as my brain was spinning in my head; although the other people in the room around me didn't appear to be as affected as I was by the intense wave of nausea.

I started to lean on the person in front of me and felt weak in my knees as my body was reacting to the blank atmosphere and ever-increasing sensory deprivation. At the verge of losing control, it was purely a subconscious reaction to want to collapse upon the ground in a desperate effort to find a physical means to anchor myself and regain my sense of balance. Moments later, a subtle hum, which was felt more than heard, began to shudder through my body. Just as I was about to collapse, the seam of a door appeared and the subsonic hum abruptly ceased.

A portal opened from the inner seam which had formed from the smooth wall before us, and the surrounding group was ushered in by a faint mental command I felt call inside my head. I was stunned to hear what sounded like my own voice compelling me to go through the doorway. Memories of the horrible events from my abductions those many years ago began crashing in, and it took all my effort to keep from succumbing to a mental breakdown right then and there. I tried to hold back the anxiety by taking several deep breaths and exhaling them slowly with any measure of control I could muster; it was some stupid yoga trick I had learned years ago, but it had always seemed to work.

The group fanned out into a sizable chamber with faint lighting covering the ivory walls. There was also a thin mist hanging in the air; much like fine spider silk lingering like a supple trail of aroma from burning incense. I turned slowly to watch as the doorway behind us closed and sank into the wall, disappearing as if it had never existed. The horde of naked citizens continued to mope about in a trance while I gradually eased my way through the thick of the crowd, which began to disperse around the room.

A few of them went straight for what appeared like a small

creek flowing with clear water, traveling straight across the back of the room; its source emerging from one wall, only to disappear into a duct on the opposite side. The people knelt there and cupped their hands to drink as if it was an automated watering trough. The mist thickened overhead, making it impossible to see how high the ceiling actually was above us. I was mildly surprised to see several oddly colored trees of a species I wasn't familiar with.

  Strangest of all were the piles of jagged crystals that lined the walls of the room. After the door shut behind us the haze began to thicken which effectively masked the interior limits of our confinement. I imagined it was designed to mimic a dream-like state to keep the occupants placid and help keep them in a zone of relative mental serenity. I scurried myself over to the edge of the crystal embankment in an attempt to inspect them in closer detail.

  There was a combination of clear and whitish shards that looked as if they had grown there in a chaotic jumble. Some had veins the color of bleached ivory running through them, while others were entirely opaque.   With mild effort, I attempted to snap off a small one with my bare hands, only to discover they were firmly cemented in place. The edges of those little bastards were extremely sharp, and I sure as hell wasn't going to go treading over them barefoot. Seeing it for what it was, this hazardous deterrent kept the occupants confined within the center of the room as effectively as if it were barbed wire.

  After making sure there weren't any beings within the chamber or watching through windows, as far as I could tell, I approached a few of the strangers wandering around to try to subtly speak with them. Regardless of what I said, they failed to react; some appeared as if they vaguely noticed my presence, but either wouldn't, or couldn't respond. I approached a man and a woman that sat side by side upon the floor by the edge of one of the odd trees; but they were also unresponsive, as if their numb minds were bound in a drug-induced daze.

Frustrated at this point, I watched as an older black woman and a thin middle-aged man approached the unusual tree, and each of them grabbed one of the oblong sprouts hanging from its thick branches. Without hesitation, they plucked the oddly colored fruit and began eating them whole. I dared to take a closer look, but their appearance was like nothing I had ever seen before. I shrugged to myself, and concluded that at least this was likely better than consuming that protein jelly my comrades had sequestered on their secret raids through the recesses of the ship.

I heard a tinkled splash and turned to see one of the men standing along the hedge of crystals, relieving himself. I gave a slight frown at how uncouth this guy was, though a quick scan of the room revealed that there were no actual facilities for the occupants to use. While he was spraying his stream of urine over the jagged quartz, I began to dread how little time this misty cage might take to fill with the smell of rancid piss and human feces deposited by its occupants. Oddly enough, I began to notice movement in the ivory rocks just as the man finished taking a leak.

He turned and walked away as if he was entirely unconcerned about who was watching him, but it was the reaction of the crystal surface that I found intriguing. Within moments, the crystals grew over the area where he had just urinated, and I was boggled by how fast they spread and wondered if they were feeding off the liquid itself as a source of nutrient, or if it was some freakish alien form of human waste disposal by sealing over it. Well, I figured it was far better to go there than to contaminate the only water supply in the holding pen; so I followed his lead and relieved myself in the same spot.

Just as I finished, I felt a faint tap on my shoulder, and almost jumped out of my skin. My first thought was that I had been caught, and an alien sentry was going to promptly drag me off into the surgery room. With a sigh, I was relieved to hear a human voice whispering to me from behind.

"You can talk now, but keep your voice down and try to keep

your head clear..." the strange man's voice trailed off as I turned to face him.

"Gotcha," I muttered back to the bearded man, noticing that he was also covered with a film of silver fleck.

"Your friends sent me to keep an eye on you," he breathed.

"I'm Tyler, who are you?" I inquired to my babysitter keeping watch over me in this bizarre playpen.

"That doesn't matter," he snapped back rudely, "and it's better if we don't exchange names within these priming pens," he spat as a defense.

I can imagine that avoiding linking a persons name to a mental image of them might be a matter of precaution, in regard to avoiding psychic interrogations by the entities which could read our minds. I was, however, wondering what the hell he meant by calling this place being a 'priming pen.'

"Where are we?" I whispered back, while trying to keep my thoughts to a dull shade. He motioned me to follow him to the back edge of the enclosure where we were furthest from anyone else. The others were either eating, or sitting, or curled up in fetal positions upon the sandy floor, fast asleep.

"There are dozens of holding rooms like this on different levels of the ship," he noted, "with nutrients infused into the air, food, and water, to keep us physically healthy. So get some rest if you need it and eat when your hungry from those shrubs," the man advised, "it doesn't matter which colored gourds you take, all that shit pretty much tastes the same."

"So you're saying there's no chance at ordering a lobster quiche from room service?" I joked, to try to take the edge off; but realized I was just coming across like a dolt, and the tense demeanor of his response was beyond serious.

"Look, pal, I guarantee you won't be laughing when you're strapped down in that medical table back there," he snapped back, and I instantly regretted my off-color sense of humor, "so I suggest that you try to avoid it as best you can by lying low and keeping your head down, savvy?"

I quickly nodded in agreement so that he wouldn't prejudge

me as a troublemaker. I realized the gravity of the situation, and hadn't fully absorb the aspect that endangering a fellow comrade might be all too easy when your captors are a race of soulless telepaths. I turned my eyes up towards his face so that he could tell I got the point of his scolding; that's when I noticed that when he spoke to me, that he wasn't using his lips. He had been speaking into my head the entire time.

"Alright then," he nodded back, "we'll speak further when it's safe again and I will help answer your questions then. In the meantime, don't bother with our lethargic friends around here," he gave a quick wave of his finger to the other patients in the holding cell, "you'll only bring attention to yourself; and believe me, you want to avoid that at all costs!"

The bearded man looked like any rugged hillbilly with an overgrown head of hair, however, I hadn't fail to notice that when he shuffled off, he acted slow and listless to effectively meld into the crowd. The one thing that bit at me was that there was absolutely nothing to do here, and I began to envy the rest of the occupants who were mentally intoxicated. I ended up biting my lip and took a seat by the tiny river, and eventually laid myself down upon the fine sand to get some much needed sleep.

When I awoke, I had no idea how much time had passed. I wasn't entirely sure of the count, but there currently seemed to be slightly fewer occupants in the priming chamber than when I had first entered, and it made me slightly apprehensive to think that the ET's were coming in and taking subjects at random while I had slept. After a long time of sitting there and finally getting up to roam the room because I was bored out of my mind, the bearded man approached me again and grazed my shoulder with his before he spoke.

"Over here," was all he instructed, so I followed him in a measured way so as not to alert the others with any sudden moves.

"Were some people taken?" I had to ask.

"Yes, a few from this group were removed while you slept.

They don't usually take the ones that are unconscious ...usually," he noted, "Also, as a precaution, don't go pacing about and letting your mind wander; you have to keep your shit together in here," my bearded nanny remarked.

"Sorry..." I responded while trying to hide a shrug of implied innocence, "what happens next?" I pushed as the most obvious question I could muster. He glanced around the room for an awkward moment before finally answering my inquiry.

"These primer cells help to both preserve the subjects and acclimatize us for whatever environment we will be injected to on our next appointment," he noted, though I was more than a little bewildered by what he was getting at, "afterward, we will be draped with basic suits and gear, which will serve as protective garments for our impending assignment."

"And what exactly is our next assignment?" I injected as a response.

"Don't know, don't care," he answered without delay, "just try to survive it," he callously turned the direction of his remark to one of advice, "and for fuck's sake, don't get alarmed if you should see them come in to snatch someone," he glared at me for a moment, until he caught my eyes to make sure I got the warning, "we'll be able to talk more freely once we're on duty," he cut the conversation short and shuffled away with that edged snippet of advice.

It felt like several more hours of boredom had passed before a strange tone began to cycle throughout the room. In a familiar sensation, I experienced a ringing in my ears as a reaction to the low-frequency noise. The rest of the sleepwalkers suddenly stopped whatever they were doing, and turned their heads upward as if they were listening to something. With caution, I edged my way to the back of the crowd so I could attain a better initiative as to what was about to go down.

On the far side of the room, a doorway emerged from nowhere and the occupants began their slow migration towards that exit, so I slowly stepped forward and merged into the crowd. The man with the beard brushed my arm to get my attention and I heard a voice in my head.

"This is it, Cupcake," he charged bluntly, "just follow along and try to keep your mind blank as best as you can until we exit the ship," he finished, before he hastened ahead and out of reach through the throng of lumbering bodies.

His words cut like a knife, and I began to feel a creeping sense of distress as I wondered what he had meant about us leaving the ship. My mind started to race and I began to hope in vain that we would be dropped back somewhere on Earth. For some silly reason I began to feel homesick for my quiet little cabin in the woods, and worried what would happen to my indoor plants without me there to care for them. How long would it be until someone came by to check on me back home when they figured out I had missed work and assumed I had abandoned my job; or would they just fire my ass with a terse phone call and send my last paycheck to my empty mailbox?

An emotional tornado overcame me as I stepped out of the mist-filled room, and the creeping despair that clouded my judgment made me question if this was a withdrawal effect from the sedating vapor that permeated the holding pen. We had spent what felt to be several days being primed to a different gravity and thickening atmosphere; which had been adjusted in subtle levels. I now felt much heavier than I had before, and my breathing was noticeably more labored as I followed the others into the adjacent chamber.

Beyond was an oblong-shaped hall, where there were piles of the dark cloth-like material that slowly spewed from a spout set high out of reach upon one wall. One of the smaller alien beings slowly combed through the room. I didn't know if it was a he, or she, or what, since it had no clothing and no obvious genitalia to distinguish it as such. The creature was holding a small crude rod which was noticeably smooth as if it had been molded from clay. I watched in fascination as it took its time weaving through the room to finally choose a woman, and it merely touched her with the small wand.

There was a small burst of light from its tip, and the elected individual turned and made her way to the closest wall where she came to an abrupt halt while a ribbed tube snaked out from an embedded funnel high up on the ceiling directly above her. This strange device appeared more organic than machine, and almost reacted as a living thing as it hovered near her head and shoulders, as if testing her proximity. Suddenly, a fine mist issued from the tube, covering her with a silver sheen as it twined around her to apply the vapor on every part of her body.

The coating appeared to be the same color and texture of the cream that Renzo had me smear upon my skin. I stiffened for a nervous moment and had to remind myself to relax when the child-size entity walked straight up to me and gazed upwards, while it noticed I already had my silvery application. I continued to stare forward in an effort to ignore it and released a silent breath of relief as it turned and continued on through the crowd of humans. It would touch its wand to whoever didn't have their metallic varnish; whereupon the protective coating would be promptly applied upon them by the coiled automation secured to the ceiling.

Those few individuals who had their glaze applied, gathered near the dispenser where the strips of dark material were piling upon the floor in a jumbled heap. A tall black man took a position beside a thick chromed pole and placed his arms at his side, lifting them from contact with this body. I almost stumbled in shock when the glossy pole shot out and enveloped his body, leaving behind a thick membrane as though he were being pressed between two giant sheets of tarp. The ebony material was suddenly sucked up through the bottom of the panels and was methodically woven across his body.

The process seemed to take just a little over a minute, and I wondered how he was able to breathe while he was sandwiched between its folds. The membranes loosened and fell away to be withdrawn at the end of the spinning cylinder, and the next person in line promptly took his place. The strips of material measured only about a hand's width, but it had been woven to fit neatly across his body with merely a few ragged spots where they had overlapped as they were mended.

I took a few steps over to get a better view of the process and I felt a tinge of apprehension that my turn would come sooner or later; and I certainly didn't want to overreact and get myself caught. A slightly chubby older man stepped forward and went through the same process, but from the side angle, I noticed something which I hadn't seen before as a thin clear tube snaked out of the ceiling behind him and adhered itself to his spine from the length of his neck down to the crack of his ass. Just as he lurched, the cylinder shot forward and applied the material which spun the excess from the pile lying on the floor upon the entire circumference of his body and limbs.

After a minute or so passed, considering the process was taking longer due to his size; the man was released and he proceeded down the narrow corridor where he stepped into a small circle raised from the floor. What I assumed was the same little alien creature I had seen before, made its way through the crowd once again and turned its unblinking gaze directly towards me. I suddenly began to feel a buzzing in my head and feared I had been too obvious in my hesitation to be the next in line. Dreading that I was about to be revealed, I strutted forward and stepped next to the chrome bar to avoid the sudden scrutiny brought upon me by the little creature.

Its large dark eyes stared at me just as the bar shot forward and I sucked in a deep breath through my nose before the membranes snapped close. I felt something cold press across my back, which I had assumed was the tube as it fanned out a webbing across my rear; however, I hadn't expected the end of it to snake itself up my anus. Doing my best not to grunt at the violation, I held onto what little air I had left in my lungs when I suddenly gasped as the oily prod snapped into place. My vision was obscured by the muddled opaque film that held me still while the material was being sucked into the mechanism at my feet. In all respects, it felt as if a swarm of ants were racing over my body as the dark cloth was patched across my limbs and torso. The strange itching sensation slowly subsided as the synthetic tissue meshed with the hair on my body and adhered to my skin. Lastly, there was an unpleasant cutting sensation at my wrists and neckline; and I tried not to appear thoroughly freaked out as I actually was, once the membrane had released me from its grasp.

Luckily, the little creature was no longer standing there to watch me at the end of the process and had continued on with its duties. I let out a muffled sigh and followed in the steps of the previous crew members, and kept a nervous pace down the narrowing hall to step within the small empty circle at its end. I stood there with my feet side by side, not knowing what the hell I was supposed to do at this stage since I hadn't had a clear view of what type of process had followed. Daring to turn my eyes downward, I observed a pool of warm dark goo begin to bleed into the circular enclosure from unseen ducts.

As the gel began to adhere to my feet, I found that I couldn't move, which sent a jolt of panic up my spine, which took every ounce of my willpower to quell. My bearded accomplice had warned me against losing my shit, and I didn't want to take the chance of being forcibly implanted or absorbed into the system as the crew's evening meal. To my relief, the gel only soaked its way up to my mid-calf and quickly began to drain away; leaving behind a thick coating glazed across my feet.

Recalling my studies on lost jungle tribes in South America which I had read about in college, I was amazed at how this process was fundamentally similar to those used by the native people who dipped their legs up to their ankles in sap from the rubber trees, as an ingenious way to make custom-formed shoes to protect their feet. After the excess gel from the device drained away, I felt a sudden jolt beneath me, and took that as my prompt to exit the machine. Turning around, I saw that my accomplice had attained similar attire and was waiting for me in a casual manner at the breach of a brightly lit door, one which had molded itself into existence upon a nearby wall.

Taking his cue, I stepped in front of him and made my way into the tight chamber where the rest of the dressed occupants

were being corralled. Within, I found a confined tube with
smooth benches lining both sides of the cylinder-shaped room.
Everyone who entered took their seats in order, side by side,
directly across from one another, while the redneck assigned to
babysit me on my first run took the bench opposite my own
inside the cramped cell. It was only when I sat down that I
realized the extent of the intrusion into my bowels, while I
grimaced and squirmed to adjust the tube protruding up my
arse without taking an effort to poke at it.

We waited there in silence as the rest of the human herd made
their way into the cavity, and the door promptly sealed shut
behind us. That was when he touched my foot with his to get
my attention, and I heard his voice in my head once again.

"Well, you barely avoided getting sacked back there," he gave
a sarcastic grin as his voice echoed in my head, "but don't
speak out loud until we exit the vehicle," he cautioned while
referring to the chamber, which I now presumed was a
personnel carrier of some sort.

The walls suddenly brightened with illumination while an
overbearing voice jolted into my head; which sounded oddly
like my own. It was undeniably the same strain of alien
telepathy they beamed into our minds; yet somehow this
chamber seemed to magnify the connection.

"*Exit craft, gather green flowers, gather white sap, avoid
black dust,*" the thundering voice ordered, "*a notice to return to
craft will be at first beacon, the crew must arrive to their craft
by the second beacon; all of the crew must be within craft by
the third beacon or they will be left behind.*" it affirmed yet
again, then the voice fell silent.

There was a sudden lurch, and my stomach started to churn,
and by the looks of it the other people in the pod around us
started to regain their senses as a white vapor began to jet
through the compartment. Through this, my guide across from
me put a finger to his lips and motioned me to remain silent.

"It looks like this will merely be a gathering mission for
biological samples; consider yourself lucky that your first drop

was not an attack run, Rookie," he offered with a snort.

I was desperate to ask what the hell was going on and what I should be expecting, so I could prepare myself mentally, but I followed his instructions and tamed my unbridled curiosity. Daydreaming in that moment, my mind drifted as I recalled the countless times I stepped outside of my cabin under a clear night sky, to gaze up at the sea of stars twinkling in the night; little did I realize one day I would be lost among them, and just how strange the universe really was.

Quarantine

My adrenaline began to shoot through the roof when an unusual electric hum jolted through the floor. Looking around me, it appeared the others felt it too, and a few other people began to show visual panic when a lattice began to form inside the interior of the cabin. Imagine if you would, a hundred invisible spiders randomly weaving a thick opaque web; which was the source of our alarm. Glancing across from my seat, I saw that my bearded guide just sat there as calm as can be; as if we were all on a Sunday picnic.

Most of the occupants merely remained in place while this fiber laced itself through the chamber, as if this was a normal procedure for what was to happen during a mission of this nature. When one of the strands directly hit me in the chest, it bounced off and continued spreading in another direction. I felt nothing from the following impacts as the strands filled the room and the entire interior was filled with a thick webbing of fat gossamer threads so dense that I could barely see the person sitting next to me.

In an attempt to move, I found the material to be relatively spongy though still easy to breathe through. This effectively held the occupants in place, much like a box full of perforated foam encased around a fragile statue. As it turned out, the trip itself was short and there was no telltale impact to reveal any landing had taken place, so I was understandably confused when the far end of the ship lit up like a spotlight. The webbing began to dazzle in the hard light with a beautiful shimmer as it quickly disintegrated around us and fell into a cloud of fine glittering dust at our feet.

I could see the far end of the ship was now open and marked with a giant lit ring around the rim of its porthole. Those crew members closest to the exit disembarked first, followed by the ones behind them until it was our turn to follow. I stumbled along with the others through the awkwardly small compartment towards the cold darkness awaiting us beyond the ring of light, wondering what I would find.

I had read several science fiction books, and as a movie buff, I had seen hundreds of films; so subconsciously, the bar of my expectations were already set pretty high. Would I stumble upon an alien world of wonders, or one of raging desert storms; or maybe hopping along like an astronaut in an atmosphere with radically reduced gravity? I even found myself filled with anticipation to catch a glimpse of several crescent moons or a virgin night sky awash with a billion unfamiliar stars. Sadly, what I was rewarded with was an unremarkable flat floor that stretched out across the belly of some dark and murky structure of colossal proportions.

I stood there for a moment in disbelief and bewilderment as I stared around. My bearded friend turned and handed me a long rod from a rack which had been mounted alongside the open doorway; he grabbed my shoulder to shake me out of my momentary shock of disbelief.

"Here, take this," he mentioned while handing me the metallic staff, "keep close and follow me," the man ordered as I turned to catch up with him.

"Where are we?" I huffed as we made our way far from the crew who were fanning out across the complex.

"This looks to be an abandoned ship or station from another race than that of our current hosts," he gathered with a quick glance around the immense building. It was comprised of dark pitted stone, and truth be told, its age looked beyond ancient.

"Why are we supposed to gather green flowers and white sap?" I threw another question his way.

"You mean the emerald buds and ivory oil..." he trailed off when he saw the confused look on my face, "don't worry about the context of the instructions they give us, a lot gets lost in the translation when they divvy out orders," he mentioned as he tapped his temple implying to the telepathic commands, "its just resource material to them, as we are merely physical labor to do their bidding."

"But why do this at all," I tried to debate with him, "I mean why not revolt and refuse to act as slave labor?" I responded as we advanced towards several mint-colored crystals growing upon a high wall. He approached the bright rocks and touched the edges along the seam of the cluster with the rod-like tool where they grew from the stone, and a light static of electricity jolted out. Once he was done zapping it, the crystals promptly popped off and fell to the ground.

"Don't just stand there, collect these stones," he ordered while showing me how the staff worked, "there are no buttons, so stop looking for one," he snapped as I was busying myself by closely inspecting the strange device, "just touch it to the rocks and it will do the rest," he granted as he picked up several of the fragments by hand and placed them upon his upper thigh where they stuck in place as they adhered to his outer suit.

I picked up a few of the stones and attempted the same feat, only to end up baffled as to how they glued themselves to my jumpsuit. I followed his lead and began severing several more crystals from where they sprouted upon the black rocky surface. Looking around, I could see many other members of our crew performing the same task at a fair distance around the chamber we occupied beneath the high domed roof. My guide seemed like a short-tempered fellow, but he finally got back to responding to my inquiry.

"Did the others let you know about the squishies?" he asked in my head without bothering to turn to me; so I noted that they had. He turned his face towards me in a slight glance, showing a troubled look lingering upon his face while he worked alongside me, "I've seen them up close in their late stage ...and I can tell you its not a pleasant way to go," he remarked, "I don't know what year you were taken or what country you're from, but our hosts don't fancy labor unions, and I guarantee they'll make use of you one way or another. You work; and you'll continue to live with all your fingers and toes. You don't, and you'll either be discarded or siphoned into protein puree," he edged that point towards me as to the reality of our situation. We collected the glassy rocks and made our way towards a farther section where another cluster had sprouted. The notion of human trafficking and forced slavery had a relevant place in Earth's history, but it still bit deeply into how opposed the practice was to our inherent human nature at our current stage of civilization. I would imagine that after some length of time without any remote chance of being returned home that the prisoners in the harvester ships would have eventually revolted, even if refusing to cooperate meant losing their lives. Compared to how we were brought up in our modern world, being stuck living under such servitude was no life at all.

"Have you or the others ever suffered suicidal thoughts, or been tempted towards it?" I asked, trying not to beat around the bush on the question, which ended up sounding quite blunt when I said it. He turned to glance at me again, but his words in my head faded beyond recognition, "I'm sorry, I didn't catch that..."

He stepped over and touched my arm again, and I was getting a little vexed about his constant physical contact. This time, however, I saw that there was a little electric spark where he made contact and the volume of his voice came in loud and clear again in my head.

"You have to stay close, the telepathy from the implants only works at close range," he informed me, "touch reestablishes the connection; at least for a short while," he stood to take a rest while observing that I was testing the spot where he touched my arm to no avail, "don't bother asking me how it works, I've got no fucking clue."

"You, you have an implant?" I stuttered in mild surprise, "Then why weren't you pacified like the others in that priming pen back there?" I inquired while recalling the term he had used as I attached more of the loose stones to my suit.

"Hell, it could have just been a faulty implant; or just as likely I became resistant to its effects," he explained, and I could understand it might work along the lines of a junkie becoming tolerant of their narcotics, or an alcoholic who needs more liquor over time to reach the same effect, "the implants can trigger the pleasure centers in our brains, so it becomes a reward incentive in exchange for cooperative labor."

Now that made sense; those types of programs had been used in many parts of our own society over the eons. I could see how it could be utilized as a temporary escape from this cycle of forced imprisonment and servitude. Humans could be weak in their methodology and self-destructive behavior from only living in the moment. It was an escape of the mind when the idea of liberation of the body was deemed impossible. It made me wonder if I was too cowardly to kill myself if I had to live like this for the rest of my natural life.

"Has anyone ever escaped?" I squeaked with a whisper while hoping beyond hope. His answer left me unimpressed.

"There have been rumors, although I doubt they're true," he stated as we picked up the rest of the green shards and headed towards another patch, "but if you try to play hero and start taking unnecessary risks, you'll never see the chance," he shot down my hopes with his level-headed advice.

The bearded man filled me in on several details, though I was slightly discouraged he wouldn't tell me his name or where he was from; stating reasons that if I ever got caught, that they could probe my mind for relevant information which could identify him in short order because of his implant. He made sure that I appreciated the risk he took by reentering the priming pen to guide me, since it was no small effort to remove the outer garment material and the tube from his bowels, just to go through the process all over again.

When I asked him what I should do when I had to take a piss, he cited that I could just urinate freely in my suit and it would be absorbed by the material. The catheter along my backside was stretched far up into my lower intestines and would recycle and expel any waste. The fiber of the suit itself further assisted to rehydrate the body and prevent water loss that escapes through the skin. It was all very technical, but nothing so far-fetched from being used in our own rudimentary space program back home.

I was interested to hear his theories to the bigger picture and I valued any advice he could give me. His attitude was more cynical, but no more so than what Renzo had displayed. I assumed the stress of this situation would eventually eat away at the core of anyone's personality, and I certainly didn't want to have an implant forced upon me to either sway or guarantee my compliance.

From what he said, it was his understanding that there were many different races of these beings from different sections of the known galaxy. Each one of them existing on a varied level of development, however, they appeared to share a common alliance in one form or another. Understandably, there were a few species that were keenly hostile and wallowed in a stage of conflict whenever they were confronted, or subjected, to hit and run tactics by opposing races, akin to guerilla warfare.

This did not bode well for the populace of Earth, since we had been foolish enough to send out deep space probes and beam messages out into the unknown without considering the consequences that there might be a few begrudged and unfriendly neighbors in the cosmos. It was human nature to act with a certain level of naive stupidity, such as calling out into space when we weren't even close to a technical level to defend ourselves against an advanced species. We were advertising ourselves in the hopes of befriending an alien civilization; and when they finally showed up, they took one glance at us and saw we were little more than a bunch of obnoxious crack-heads who would only spell trouble for the rest of the neighborhood.

Our warlike demeanor didn't make such a great impression either, and once thermonuclear weapons were placed on the table, their attitude about us changed dramatically. After my first contact all those decades ago, I had spent a great deal of my life researching the subject of aliens and UFO's, only to realize that there was evidence from renaissance paintings to etchings from the orient, and all the way to cave drawings across the world of antiquity which recorded these cosmic neighbors, revealing that they had been visiting our little blue planet for quite some time. I could imagine that human civilizations were seen as immature and callous in our early stages of development; but my nameless friend was quick to correct my deluded method of thinking.

From what he had gathered during his time in their midst, was that there were many other worlds also brimming with human life in a variety of stages of development. For instance, he was equally adamant that our combined civilizations on Earth would be far better off if our societies returned to the pre-industrial age; and expressed his anger about what mankind was doing to harm the ecosystem and the irreversible damage to our own environment. When he mentioned that, I could see how he could be a hippy tree-hugger since his personal appearance fit the part; but he was certain in his own mind that many of the contactees would have never been taken if our society had acted more responsibly. Regrettably, I couldn't bring myself to disagree with him on that point.

Our conversation was cut short when we heard a scream echo in the distance. Stepping out to take a look, we could see there were several of our crewmates in the distance making a hasty sprint back towards the transport ship, even though the first beacon had not yet sounded. They had dropped their tools and were screaming wildly in fear as they ran. For the first time, my guide spoke out loud; although it didn't sound like English.

"Filho da puta!" he uttered as he stepped beyond my position and glared into the darkness towards the source of the excitement.

There were other members of our crew who had fanned out among the open building, though several were making a mad dash for the shuttle we had arrived in. I came up beside him to see what the commotion was all about. There were three individuals stumbling over one another as they made a bee-line back towards the transport vessel. Behind them, I could just barely make out a handful of small creatures chasing them, though they were hard to see because of the dim lighting.

"Grab everything, we've got to get back to the carrier!" my guide said in my mind after taking a second to touch my arm as he reestablished mental contact. I wished I could do the same, but without an implant, the telepathy only worked one way.

"What are those things?" I stammered while hastily collecting the rest of the stones just as a loud reverberating tone began to emit from the ship.

"That's the evacuation alarm, we have to get back, now!" my guide shot back with a raised mental volume. This guy came across as tough as rocks, so I wasn't going to argue with him.

Luckily I was in decent shape myself and could handle the short jog back to the cylindrical ship we had arrived in; though with a scan around the area, I couldn't see any opening to the exterior of the building to explain how the ship itself had gotten inside this colossal structure. Running side by side, I tried my best to get a look at the small creatures which ran on all fours. One of the things leapt onto the back of a large man who was lagging behind the rest of his comrades, while they continued to scurry ahead. The man fell and began screaming like a child as the thing clawed at his head and a cluster of similar creatures in their pack added into the scuffle around him. They weren't drawing any blood as far as I could tell, but it still looked like he was taking a thorough beating.

A handful of others from the pack of beasts zipped past the fray and continued the pursuit of the crew members trying to escape ahead. Above us, there was a brief flash of light and three bright orbs emerged into view and formed a triangle as they hovered high above; spinning together slowly as if they shared a common axis. Suddenly, one of the lights separated from the formation and sped off towards the lead end of our personnel carrier. As it came into view, I could see that it was a metal orb the size of a small car, and had a glowing ring of lights which produced an aura around it.

I figured the craft must be some sort of defense drone because it took the lead in front of the retreating humans as a thin beam of light shot out from its center; hitting the ground in front of the foremost creature approaching our ship. The ray was sharp like a laser beam, but much wider and radiated a bright white. The creature came to a screeching halt just before entering the tight spotlight as the orb hovered there far above it out of reach. The drone drifted gently as if in a light breeze, although the targeting of the light beam it emitted remained steadily fixed.

In its glowing radiance I could finally see the wild animal. Strangely enough, it closely resembled the child-sized Grey alien I had seen within the ship before we had been deposited here. The creature was of the same stature, but there were some significant differences in its appearance. For one, its skin was an oily black and it possessed multiple ridges along its forehead; also its large eyes were colored a horrible bright blood red. It cowered there from the hard ray of light as if it knew it was a weapon and that the beam could be turned upon it at any moment.

Glancing back, I could see that the man they had taken down was no longer moving and the rest of the creatures began to pace like hungry wolves at a safe distance beyond the column of light. The sound of the alarm rose in volume as the rest of our crew returned to the relative safety of the ship and scampered inside. They reset their rods back in their holders upon the door as the green stones fell from their suits the moment they passed through the portal. Many others were also carrying translucent sacks of a vanilla-colored gel with thick bundled fronds similar to bleached seaweed. These dropped items were sucked up through a vent at the bottom of the sectioned hatch and disappeared from view.

"Remember, don't speak out loud once we get inside," my bearded accomplice warned as we approached the entrance and saw the nervous faces on the rest of our crew.

When we came within the presence of the doorway, I felt a static tingle across my body and the stones unglued themselves from my suit and fell to the floor, where they were promptly vacuumed up through the vents at our feet. Jumping aboard, we took our original posts where we had sat before as the rest of our squad fell in behind us. Moments later, the portal cycled shut and the alarm ceased. Once again, the strange spongy webbing began to form within the ship while I shot a forlorn glance towards the empty seat of the man we had left behind.

I was desperate to know what those feral creatures were we had encountered and why they had attacked our crew, but knew I couldn't speak until we got back on board the mother ship. As the safety webbing thickened to blot my vision, I closed my eyes and began to drift off for some much needed rest. The atmosphere vapor lining my lungs made my breath feel sticky and wet, and the gravity changes left me with an almost drunken feeling of exhaustion. I never felt the inertia as we lifted off on our return trip to the Harvester, and faded off into a listless state as I thought back to the quiet life I had left behind in my little home out in the woods.

As a contactee, I had experienced several abductions as a child and onward for many years which stretched well into my teens. It all started after my parents experienced what they described as a paranormal episode of missing time while on a trip along a desert highway. When they first told me about it I thought they were just pulling my leg as a joke to get me to believe some wild story, so I had shrugged it off as more nonsense that adults were known to lob around in their overly deceptive world. However, I became a believer when only a few days thereafter, I was also taken.

I had been abducted from my bedroom in the middle of the night by a pair of tall gray beings, and held in a small chamber similar to the white room where the rest of our crew had been placed before being released into the crystal-lined priming pen. If I had to guess, I would say it was probably some type of sterilizing process before I was brought into the piloting room of a saucer-shaped craft.

The control room was located on the uppermost ring of the small craft, which itself only took up a mere third of the circumference. The gray creatures had also spoken without audible words and communicated through direct thought, just as these Overlords had within the harvest ship. There were two of them piloting the vehicle while a third acted as my accommodating guide, who held my hand while it showed me maps and images, including a message they had for my species. Many decades later, I came to the conclusion that I hadn't been specifically chosen for the abduction, but that I was merely a side-note from my parents kidnapping upon that lonely desert road, which had happened all those years ago.

I can only presume that they had been implanted and were tracked back to our home, and I was distressed to discover that I was literally unable to talk about the experience to my own mother the following morning. My life became a jumble of confusion and anguish after that episode, as my perception of the world I had known was thrown out of kilter. Skipping every two years, during mid-summer, I was contacted again and again; although the following visitations were far more disturbing.

Being paralyzed, and poked, and prodded, and studied without any form of consent or communication became a traumatizing experience. By the following visitation years later, my mother had been diagnosed with an overly aggressive cancer which ate away at her body, and as for my father, he had lost his mind and moved to the other side of the country after their resulting divorce. Less than a decade later, she passed away from a dreadful combination of brain and lung cancer, and I began to turn the blame of her death towards our extraterrestrial visitors.

Every two years during mid-summer I would set up a variety of gimmicks using traps and tripwires set throughout my home in an effort to give me some sort of warning whenever those beings arrived. Needless to say, the efforts of my ingenuity never seemed to work; for the beings came and went without restraint. Even though I bolted down the house tight, I finally saw how they got inside one morning when I awoke from another such visitation to witness a glowing green portal a mere arm's length from my bed.

Needless to say, I was unnerved when the glowing doorway suddenly blinked out of existence before me. Reaching out to verify that nothing was there, the lingering static electricity of its presence had made the hair on my arms stand on end. From that point onward, I felt as though I had lost my mind; wondering if I would be locked up in a mental institution if I reported my experience to the police or state authorities. After years of diving into endless research and educating myself on similar paranormal events and the repercussions abductees faced, I was glad that I hadn't exposed myself to their scrutiny.

There finally came a day when I packed my bags and moved a thousand miles away, and from that point forward in my life I was always on the move, never living in one place for too long; for it always seemed as if I could never find a place I truly found comfortable enough to call home again. Since the day I left my childhood home, I hadn't experienced another contact for several decades until the very evening I was swooped up into this nightmare. I had lived most of my life trying to make sense of it all, but now that I was here, I felt even more confused. I imagine most people would have reacted much differently, while fearing for their life and the loss of everything and everyone they left behind; however, that only applies if a person actually bothers to forge relations worth missing. As for me, I was a loner.

Admittedly, I was more than a little uncomfortable with myself when I realized that I didn't actually feel a sense of loss; but felt more like an overshadowing acceptance of the situation. I don't know why, but somehow I always felt in the back of my mind as though I knew it would eventually come to this. As it turned out, I had wasted most of my life selfishly searching for answers when my time would have been far better spent pursuing the right questions.

Society of Slaves

While growing up I had noticed that many seniors, who should have been otherwise occupied with enjoying their golden years, were instead distinctly bitter as if they were angry at the world. Over time their pessimism rubbed off on me like a contagious disease; though I tried never to fall into that negative perception of life. Maturity comes in all forms, but becoming responsible for one's own actions is in the top tier of that category; which undoubtedly is why I, like many others, was frustrated by the conduct of governments and regimes which seemed to escalate ever-more out of control.

Most human beings felt like puppets drowning in a flood of propaganda as we were told what to do, what to think, and what to say; only to feel helpless when the powers that be, began waging wars against foreign nations and committed atrocities with loss of life on a phenomenal scale. I wasn't an idiot though, noting that human history had proven that we had a bad habit of repeating our mistakes over and over again, without end. Researching lost cultures of our ancient past, there was compelling evidence which showed that mankind had inhabited our little planet far, far longer than those accepted by our modern religious doctrines.

I had the humorous experience of once asking a religious fanatic how they could explain the presence of dinosaur fossils, which were millions of years old, if their holy text claimed the world had only existed a few thousand years. In response, he claimed their bones were put there by the devil to confuse us ...hah, wow, just wow! By far, the vast majority of the human race currently lived in what was considered poverty, but what truly amazed me was the way our social order had been groomed to view anyone existing in a pre-industrial lifestyle who didn't possess the latest computer, television, expensive house, fancy car, or stylish cell phone in our day and age, was somehow considered as destitute. Even those merely living a simple life off of the grid was somehow frowned upon, and were considered to be wasting away their life.

Taking a step back, I realized how most people lived their lives with either their head up their ass or buried in the sand, and never bothered to think outside the box. In all respects, what my bearded guide had claimed about the human race being better off in a pre-industrial age, was basically true. Human society had become exceptionally efficient at creating waste and pollution, and social norms established a habit of chastising anyone who complained about it.

I had found it interesting to read about ancient Greek scholars who claimed that every dozen millennia or so, the Earth experiences a great cataclysm which upturns the world we once knew, whereupon mankind must begin again as children. That in itself might sound like a pretty colorful myth; that is until ancient technologies and unexplained artifacts were found buried in places they didn't belong. Stranger still, both the mainstream scientific and religious communities help to brush the significance of these unique findings aside, and such discoveries go unreported, and thus, are entirely unnoticed by the population at large with our authorities basically stating: *'nothing to see here, folks, just move along.'*

Sadder still, the number of people who are awake and open to such ideas are wistfully small compared to the size of our population. Having delved into the UFO community, I warily tested the waters before diving in head first. Shining like a torch in a windstorm, what I saw of the topmost wick of their movement were those in our society who cried out for disclosure and transparency of the truth from the upper echelon of our governments and military, demanding that they unveil their elaborate cover-up of hiding the existence of intelligent life outside our planet. However, I soon learned that a vast majority of people didn't understand that the very core of the disclosure movement was enveloped around the release of life-altering technologies that would fundamentally change our society as a whole, but were instead kept shrouded in secrecy for nothing more than the sake of profiteering by the elitists which promoted to control mankind as a society of slaves. Funny how it seemed like the tables had turned, only to realize here I was filling that same role. Telepathic control was already forced upon our society through the elaborate schemes of media advertising. Go to work, pay bills, spend money, watch shows, consume, buy, buy, buy! However, in the rare event when an individual wakes up from this endless grind they experience a mental breakdown. Once you step back and recognize you've become a slave to your possessions, you can turn a leaf and start to see the world in different colors.

It was hard, and I mean tortuously difficult not being able to speak to anyone about my abductions. There existed a stigma of being labeled either mentally ill or delusional by your peers. Like tape across a hairy back, removing that label is far more painful than to avoid having it applied in the first place. Thus, most contactees choose to hide their dark secret and bury it away. Regrettably, that can frequently lead to broken homes, fractured marriages, and a rash of suicides; because society refuses to recognize the source of the malady.

Well, here I was on an alien vessel being forced into slavery; how crazy was that! It would break most minds, but it's hard to crack someone open when their lives had already been shattered long ago. Oddly enough, I found the whole circumstance I was in to be quite interesting. I was shaken out of my wistful daze by a hard shove against my leg.

"Time to wake up," my bearded nanny nudged, while I opened my eyes to see that our transport had already docked and the protective webbing, which held us securely in place, had since dissipated, "follow me and don't lag behind; we'll see if we can find our group."

The other occupants filed out of the vehicle and we found ourselves funneled through a circular hall shaped like a ribbed cone. The bottleneck of the corridor only allowed the passage of one person at a time in single file; and was apparently designed this way to administer a series of decontamination phases and return our metabolism back to its average medium. Beyond was a narrow hall flooded with a dark blue glow which made everyone's skin and hair illuminate with a flurry of colors like some evolved UV light. During the course of this, I was forced to exhale to the point I became dizzy as all the air was suddenly sucked from my lungs; while doing so, I observed a thick vapor escape from my throat.

The people in front of me were also gasping for air as they recovered from whatever gas had been expelled from our lungs. Fortunately, there were no alien sentries at the end of the process as we were ejected into an enormous hall. The walls consisted of an aged metallic gray with spattered swashes of patina marked upon its surface. I had to manage a quick pace just to keep up with my guide as I watched the top of his furry hair weaving its way into the crowd and disappear.

I was startled to see hundreds of people all mulling about the chamber; some were speaking to one another with their voices, as others stood staring while locked in telepathic conversation. There were a few, however, who simply stood alone with an empty glaze in their eyes or stumbled along in a catatonic state. At least everyone here was clothed and there was a measure of social exchange taking place among the occupants. I finally caught up with my bearded companion and saw him standing among a few familiar faces near the middle of the chamber.

"Ah, Tyler, glad you found us," Aaron blurted out to my surprise as he waved me over, "don't worry about speaking out loud here, this is the main assembly tank and it's not monitored by our hosts," he advised.

"There are too many people here and it overwhelms the clarity of their mental communications," the bearded man confirmed, "our minds are too chaotic, and it may be why we only see a handful of them at any given time since they find it difficult to endure our presence," he finished.

"Renzo and Candice are farther down the line," Aaron stated as he pointed across the enormous chamber, "and the 'Marks' are at the very end of the containment level. The hybrids tend to hang out together, and it would likely draw suspicion among them if they were to mingle with us lowly human life forms in public," he smiled jokingly.

We found Aaron, who placed his hands together and offered a courteous bow to my bearded friend while they were locked in private mental conversation before he eventually turned and disappeared into the crowd. I watched my chaperone stroll away without having the chance to thank him for his help. Inspecting our surroundings, this holding level was designed with an overabundance of headroom. It was several hundred meters long and well over three stories high, yet there were no stairways or additional levels, nor even furniture such as chairs or tables to use as far as I could tell.

"Follow me, let's go find the others," Aaron gestured for me to accompany him as he headed off in the opposite direction.

We wound our way through several small groups who stood among the various individuals that appeared to be in some kind of trance. As I made my way through the crowd, I couldn't help but notice that nobody here appeared to acknowledged my presence, making me feel as though I didn't exist. It then occurred to me that without an implant, which allowed the elemental means of telepathy, there was the chance that I was not registering to them on a psychic level. If minds didn't touch, it was comparable to people who avoided eye contact and didn't wish to be disturbed. One of the most basic forms of human communication had been replaced with a higher order, which had prioritized mental recognition above all others.

It didn't take long to find our friends, who were busy talking to a pair of women who wore serious and shaken looks etched upon their faces. Renzo turned to greet us as we drew closer. The two women were speaking with Candice in a hushed tone as if they were afraid of being overheard; although Candice tried to assure them to ease their concerns.

"These two ladies are sisters who just arrived from another harvest ship," Renzo stated as he nodded over to the pair of women in their black jumpsuits and wearing the same silvery cream upon their faces that we adorned, "from their story, they had apparently avoided implantation by creating a distraction and slipped into the group which had already been modified," he amused at their ingenuity.

One of the women started to feel weak from the stress and began to sit down on the floor, though Candice quickly advised her not to.

"I wouldn't do that if I were you," she advised, "the frequency of energy that is used to induce artificial gravity within this chamber can cause a great deal of discomfort when it comes in contact with the rectal apparatus in your suit," she warned.

"In other words, you'll probably lose control of your anus and it will make you feel like you're flushing ten gallons of diarrhea while your intestines are coming untied at the seams," Renzo added in for flavor.

The women both looked at him in horror while Candice elbowed him in the ribs for his crude tongue. However, she admitted those were the symptoms they might expect should they not wish to follow her advice. I thought that was an informative insert into the conversation, as I had felt like sitting down myself, but noted with a quick glance around me that everyone else within the entire chamber was in fact standing on their feet. A few were leaning on the walls, but nobody was lying down to take a rest; which I had found a little odd at first.

"The others have implants which are currently stimulated into a sense of alertness, so to speak," Aaron interjected, "and those people walking around like zombies are enjoying a euphoric drug as a reward for meeting their work quota on their previous mission," he announced.

"How was it they became drugged like that?" One of the sisters asked, in worry that they might also end up in a similar helpless state.

"Actually, the chemical mix is already in your glands and released by the brain in measured amounts, its merely manipulation of those pleasure centers that allows our alien hosts to portion out any given quantity they desire," Aaron advised, "it's all self-contained in one's own body, so there is no way to use it as a form of contraband or black market trading between the prisoners," he added.

"It's actually quite ingenious if you think about it," Renzo added as the two girls gave worried glances to one another. One of them dared to ask the most obvious question.

"So, we are prisoners here?" she mumbled with tears beginning to well up in her eyes, but Candice quickly wiped them away and shook her back to her senses.

"Don't ever lose your emotions in public, that is the one thing that will give you away for certain," she snapped at them both, "yes, we are all captives here; so suck it up and deal with it or you'll get caught and have those implants jabbed in you, and you will be under their control; got it!" she barked quietly at them under her breath so as not to create a commotion. Both of them nodded in unison while Candice reaffirmed they didn't wish to become like the other abductees, and the sisters again shook their heads like puppets on a single string. Renzo waltzed over to both Aaron and I, and leaned in towards us to whisper his intuitions.

"Eh, I don't think they'll last a week," he muttered callously, "and my advice to you is not to be around when they go down," Renzo whispered as he turned his gaze towards me.

Aaron admitted that what Renzo said might have sounded cold-blooded, but he's seen it happen more often than not. Getting yourself emotionally involved in newcomers who don't possess the character strength to survive here can become a real danger, especially if they expose accomplices when they suddenly find themselves cornered. In such situations, you have to discard the idea of taking responsibility for anyone else in this mess, especially if they can't keep their own shit together. Unfortunately, as cold and heartless as that sounded, I had to admit he was right. This was an extraordinary situation which held little leeway for those who might botch things up for everyone else, especially if they lacked the willpower to keep a level head. Honestly, I began to wonder just how long I would last before falling apart. On that subject, Aaron made it clear, that if I ever lost control, then I should not expect to rely on any help, and hoped that I would have the honor not to endanger the rest of them or take anyone else down with me.

As I looked around the chamber I saw many different people of different races, and it struck me that their telepathic abilities allowed them to read each other's thoughts by translating past any language barrier; which further preserved the peace and alleviated any confrontations. The human mind was addicted to our own sense of privacy; but there clearly existed a certain level of serenity in this mind-to-mind communion observed here. For but a brief moment I began to wonder how bad it would be to be placed under the influence of the implants; and if it was solely a means of control, or possibly an enhancement to expand a wider potential in ourselves.

Above all else, a sense of freedom was the driving force behind the human psyche; but so was the sense of position and hierarchy which was embedded into our society. One of the things that got me in a lot of trouble in my career with previous jobs was that I saw everyone above and below me as equals straight across the board. I would stand up to my boss or company's CEO and speak my mind whenever I disagreed with one of their ill-designed or flagrantly asinine ideas; which almost always seemed to place more workloads on the staff and only benefited the upper managements pockets in the end. My attitude of fairness and equality in business did not go over well with the executives who weren't used to someone questioning their orders. Eh, fuck them! I had learned from experience to always, *always* question authority.

"We should meet up with Mark-1 and 2, shortly," Aaron advised as he noticed me taking my time eyeing the room, "the hybrids have better insight as to what the next assignments might be on the table, and when we may have time to slip away unnoticed to rescue any new arrivals recently placed in stasis," he offered while taking a stand beside me, "...So, what is it that you see out there, Tyler?" Aaron asked while he noticed me casually scanning the crowd.

I took a moment to consider his question, and wondering if he was judging how well I was balancing my mental shock to this situation. I tried to be as honest as I could in my reply.

"It's really not what I see, but what I don't see that has me thinking..." I trailed off in thought. Taking that context, he added his own perception.

"There are people here from every corner of the globe, many of them speaking a different language; but thanks to their implants they are able to communicate effortlessly to find common ground," he added while pointing towards different clusters of contactees, "some here only speak French, or German, or Russian; hell, I've even met one guy that spoke Swahili!," he chimed with a quirky grin, "But among this vast assortment of races you won't find any true religious zealots or anyone morbidly obese, because they want healthy specimens in both mind and body," Aaron added.

"Why does a person's religion make any difference?" I blurted out without fully considering the question.

"From what I've gathered by what the hybrids told me, is that on a fundamental level, people who are overly devotional to such fabrications of their minds inherently lack the ability of logical thinking required to survive this adaptive environment," he stated, "it doesn't matter if a person is obsessed with a fictitious god or fabricated doctrine they follow. It's not the drug use or even excessive intake of food, it's their addictive mentality they find as a critical flaw; but there is a darker side to it all as to why we were chosen," Aaron admitted. His last words left me puzzled.

"What do you mean by a *darker side?*" I asked with a confused scrunch of my brow, "It seems that being free of drugs and specimens of a relatively healthy physique would be considered positives on any scale."

"Our friend back there stated you were lucky enough to be on a resource excursion on your first outing," Aaron mentioned while referring to my mysterious bearded guide who helped me through the priming chamber, "however, there are far more dangerous missions we are expected to perform for our alien hosts," he noted while his mood drifted to a more serious tone. On that note, I took a moment to tell him about the oily black-skinned creatures with the red eyes we encountered that attacked our crew members. Aaron listened intently as I described the environment of the ship we were on and the glowing orb that came to our defense, and how it staved off the pack of beasts with a beam of light. He nodded quietly for a moment as he contemplated the events that followed and recalled what he had heard from other members among the human captives.

"Whoa ...consider yourself lucky, from what I've heard those wild little monsters are highly toxic," he stated, "they were specially bred to work in septic environments which are poisonous to others, but the toxins inherent in their systems ultimately affected their mental capacity and their breed went feral," he noted to my look of surprise.

"What," I mumbled in confusion, "...you're telling me they were bred that way?"

"I thought you would have figured it out by now," Aaron replied, "our host's utilized biometric technology to manipulate and augment DNA strands in an effort to gain their desired results. The hybrids, like our friends the Marks', are offspring from such stocks designed towards a specific project or task."

It sounded crazy until I took a moment to think about it. Back on Earth our farm and meat industry were bio-engineering crops and cattle to become more resilient to disease while also tempering them to be more productive. Genetically modified produce had caused a huge commotion among the general population, which had considered its use as unnatural and drew warranted attention towards its possible dangers. It all sounded like some deranged creation from the lab of a mad scientist, but the truth was we had been doing it for decades. Most people and many specialists in the field were rightfully worried about mutations that might escape such controlled environments and throw the entire ecosystem of our planet out of whack. There had been more than enough horror films made on the subject, which only fueled the fears of the public.

Many people didn't approve of scientists playing God, especially in the arena of eugenics. I could only imagine what an advanced intelligence might be able to do with it. These beings were at a stage where they could integrate both carbon and silicon into usable technologies. Having considered that I wondered why our experts separated Animal, Vegetable and Mineral; when all of these categories were actually living and growing substances. If one could step far outside the box to see how they were combined, they would find that its applications were endless. Honestly, the potential of it was beyond my comprehension; but that's probably why I loved the imagination and wonderment of science fiction so much.

Candice stayed behind to console the two sisters who were on the verge of a breakdown, while Aaron, Renzo, and I went to find Mark-1 and 2. The far end of the enormous chamber was noticeably darker than the rest of the cell, which is where we approached the border where the hybrids had quarantined themselves from us lowly humans. At Aaron's direction, we waited for a moment at a distance, and turned to make our way back into the crowd when he gave the sign. At this, I turned to notice that three of the hybrids separated themselves from their group and began to follow us, which got me worried.

Not to sound racist, but they all looked alike to me. The three bald-headed beings closed in on our trio as we stood just inside the fringe of the all-human crowd.

"My apologies for the apparent segregation," I heard a voice in my head announce, though I was a little surprised since Mark-1 didn't need to make physical contact to achieve a mental connection. I clearly jumped at the sound of his voice, and Aaron placed his hand on my shoulder to calm my apparent dismay. Aaron turned back to Mark-1 and 2, without making a sound, so I presumed they were speaking telepathically.

"We have brought a friend," Mark-2 announced, "he is willing to take the designation of Mark-3, if you desire," he noted to the rest of us. I was a tad surprised how quickly Aaron offered his trust to this new recruit, but I imagine that the hybrids were beyond acts of betrayal and other unsavory human traits.

"Greetings to you," Mark-3 introduced himself with a slight bow as he joined our group.

"We will address Mark-3's situational issues once we can convene again at the cube," Mark-1 stated as he referred to our hidden sanctuary below deck, "there is, however, a matter of urgency that we were made aware of recently. There is an upcoming conflict posted on the data stream that is considered to be flagged for a hostile confrontation within the next five cycles," he stated in a flat tone. Aaron's face washed over in a grim repose as his companion mentioned this news.

"Uh, how long is five cycles," I blurted out loud, "Is that like a year or a month, or what...?"

Without answering me, Aaron took Mark-1 by the shoulder and they both turned away from the others; apparently to conclude their dialog in a private conversation.

"Don't worry yourself about it," Renzo cut in, though he also failed to answer my inquiry, "Two, are you sure certain of this information?" he asked.

"Most ...certain," Mark-2 stumbled in thought as he searched for the correct word, though I had to remember that translations were variable to the listener, "assured, affirmative, yes," he finished ascertaining the correct phrase.

"Yes, but how long is a cycle?" I pressed again to no avail.

"Whom are we facing?" Renzo inquired as he left Mark-1 and Aaron to their private deliberations.

"....*" a faint hum echoed in my head as I saw flashes of light and blinked my eyes wildly as I thought I was about to pass out, "my apologies, it appears their verbal designation is not known to you," Mark-2 addressed towards me.

Stepping out of character, Renzo was courteous enough to inform me that their form of telepathy relies heavily on images to translate information in a faster and far more proficient manner, but it has its limitations. Aaron and his hybrid friend turned back to us and made an announcement I didn't care to hear. From the report by the hybrids, a large number of our human crew would be drafted for a duty battalion to lay a counter-assault against an alien race who had trespassed against our hosts.

"A race they call the 'Anu', as you pronounce it in your speech, have violated a territory treaty against a disabled Overlord reconnaissance ship, and must be driven back in order to reclaim their lost vessel," Mark-1 clarified for us, "they are even risking the hybrids on this excursion in an attempt to rectify the situation."

"You mean we will be going to war against another species and they're expecting us to fight for them?" I blurted out as my words caught in my throat. The last thing I wanted to do was to be involved in combat, and the way Mark-1 made it sound was that they pretty much considered their human counterparts as expendable.

Renzo advised me in so many words, that there would be a training drill on the use of the Overlords weaponry. Such confrontations were few and far between, but Renzo himself was one of the survivors of such a raid. He had once been assigned to a squadron on a strange white world riddled with yawning chasms, which cut deeply into its ivory surface. The planetoid itself had a large moon that spun on a wide elliptical orbit that frequently brought it precariously close to its host planet.

At the bottom of these chasms flowed raging rivers, pulled by the ebb and tide of its celestial counterpart. Once every period, the angry currents lurking below would rise as the swell of gravity would surge to flood the surface by hundreds of feet in a display of its remarkable high tide. The dwellers of this world had adapted to these extremes by fabricating towers molded from the pale stone upon its surface, which were hollow and adorned with transparent domes. This unique

design trapped a breathable atmosphere within these sub-
aquatic sanctuaries during the cycles of its rising seas, until the
waters once again subsided beneath the surface.

It's native species were adapted to living on both land and sea
and were, in all respects, a graceful merger between amphibian
and reptile. These beings were distinctly larger than the
average human and were covered in fine scales that glistened in
the warm light of their twin suns. They were unmistakable in
their appearance, as one might imagine what a humanoid might
have evolved in to from the ancestry of dinosaurs; had those
magnificent creatures not met their demise on ancient Earth.
Renzo had been assigned to a squadron deployed to achieve a
single mission with orders to sabotage their domes.

The human crew had been suited with breathing devices and
instructed to apply markers onto the exposed areas of the dome
vaults at the initiation of the high tide. Renzo and his team had
been dropped from armed vessels into the rising waters, one
crew member per target. They were to apply a simple
triangular marker onto the exposed sections of each structural
dome and await extraction on the ocean surface. He could only
deduce that there was something in the water itself which
interfered with the operation of the scout ships; and thus,
required this alternative plan to meet their objective.

They were told nobody would be present in the domes
themselves. However, that allegation turned out to be a lie.
Dropped on his target, he was instructed to hold onto a silver
rectangle box with a looped handle, and Renzo couldn't help
but joke to himself that it resembled a small beer cooler.
Stepping from the vehicle and into a light source, the carrier
device slowly descended within the beam until he hit the
water's edge. Frankly, he was half tempted to let go of the
handle during his descent just to see what might happen; but
fear and common sense kept him from such recklessness. The
silver device remained floating above as he ducked below the
surface waters and made his way to the strange habitat now
submerged below the rising ocean.

Renzo couldn't help but pause at the beauty of his surroundings as he floated in the crystal sea glittering with rays of sunlight cutting through its brilliant turquoise waters. There was life here in the form of delicate creatures swimming to and fro through the wild currents and eddies. For a brief moment, he felt at peace, suspended in this exotic aquarium of dancing lights. Once he reached the dome, he pressed the packet to its shell as instructed, and prepared to return to the surface for retrieval. Peering below into this alien dwelling, he saw two reptilian creatures sleeping within. They were laying head to foot while encircling a glowing stone, and appeared to be in a state of hibernation, entirely oblivious to their human visitor lingering outside their window.

Renzo realized the deceit too late and made an effort to remove the target marker he had affixed moments before. However, his attempts at prying it loose were in vain, as the water itself acted against him to leave his hands slipping across the smooth surface of the dome. He had no wish to cause these innocent creatures harm, and tried to beat against the transparent dome in an attempt to warn them, to no avail. The creatures were dormant and his presence went unnoticed. He had no animosity against these entities whose world they had invaded, but he was a slave to the Overlords for his own survival and risked being left abandoned on this alien world to face his own fate if he failed to comply.

Life on the harvest ship was chancy enough since he took the risk of being caught and reprocessed, or placed in suspension. On one occasion, Renzo was out on an excursion from their sanctuary beneath the Cube, when he had stumbled across several stasis pods. There, he discovered a vast array of animals held within these capsules, such as one which appeared to be a mountain bear, and yet another that contained a domestic dog, all pressed between transparent sheets of some type of thick sheath as if they had been vacuum packed for preservation while saturated in a milky liquid.

One particular sack contained a human, or what was left of

one. Their gender was indistinguishable from the condition it was now in; having been left and forgotten for a great period of time. In these late stages, this unfortunate victim's bones had effectively liquefied into jelly and their organs pressed together without the assistance of skeletal support. Though he was left stunned and disgusted by what he had seen; a morbid fascination overcame him as he peered into the alien container to get a closer look at this corpse being absorbed by the ship. Within the sheath, an eyelid suddenly blinked open and turned its varnished gaze towards him as he leaned in, mere inches away from his face, while the fine muscles of its softened jaw began twitching as if trying to speak.

It was a horrifying moment Renzo would never forget; for the image of it still haunts his dreams to this day. Even though there was no voice from this poor soul, all he could imagine was hearing its silent cries echoing over and over again in his head, begging: "...*Help me.*"

He had stumbled away from that living nightmare in a daze, knowing that the words of that dreadful plea were but a reflection from his disturbed mind. Renzo cracked that day and was never the same person since. He didn't fear death, but he would never allow himself to go like that.

The irony of it was that he was now the curious looking alien trespassing on a sovereign world; peering uninvited into the lives of other beings who slumbered in their abode; oblivious to his intrusion. He was momentarily free from the Overlords captivity, although once his oxygen apparatus ceased to function, he would either suffocate from drowning or choke to death in this foreign atmosphere. It was just as likely these scaled beings would capture him and dissect his body into pieces in their curiosity to see how humans work. His soft brownish skin, along with his hairy head and small eyes would be exotic and freakish abnormalities to these reptilian creatures.

His oxygen apparatus beckoned for him to resurface, so he turned and made his way to the open sky. Finding the buoyant silver device, he held onto its handle as the waves lashed across the surface. The winds above became increasingly violent with the approach of the enormous moon, which lingered like a giant looming above in the bright amethyst sky. In a flash, the glowing orb of a scout ship seared through the clouds and positioned itself directly above him.

From it washed a trail of blue light, which tugged on the silver transport device as it began to rise into the belly of the ship. Ascending in the glow of the beam, Renzo found himself safely back onboard; only to turn and watch helplessly through the portal as a solid white ray of light shot out from his vessel and pierced the water below. Moments later, a deluge of air and gas bubbled to the surface from the ruptured dome; and Renzo felt grief for what he had done and the beings he had aided to murder in their sleep. After that particular mission, Renzo noticed that several of their crew had not made it back to the ship; which had likely died as the sunken domes ruptured or their bodies had been beaten into submission by the raging currents on this strange alien world.

He never found out why his hosts had attacked the Reptilians in such a cowardly manner; but whatever campaign the Overlords had in mind for them in this upcoming tour, it was certain to be treacherous. It was these personal sacrifices of character we traded for our own survival; which is likely why they had chosen mankind for such ventures, for our species could always be relied upon to act with selfish conformity and fearful obedience. After all, our societies had already groomed us to think that way, and we weren't about to change our nature.

Influence

After many questions and much grief, I finally discovered that what they had referred too as a cycle period on this harvester ship was of no real defined set of time; but actually a reference to when the captives were herded from one section to another. It was during these semi-chaotic periods that so inclined individuals, such as ourselves, could slip away unnoticed into the elaborate venting system and find our way back to the Cube. This also allowed for the rare opportunities to scavenge for supplies and add new recruits into our secret rebellion. Aaron corrected my opinion on that caption, pointing out that we wouldn't be throwing a revolution anytime soon. From what the hybrids told us, there were far more human captives onboard than there were actual numbers of our alien hosts, who controlled the internal operations of the ship.

Mark-1 stated that one of the revolving rumors among the hybrids was that these intergalactic vessels were far older than we could imagine, but it was widely speculated that the full measure of its technology had been lost over time. The Overlords who now controlled this ship and others of its kind did not have full knowledge of its functions. If some system should ever break down, they relied heavily on the biological repair operations of the vessel to fix itself. Although it was designed to do just that, there had been rare occasions when there was nothing they could do if a critical system became severely damaged. The knowledge from the original builders of these types of craft had been lost to the ages and they were at the mercy of the ship if they should experience any catastrophic failures.

In a way, this made a bit of sense, as I recalled that my grandfather used to have one of the first editions of classic cars back in the early '50s. If anything broke on the vehicle, it was simple enough to fix if you knew how; but what the auto

manufacturers came out with nowadays were comprised of
bundles of computer chips and erroneous sensors. If your car
stopped working, you had to bring it to one of their goddamn
shops to get it fixed no matter how simple the repair; there was
no doing it yourself in your garage anymore. Truth be told, I
figured car companies designed their vehicles that way on
purpose so that consumers would continue to be reliant on
them to fix their own products.

I remember going out to dinner one time with my well-to-do
friend and some poor fellow parked beside us in the lot had his
battery die on him. He had jumper cables in hand so we lifted
up the hood for the very first time of my friend's fancy new car,
and for the life of us, we couldn't even find the goddamn
battery. We didn't even possess the special tools it would take
to open the engine compartment which looked like it was
sealed up like a tank. All three of us stood there baffled and
just shrugged our shoulders, and we had to leave him there for
someone else to assist.

That episode was pretty much a prime example that showed
how modern technology was making us far less self-reliant. It
used to be that components were pretty straight forward. If the
connection on your corded phone was going goofy, then you
could open it up with a screwdriver and fix the loose wire; but
the average person simply couldn't pull that bullshit nowadays
with all the microchips and wireless communications boards
packed into cell phones. More than once I've asked myself; are
we actually making life better with all this crap, or just
distracting ourselves from the importance of what really
matters? Sure, it was a deep question; but I liked to think of
myself as a philosophical type.

We had all slipped away during the following transference
cycle and made our way back to the Cube and found myself
increasingly interested in learning the functions of the ship I
had seen thus far. When I asked Mark-1 about the enormous
silver box positioned above our little sanctum, he could only
offer wild speculation as to its purpose. This was a matter that

I found unsettling, solely for the reason that if we were ever going to escape this life of servitude, we would have to gain better knowledge as to the operations of the ship. For one, I wouldn't want to hop into an alien escape pod only to discover too late that the atmosphere within might be too toxic for our frail human lungs to endure.

From what the group stated, there were a great many things on this space barge that could kill you. Asking the hybrids, I wondered if they were knowledgeable of a written language these aliens used so we could at least have a half-assed chance of identifying tools or vital sections of the ship. Both Mark-1 and 2 were present and shook their heads to mimic their human counterparts.

"Even if you could interpret visual symbols, there would be no way to translate their meaning into your limited language," Mark-2 offered as a tribute to my utter ignorance.

"Well, aren't there basic symbols we could memorize for what's useful or what's dangerous?" I pleaded as I tried to offer a shade of logic to my obtuse inquiry. I was thinking of simple things like food, or water, what might be hot, cold, or poisonous, and other basic crap one might find on any label or sign. Though again, I was thinking purely in small-human-mind terms as far as they were concerned.

"Such symbols you are inquiring about rely on weaving emotions and visual clues to identify a specific function or object in a way you simply would not be able to decode," Mark-2 offered again.

Aaron tried to console my rising exasperation; and reminded me that even on Earth, with our hundreds of modern languages, that there were far too many variables to consider. Mark pressed the insult further by stating that I was utilizing a two-dimensional question to decipher a five-dimensional problem. Then again, these two hybrids had never been on Earth themselves to view the signs we commonly used for international identification by people of almost every language. Still, he was proficient at making me feel like a real retard for trying to make my point.

"We have a symbol of flames for what's 'flammable' and one for male or female bathrooms; or a skull for what's deadly or poisonous..." I tried to press, but he was apparently immune to my idolized argument.

"There are several thousand species in the relative universe known to us in this era; of which, a vast majority whose 'head' appendage, among those who possess them, differ vastly from that of a human. Besides which, even if they had never actually seen a human head without its flesh; they might very well fail to recognize what a skull was; let alone its meaning," he stated bluntly as a look of disdain began to well in my eyes, "Even with my limited knowledge, I am aware of well over three million flammable elements; and how would anyone recognize a 'flame' if they have never seen one burning within an atmosphere customary for your species?" he related, although he started to sound chastising by the way he said it.

"Look, dude, you're overcomplicating the question," I nudged in as a reply, "is there anything in their written language we could use to our advantage or not?"

"I hate to answer a question with a question, but did you also realize that there are androgynous beings and those with more than five or six genders. There are even life forms which reproduce by means you would find relatively impossible," Mark-2 took a position of defense, "and from what I understand of your modern culture, there are not even bathing facilities or actual 'baths', as you title them, within your so-called public bathrooms!"

"You mean restrooms..." I tried to correct, so as not to sound like an idiot; at which I failed entirely.

"I beg to ask; do your citizens actually 'rest' in these rooms; in order to sleep or relax and recuperate?" he flung back at me. I just stood there with a stupid frown etched upon my face.

"...No," I finally admitted with a scornful frown.

"So, as to make my point; it seems that even your so-called commonplace language symbols are a complete ruse," Mark-2 cited as his hybrid twin nodded in agreement beside him, "...now take that pattern of confusion and multiply it a thousandfold if you wish to apply it to your current inquiry."

The hybrids had made their point while Aaron looked on; seemingly enjoying the absurd humor of our conversation. Apparently, it was quite a rare occasion to have someone impress him in such a manner and juggle an array of such out-of-the-box modes of thinking; even though I had respectfully lost the argument on all grounds.

"I have to ask Tyler," he leaned forward as the hybrids left to the other side of the platform, "did you happen to know what your IQ rating was in college?" In response, I had to think long and hard for a moment trying to recall my scope of education.

"Well actually, it was well over 140 before I even entered high school," I admitted, though not trying to brag about it, but just stating the facts.

"And how would you account for that significant ratio, Tyler," he inquired, "...did you realize that score places your base intelligence in the top 1% of our entire world population?

"Um, no..." I admitted and was frankly surprised by this.

"So, let me ask what job you had before being swept away here to our grand alien resort," Aaron inquired, "were you an engineer, or in any doctorate or scientific field?"

"Uh, no..." I blurted again, sounding like a broken record, "I was just managing a stupid little restaurant," I admitted with a sense of embarrassment.

"So my question is, what was a person of your level of intelligence and analytical frame of mind doing working at such a low scale job; when you have such a higher potential?" Aaron asked as he pinned me under a spotlight. I could see by the look in his eyes that the question wasn't geared to be insulting; but that he was trying to underline the answer I was about to give.

"Well, actually it might be because I got an encyclopedia set as a gift for the holidays one year when I was just a kid..." I began; though Aaron cut in a quick question which carried the sting of a razor as he said it.

"And I assume this was after the time you began experiencing contacts?" He framed his inquiry, and I nodded in agreement, "please, do go on..." he offered in return with a gesture for me to continue my story.

"I know it might make me sound like a nerd, but I thought those encyclopedias were the best gift I ever got at the time; since we were fairly poor and unable to really travel much, I learned about the world by reading through every single edition of the entire set, A-through-Z," I smiled unconsciously as I remembered my desire to absorb information. This, of course, was in a time long before there was such a thing as the internet, and such vast access of information wasn't available at one's fingertips on the scale it was in today's world.

"So you had a genius level IQ prior to High School, and how did your studies go from there?" Aaron asked as he led the direction of our conversation.

"Well, I graduated two years ahead of my class at the age of 16," I shrugged, not trying to seem like I was boasting; because I certainly wasn't, "I was jumped up in credits and grades and took several summer school classes to get it over with."

"Did you go to college from there?" Aaron urged that I finish; though he offered a softened glance and a shrug as a response to my wistful answer.

"Well, no; not right away. That was a time close to when my mother died from contracting her mysterious cancer, and I was on my own after that, since I was only 17, and work was hard to find at that age," I blubbered with a noticeable edge of remorse cutting into my voice.

"And would you say your demeanor changed after your mother passed?" He asked.

"Oh, absolutely," I admitted without hesitation, "I can guess you can say I was a strange child, but I never saw myself as smart or exceptional. I just felt..." I tried to search for the right words as Aaron hijacked my train of thought.

"That perhaps you were somehow out of place, and even felt a little detached from everything?" Aaron added while the familiar content of his words rung like a bell.

"Yeah, something like that," I had to admit to myself; now realizing the oddity of my teenage years. I had been labeled as a Savant, but honestly, there were far more times in my sorry life than I could count when I was left feeling like an idiot, more than anything else. I didn't *feel* special; I just recognized that I saw the world from a different perspective than most.

"Believe it or not Tyler, your story runs along the same line as Candice, Renzo, and myself; and pretty much everyone else you saw back there in the holding areas," Aaron stated as he consoled my apprehensions while revealing that there were many others who had suffered the same fractured views in their own pitiful lives, "Abductions happen to people from all walks of life across the globe, but there is something unique about the people who get snatched up by the Harvesters that most all of us have in common."

"...That we all got sick of the rat-race, and saw it for what it was," Renzo edged in after overhearing our conversation. I had to admit that I identified with what he had said. Most of modern human society could be viewed as one giant clusterfuck if you looked at it from a certain perspective. We had seen past all the bullshit and artificial perceptions, and broken them down to their simple components. The truth was, I never saw the purpose in over-analyzing anything and possessed a certain level of clarity, and admit that I had spent my adult life confused to the point of being aggravated as to why most others couldn't see it.

That sudden realization hit me like a brick. We were on a ship full of contactees who had been plucked like weeds from our world because we noticed something beyond the norm outside of the usual spectrum. The real question was why? Did our alien hosts perceive us as merely deranged loners who wouldn't be missed; or were we somehow a danger to them and the world around us, or did those few of us represent a risk that might jeopardize their agenda ...whatever that might be. It was aggravating not to have the answers laid out plain and simple, but it was difficult to analyze something you couldn't fully understand.

"Are you afraid to die, Tyler?" Aarons tone turned lightly inquisitive, despite the seriousness of his question.

"Well, it's something we all have to face one day or another," I responded bluntly while shaking my head to answer.

"And how would you fit a square peg into a round hole?" he continued to interrogate with an odd set of questions. With a shrug, I just blurted my answer without thinking.

"Easy, just make the hole wider," I remarked.

A stupid look of satisfaction washed over Aarons face as he smiled at my response; as he noticed I finally got the gist of what he was getting at. The clue he was trying to point out was that all of the fellow contactees on the harvest ship shared a basic cohesive perspective, which varied greatly from the rest of the human race.

"You see, Aaron smiled, "you instinctually chose to change the perimeters of a given objective, rather than alter the objective itself to fit what it was not designed for."

Honestly, it took me a moment to wrap my head around that philosophical analogy. Aaron confirmed with Renzo that there were several thousand human captives mingling in the multiple melding chambers present within the belly of the ship, and concurred with the reports that a vast majority of them had previously resided far away from large cities and lived out in the country by choice. After admitting that I had also lived in a cabin out in the boonies when I was taken, it was my assumption that this was only relevant because it made abductions easier to perform unnoticed in such remote locations. My presumptions were entirely wrong.

"All three of us here also had jobs and careers in large cities, but felt an overpowering unease which led us to seek more solitary lives," Renzo related with a hint of reminiscence lingering in his voice.

I had to concede that I was uncomfortable in big cities; but felt it was a result of my loathing of all the concrete and pavement rather than with the incessant noise and the rowdy crowds. The result was that subconsciously or not, in our individual life choices we had effectively separated ourselves from the herd.

After a moment of deep thought, I knew he was right. I didn't care about money, or fame, or acquiring possessions, which the rest of the masses were infatuated with; I wasn't co-dependent and was perfectly happy being alone. I even felt a little guilty about that, thinking that I was just physiologically bent towards being anti-social; but the underlying roots of that motivation were germinated by something else entirely. The abductees represented the minority of the population who sensed a growing anxiety and distaste for the direction that our society, and our species, as a whole, were heading and resisted becoming a part of it. If so, then why were we granted the unassuming honor to serve as slaves upon an alien harvest ship? The answer to that was equally confusing.

"Every person you have seen here on this vessel has been influenced on one level or another to defy a certain method of thinking," Aaron granted as an answer to the questions welling in my eyes while I was searching for answers, "our religious convictions are relatively more relaxed or entirely non-existent, because we see beyond such wrappings as shells gilded with worthless propaganda. We see the value of life in ways others find trivial, and a connection to the elements on a ...well, on a more elemental level," he finished with a shrug.

I had to confess that the core of what he was saying rang true, and that my daily life had been tainted by the madness of those people who ran our Governments and their needless wars, including the baseless violence they perpetuated. The masses were prodded and swayed by deceit, and influenced to follow the personal agendas of those few who held the reigns of power, contrary to the will of the many. Fundamentally, anyone could take a step back and say *'No, I'm not going to participate in this'* and stop the immoral conduct in its tracks.

However, our society put up these illusionary fabrications of power in the hands of puppeteers; and anybody who dared to raise their scissors to cut the strings were quickly silenced as punishment, and furthermore, were made an example of to all others who might have shared the same idea of freeing ourselves from our suffocating suppression.

The most bewildering thing I simply couldn't absorb was the lack of honor in those who were lifted to such positions of power; and how they turned their offices towards serving themselves, instead of using that rare opportunity to make such positive and necessary changes for the many. In all honesty, I squarely put most of the blame in those who closely encapsulated such deceit and corruption; who in turn, did nothing to stop the madness. If I had things my way, all politics and military would be wiped from existence; for I saw no need for it as others might. We were all people sharing the same planet together, and there was no need to divide it.

Even with that insight, Aaron himself wasn't quite sure if our Overlords saw us as a benefit or a hindrance to their overall scheme of things. Regardless, these creatures had a unique perspective to see everything as a resource that could be utilized in either one form or another. I wondered if such a heightened overview was the result of untold centuries of evolution, or if they had once been similar to mankind at a certain stage of their development; both ornery and cruel.

From what the hybrids had exposed beforehand, was that any communication between humans and our alien hosts would always be crippled; since we were unable to understand or perceive the delicate shades of their true intent. Thus, as humans being human; we would always presume the worst and fear the unknown. Our species had a particular talent for that.

Candice, herself, thought it was a real hoot that all of us in the servant class of this harvest ship possessed the same hippy tree-hugger sense of enlightenment; but that our only reward in the end for that ideology was to risk our lives serving as slaves upon this space barge. Aaron tried to argue her point, as he remarked that he didn't truly believe such widespread grooming would be for the sole purpose of being recruited as mere meat-shields for some intergalactic warmongers. Although, he grudgingly admitted that he lacked any proof to support that viewpoint. Aaron had seen a lot of humans on this ship die needlessly, and he personally struggled to make sense of it like the rest of us.

The hybrids had been meant to fill a crucial role in the Overlords strategy, to prepare humanity with a new set of tools in an effort to help redirect our course of evolution. The clones aboard this ship, however, were not yet perfected and would fail to blend into the human society in their current state because of their outward appearance. Vicious racism was an enormous hurdle that had plagued our species for countless millennia, and introduction of hybrids at this time would only backfire. Thus, new generations with more linear human appearance were being processed, and early-stage specimens such as Mark-1 and 2 were retired from their original strategy and repurposed to serve the needs of the ship's crew. On these galactic vessels, nothing went to waste.

This left the hybrids with their own dilemma as they strived to survive by their wits and prove their value in servitude to the Overlords. They recognized themselves as merely a biological resource to a dominant species and did not contest that fact, and for some reason that irked me more than it should have. Being subservient to another had always yanked my chain, and it made me wonder as to why the Hybrids, with their clearly expanded level of intellect, had not challenged their captors to secure their own freedom. When I confronted Mark-2 with that question, his reaction was one of confusion as to how I could even concoct such a suggestion without possessing the faintest idea to the scope of their situation.

Rebellion, it seems, had been bred out of them. Logic and rational thought was their dominant impulse to exercise in any situation. They held no animosity for their treatment, for they were well fed, and cared for, and sought no desire for personal gain, which was simply not in their nature. They saw mortality in a entirely different spectrum than most; because they did not cling to such weaknesses as fearing the unknown. To them, death was only a cycle in the most simplistic terms; far removed from the provisions dictated by the gilded fantasies of our world religions.

Candice had left the two sisters behind in the melding chamber with instructions to not bring attention to themselves. If we were going to be set on a battlefield, there was likely little chance they would survive. Most abductees who lacked implants got themselves killed within the short term; I planned on not adding myself to their ranks. If there was a way out of this, I was going to find it.

On Aaron's suggestion, I was to accompany Candice on one of her excursions to scavenge supplies from the far corners of the harvest ship. I jumped at the chance since I was curious as hell to explore the structure of this alien vessel and learn what I could to heighten my own chances of survival. Once outside the sanctuary chamber, she made it clear that I was to follow her lead and every instruction to the letter; and I agreed. Both she and Renzo were far more intense than Aaron ever appeared to be, although I didn't know the full stories behind their history; either in their previous life, or how their experiences might have molded them during their tour upon this ship.

Once we climbed through the tubing and onto a service deck, we made our way to a disposal area where newly acquired abductees were stripped of their clothing and personal items before being placed in their selective groups or packaged into suspension sheaths.

"Do you have any idea why I was chosen to be placed in stasis?" I whispered to Candice as she tiptoed through the corridor in front of me.

"Most likely because you're goofy looking, and you suck at following instructions," she quipped back at me with a dash of venom in her tone. Clearly, she didn't like me being too talkative while we were performing our reconnaissance.

"Sorry, I was just..." I began to blabber apologetically, feeling like I had said something wrong. The one thing I had figured was important to hold onto would be a sense of humor and friendship, but I guess I was expecting too much.

"You saw those two sisters from before; the ones we left behind in the melding chamber, right?" she snapped with a drop of bitterness.

"Yeah, what about them?" I replied.

"I didn't get too chummy with them because they lacked any capacity to maintain a rational attitude in order to survive this place," she breathed quietly, "the number of us who are free of implants are few and far between, and we only survive by exercising caution and practical thinking."

Her words made perfect sense, since it was obvious that this situation was unprecedented, and that the level of shit could get neck-deep in a heartbeat. Candice weaved us a trail through several corridors as we climbed an uncountable number of levels, until we eventually arrived in a small chamber located next to some sort of bay which contained a cache of spheres of all sizes set within the walls.

"What are those things?" I asked, dumbfounded.

"You must have seen photos or heard stories of glowing spheres or foo-fighters before..." she led on. The truth was, I actually had. I, like many other contactees, spend a great deal of our lives researching the troubling mystery behind our experience with alien encounters; but unfortunately, this usually led down a rabbit hole which always produced more unsettling questions than answers.

"I think so. So these are like smaller ships they send out on recon?" I inquired without trying to sound too much like an idiot, "Some of those appear far too small for any creature to fit into."

"That's because they're drones," she replied, "unmanned vehicles we believe they use for surveillance and tracking specific targets."

"Targets like us?" I suggested with unease.

"Like presidential and military transports; or anyone of particular interests such as molecular or nuclear scientists, etc," she explained. Asking her how she knew this, it was her presumption based on data she had collected before she had been harvested.

"And what about the larger ones?" I asked with interest.

"Merely bigger drones, although they possess a cabin to carry one or two of those bastards, as far as I can tell," she granted.

They had tried to get their hybrid friends to verify this hypothesis for them, but the clones revealed they were not specifically instructed on the workings of these airborne vehicles or how they functioned. That made practical sense on a certain level, that the Overlords had refrained from educating their subservient hybrids on particular vital functions of the vessel and these scout ships, which could respectively become a security risk to their hosts. I wanted to look inside of one and see how it worked. However, Candice warned me that being a curious cat on a Harvester could eat up all my nine lives in a heartbeat; and was warned not to wander off on my own.

"I don't understand why Aaron is so worried about the pending encounter," I stated bluntly, "wouldn't it be more practical to simply hide within the sanctuary beneath the Cube until the conflict is over, and then blend back into the group after the danger had passed?" The plan made perfect sense to me, but her hard glare didn't make me feel any better about my so-called bright idea.

"For one, just because our fellow crew members have implants doesn't make them any more disposable than the rest of us; we have to look out for one another," Candice chastised me for my craven selfishness, "and two, if by some unfortunate chance this ship should sustain damage during a battle and they are forced to purge the energy core, then it's lights-out for anyone hiding in the sanctum!"

Candice had a talent at making me feel like a dolt, so I concluded that it would be far less scarring to my ego if I just shut the hell up and let her offer advice on her own initiative.

The stripping room we had entered was formed like a half-circle with curved edges rising along the floor. There were trousers, and coats, and assorted junk tossed around like so much trash. She made the rounds up here frequently to see if there were any new items dropped by recent victims. Something useful like a pocket knife or anything else that could be used as a tool; so she sent me rifling through the pile on one side of the room while she took the other.

Personally, I was kind of hoping to find a snack bar or a lunchbox, since the embryonic fluid in my system had started to wear off and I began to feel the sting of hunger, and wasn't terribly keen on eating that goop the hybrids had stocked for us. I was surprised to hear that we were usually only given nutrients within the priming chambers, like the crystal-filled room where I had met my nameless guide. Liquids were reclaimed to a certain degree, and nutrients delivered by microspores were fed into the melding chambers, which were absorbed by the suits we all wore.

It was becoming ever clear that these second skins we adorned kept us alive in more ways than one. The hybrids, themselves, were provided with additional supplements, and it was the Mark's who helped supply the excess stocks to our group back in the sanctum, as that particular section of the ship was cut off from whatever vapor that was used to adjust our dietary needs, which were filtered through our uniforms. Within the piles of garb, we found a few minor items like a car remote and a dead flashlight, which Candice saved for Renzo, who was handy at electronics, and could possibly make something useful for us to jerry-rig this alien tech. I was still curious as to how those drones in the bay operated, but Candice wasn't in the mood to do a great deal of explaining.

"When they are activated, plasma ripples over the orbs skin, lighting it up like a giant lamp," she stated, "from what I've learned, some of their ships are powered by an electromagnetic liquid core which counter-flows an energy field around the entire vehicle; isolating it from any localized gravity wells."

That sounded fairly complicated, but I could just imagine all the cool shit any aeronautics engineer could make out of a liquid magnet. I would ascertain that they utilized something far more complex than mere radio waves to control these drones, or whatever it was they were using for interstellar communications. Candice told me I could go jump in a lake if I thought she was going to try to explain that one. Although, it had been Renzo, himself, who once told me there was more to this than the eye could see; let alone what the Hybrids weren't telling us.

While rifling through the piles of clothing we heard a low hum begin to course through the flooring beneath our feet. In a flash, a small ball of light shot past our location and down the corridor we had taken. A worried look washed over Candice's face as we stood there stunned by what had just happened.

"What the hell ...was that a drone?" I dared to whisper to her, though she was already starting to pick up her pace as we began heading back to the sanctuary of the Cube.

"That's it, this field trip is over, kid," was all she cracked towards me as we began to backtrack our way to the sanctuary. We were caught off guard when a large shadow emerged at the end of the curved tunnel where we were heading. It appeared as if the end of corridor was filled by a moving wall, and we found ourselves squarely in its path.

"Here, get in!" Candice barked as she motioned for me to prostrate myself into a hollow on the outer edge of the concave floor. We both crammed ourselves into the small space and I began to wonder what grand idea this was of hers as we watched the black shadow approach. With a pulsating hiss, a thick section of metal passed over us as it consumed the entire hallway where we had just stood moments before; and slowly continued on its course through the corridor.

"What was that?" I blurted quietly as we lifted ourselves out of the tight coffin in the flooring.

"It's some sort of automated sanitizer," she answered, "but that's one housemaid you don't want to be in the path of,"

Candice warned.

I would imagine so, as it slowed to a crawl in the area where we had been searching the stacks of discarded clothing and trash. I could see strings of electricity snake from it around the debris lying upon the floor. Candice grabbed my arm as I stood there gawking at the fireworks, and we led ourselves back through the storage bay for the orb drone ships. Traversing across the small gangplank, we saw that there were now several small orbs missing from their sections, leaving empty dimples where they had once been docked.

A handful of the orbs both large and small were slowly rotating in position; which we took as our cue to make ourselves scarce. I was wondering if we had been detected somehow but did note that the glowing drone which had zipped by us earlier, hadn't given us a moment's notice. Candice, on the other hand, was desperate to make it back to the sanctum to report what she had seen. As we retreated through the familiar sections, a blue radiance began to light up the walls around us.

"Oh shit!" Candice blurted, and I was just about to ask her what was going on when we were both suddenly slammed to the floor. The next moment, the ground abruptly pushed away from us and we found ourselves floating off the floor, completely helpless. I tried to call out to her in a panic to inquire what we should do, but no sound came out of my mouth when I spoke. Seeing her face, she too was trying to tell me something, but we were caught in an atmospheric pocket void of all sound. I had never been weightless before; and though it wasn't entirely unpleasant, I could feel a wave of nausea starting to surge through every point in my body and couldn't help but clench my eyes shut as my vision started spinning uncontrollably.

The floor slowly began to greet us once again as we were laid gently onto the deck; and as my ears popped, I noticed I was sucking in a gasp of air which had been entirely drained from my lungs in that captive moment. We both laid there trying to get our bearings when a sudden arc of charged electricity danced through the corridor. Frightened as we were, it was too fast to outrun and overcame us in mere seconds as it passed. We both came out of it neither worse for wear, although it stung like a bitch wherever it touched our suits as it flashed over us. Within moments, the gravity was back to normal, and Candice stood up in a rehearsed motion to brush herself off.

"The ship just jumped, let's get back," she spat.

"Jumped ...jumped where?" I blurted like an idiot in pursuit of Candice as she raced ahead.

"Likely to another star system," she answered without pause.

Misinformation

We got back to the Cube and realized that the space jump went mostly unnoticed within the sanctuary, since there happen to be several redundant safety protocols which actively stabilized every system linked to the energy core of the ship. It was a long while before Mark-2 returned with news from the melding chamber where the other abductees were currently being held.

"Sirs, and lady," Mark-2 began, while practicing his social etiquette, "this vessel has been reestablished at the outer edge of a solar system where our ground troops will be deployed. From my intel, there are four sentient species at a current state of conflict within this region of space."

His words pretty much described the tensions between countries anywhere on Earth any given day of the week. If we were to be a part of this mission, we had to get ourselves back to the main group and await deployment. Personally, I was more than a little concerned about jumping willy-nilly into an alien war; but there was no honor in hiding like a scared rat in the belly of the ship. On the other hand, there was no honorable sacrifice in dying either, as Renzo pointed out; but hopefully it wouldn't come to that.

"Tyler, a word," Aaron added in haste while the rest of the group packed away any useful gear and making their way back to the melding chamber, "as I've showed you before, this is a power node," he stated while showing me a golf ball-sized metal sphere, "there is a chance that we might be assigned weapons on this excursion, and if you see any extras of these lying around, you snatch 'em up, got it?" he added with a slap on my back.

I nodded in agreement and followed him back to the chamber vents, where we slipped back into the crowd one at a time. Not long after, a white glow lit up the upper half of the room forming a level plane of laser light from wall to wall. As if this was some type of cue, the rest of the implanted humans took a position against the walls when a fine vapor began to seep from various pores in the molding. Once it flowed around us, I could feel the skin of the suit I was wearing begin to soak up the gas like a vacuum. Shortly thereafter, I felt a sudden rush of energy as if I had drank an entire pot of coffee along with a dozen lumps of sugar. I felt oddly alert, and the grinding pain from my hard fall earlier began to quickly melt away.

As we were all poised along the perimeter of the chamber, something that looked like a misty hologram formed in the center of each of the three separate sections of the room. Glancing side to side, I could tell that each image was different. The one before me showed a white ball with a small indentation on one side. The figure down the next section over was of a long silver rod, cleanly cut on both ends. The one the farthest from me was red and translucent, and I couldn't make out what it was showing; but I didn't want to wander off and appear out of place since everyone else in the chamber was standing vigilant and concentrating solely on the image displayed in front of their specific grouping.

Once again my own voice echoed in my head with words that were not my own. Simple one-word instructions which were repeated over and over; "*Search, study, observe, function, heal*," were issued like affirmations at a church communion. While this was going on, the image spun and showed how a smaller ball which appeared identical to the power nodes Aaron had been speaking of, was inserted into the cupped part of the ball. This was then passed over the image of a three-dimensional simulation of a human apart from several alien forms; though their models were lacking any definitive details. The image displayed a human arm separating from the body and how to use the white sphere upon the wound.

Needless to say, this representation got me a little antsy as to how violent this mission was going to be. The image next to our group showed the silver rod being pointed at structures and a blue dot would appear. However, I could not hear the commentary of the other holograms; only of the one before me. Assuming as much, we had already been indiscriminately assigned to squadrons based on our random location in the chamber when the session of instructions began. At the far end where the hybrids were positioned, there was a wall of white light which appeared to stream a line of data which I could not make out from where I stood.

Just as suddenly, all of the simulations changed into mirror images of something that looked like a helmet which clamped from behind like a clamshell around the figure of a human head. Within this were images of colors, and again the voice repeated its incantation; "*White form is friendly, yellow is adversary, green is wounded,*" it repeated, then changed its chant to "*attack yellow, end yellow, stop yellow,*" the Overlords drilled into our heads. The instructions were simple enough.

The rest of the group around me suddenly turned towards the wall in unison, and I felt like a chorus dancer on stage who had forgot their routine as I spun to mimic their movements. From over my shoulder I looked out of the corner of my eye to watch a glowing orb emerge from the ceiling of light as it floated throughout the length of the room in eerie silence. I felt unnerved that this drone might be scanning the implants, so I felt a wave of urgent relief when a wide doorway formed in the walls before each of the three groupings. I made sure I was one of the first ones through to put some distance between me and that hovering drone.

The pathway before us was short, and the walkway terminated into what appeared to be another fitting room. This one however, was far more organic in nature. Streams of red and orange tendrils flowed from ports in the ceiling high above and I tried to glimpse around the entry to see if there were any of those little Grey beings to give me the stink-eye, as I had received from one before. I fell back a little in line so I could take my lead from the people in front of me who were receiving instructions through their implants, and they began to take separate positions in groups of three as they stood back to back underneath these writhing florescent tendrils.

I took my post and tried to mirror the group beside me, and stood there like a dolt as I saw Renzo walk past while I threw him a nervous glance; and feeling a tinge of relief that there was someone recognizable in my assigned group. Apparently we were being drafted as the field medics on this little safari. I truly wasn't ready for the bright strings of spaghetti that seeped over my head and began to crawl its way up into my nose. I was about to choke and lose my poise when the tendrils coursing through my nasal passage and down my throat felt as if they suddenly melted; leaving behind this strange glaze that felt unnaturally slick. I fought like a bastard not to pick my nose and try to snort some of the gunk out when the others around me suddenly turned and began making their way towards a tall black cylinder.

It was a real struggle not to sneeze as I scrunched my nose trying to fight off the urge, then I noticed the person in front of me walked straight into the metal cylinder as if it were immaterial. I was a little amazed, but equally worried about not being able to see what I was in for. The first person who entered, never stepped out, as a second followed behind in their place. It was confusing to explain where they went, as I peered around the device to see where they had gone; but saw nothing there that relieved my rising curiosity.

My instinctual impulse was to run away and fight to protect myself from the unknown; so it was a mental effort to step into this alien apparatus and maintain my self-control, where I was robbed of all senses when it enveloped my body. At first, the blackness that engulfed me was total, but after a moment my vision cleared to reveal that I was in a sphere of soft light that was moving through a turbulent liquid substance. As psychedelic as it was, the ride was quickly over and I was left standing in a pure white room, where one of those clamshell helmets I had seen before, was attached to a securing rod above my head. A ring of light suddenly gleamed on the floor as a clue as where I was supposed to stand, so I took my position.

There was an uncomfortably long moment of silence when nothing happened, and I began to get worried as to the momentary lack of action. I didn't know if there was some sort of mental instructions which I simply couldn't hear, so I stubbornly stood my ground. A moment later an Overlord's voice echoed in my head, instructing me not to close my eyes. With a subtle sigh of relief, I saw the helmet lower behind me and it began to clamp around the back of my neck to fold itself over my face. In reality, it was tremendously difficult to force my eyes to stay open. Like an ass, I blinked several times; not knowing if I had screwed up whatever synchronization was going on within this alien device.

The interior of the helmet was opaque at first, but quickly became transparent after a few seconds, and I was astounded at the change in my visual perception. A portal opened in front of me, and I stumbled as I took my first steps. My field of view was now notably wider, and the structures around me altered from two dimensional to something almost translucent. Attempting to get my bearings was keenly harder than I had first imagined, and I couldn't help but grab the wall to catch myself from falling over. I was forced to place one step in front of the other while adjusting my equilibrium, as this was something I had never experienced before; so I took it slower than usual as I stumbled like a drunken idiot while following the path which took me straight into the leading edge of a cigar-shaped alien craft.

The top and bottom of its end was scissored open, and saw there were a few other human crew members in there before me, standing side by side in front of several thick silver poles which lined the entire interior of the vessel. At least I assumed they were human, since they were wearing the same black one-piece ragged leotards; but the helmets made their undefined heads appear like unpainted mannequins. With curiosity, I began to raise my hands to feel the helmet I had been fitted with; realizing I also looked the same with this form-fitting gear over my head, but just barely fought the compulsion, as I imagined Renzo might be watching from somewhere and would certainly not approve of me fidgeting about and bringing undue attention to myself. Needless to say, there was absolutely no way of identifying anyone except by subtle hints of their height and body weight; which unfortunately, were details that were blurred by the altered perception of the optics in the helm.

I took my position next to a pole in a stance similar to the others as several more crew members filed in behind us. Once the final person boarded and took their post, I noticed that by the number of empty passenger slots that there was ample room for hundreds more personnel to fill the ship on this level alone. The rampway cycled shut and another telepathic message offered a command in one simple word; "*Sleep.*"

'Well, this is fucking great,' I thought to myself. I can tell you, it was a long time standing there in anxious discomfort as I tried to wait for whatever came next. Even if I could doze off from boredom, whatever stimulant was in that mist my suit had absorbed earlier was keeping me wide awake at the moment. Without an implant, I was not so easily susceptible to whatever powers of suggestion they controlled us with. I stood there waiting for the cushioned webbing to fill the cabin to help me stay upright, but my wish for relief never materialized.

Instead, the chamber filled with a type of gas so thick that I could see eddies of the air currents blur around us while the pressure in the crew cabin rose to an uncomfortable level. Just as quickly, the metal poles beside us swerved to our backside and attached themselves to our spinal columns. As alarming as it was, I found it did help to keep my body erect and locked in place while giving blessed relief to my aching muscles. Eventually, I managed to doze off again.

I awoke long before we landed and was amazed to see that the chamber around us had expanded outward several-fold. It was becoming ever more apparent that these ships were made of a unique composition of a material, which had the appearance of metal, but could mold and form at will to meet any desired design. The room around us was now much wider and all of the rods attached to us had been rearranged into a single file. Without any form of notice, the floor beneath us opened while the supporting rods upon our backs transformed into translucent beams of light.

I almost yelled out loud as the floor dropped away to open space, and we were held helplessly suspended above the void. I pissed myself uncontrollably from the fright, which did no damage, since it was immediately absorbed by my suit. Stars glittered there in swaths of purple and white as they glided across the open sky below us. The ship encroached onto a world far removed from my knowledge of our solar system. It was a planet speckled with vibrant hues and thick clouds swirling in pockets. For a moment, I thought I saw another ship zip past us below our line of sight as my feet dangled into nothingness.

In leaps of speed, the ship jolted forward; though we did not feel the kinetics of these surges over the great distances the ship covered while we entered into the atmosphere. In all sincerity, I was stunned by the beauty of it all. It was one thing to sit and watch a film about space exploration, but to be enveloped by this sense of awe and wonder made my body react in ways I couldn't anticipate. Instead of fear, I felt this strange urge to be dropped into space so I could be absorbed by its magnificence.

Rays of angry light began flashing through the clouds as we approached the surface, while inside the ship, a thin cylinder device floated past us where we were held tethered. The object dispersed a bundle of ivory spheres, each the size of a large orange fruit, and these objects adhered themselves onto our suits. After it finished allotting the medical devices, the cylinder finished its pass, by switching sides and delving out the power nodes Aaron had been so keen upon securing. These also glued themselves to our suits just above our elbows.

Once it was done, the cylinder shot off and quickly vanished into the bowels of the ship and my attention was drawn back down to the terrain, which rose up to greet us at terrifying speed as our vessel descended. In one linear motion, the illuminated rods securing us, shot us down onto the planet's surface and instantly dissipated. Within that startling moment, we were all left standing on the ground. Looking straight above me, I could see the true size of the massive cigar-shaped vessel just before it blinked from existence as it sped away beyond the upper atmosphere. Now that we were here, the reality of our situation on the ground war set in, as a similar spaceship discharged a group of our armed human soldiers a few hundred yards from our current position.

Following the other medics lead, I removed the sphere from my right arm and the energy node from my left; and set it within its dimpled compartment upon the device. The ball gave off a slight rhythmic glow, and with my free hand, I gingerly felt at the strange helmet which had been molded to the contours of my face. It was becoming shamefully obvious that the others didn't seem to have any difficulty maintaining their balance the way I was currently suffering, due to the way the helmet enhanced my senses. Far ahead of us across the rocky terrain, we saw another of our drop ships set down another squadron of troops near the edge of an enormous vessel that ate up a vast portion of the horizon.

I was able to look around me for the first time, but the gear attached to my head caused my vision to absorb many more spectrums of light than I could have ever imagined. I could even see the heat signatures on the ground left behind from my fellow soldiers. The sky was ablaze with streaks of light that shot through swirling clouds, but the brooding landscape which stretched around us was broken and rough. Bands of thick metallic ore twisted through the sediment and there were oddly glowing spores that wavered gently in the mild wind which swept the surface. The scenery would have seemed peaceful if it wasn't for the stampede of our ground troops scurrying upon us to set up a perimeter.

I was expecting that my human comrades would show up on the helm display as a white aura or something that designated them as friendly, but there was no such visual tag. The leading attack group had been given a different set of instructions; so I huddled there with the rest of the medics who had formed a central circle behind the protective line of our troops armed with their long silver weapons.

We stood there poised for quite some time until a shrilling alarm lit up in my helm, which could not be ignored. Suddenly, a vertical red line shifted across the face of my helmet, directing my attention towards a specific location. Our armed troops bolted into action and made their way directly towards the designated target, while the group of medics I was in fanned out behind them. Without an implant, I couldn't ascertain what information was being broadcast to guide them.

I looked around at the winding chasms and labyrinth of tall boulders which stretched out as far as the eye could see, and wondered how easy it would be just to make a run for it and escape this madness. Searing streaks of light rained vertically through the air, directed at our departing vessels which accelerated beyond the reach of enemy fire with a blinding flash, and they were gone. Giant black orbs replaced their presence as they barreled through the turbulent sky. One of these giant balls of death swerved in our direction, and I braced for the inevitable fate that would befall us.

I crouched there, waiting for the alien ship to target us and have our sorry lives ended in a flash of hot light; but the ship continued on its course over our position as if we weren't even there. The massive craft looked ancient, as I observed deep scars upon its surface. Along its circumference was a wide groove rimmed with faint lights etched within. I held my breath as the sphere passed over us, fearing that it could crush us all if it suddenly fell from the sky. I was confused for a moment as to why it could target our personnel carriers, yet was completely blind to our presence on the terrain below.

As if responding to a silent signal, all the medics stood in unison and peered off into the distance. Just out of sight beyond the forest of stones, bright blue flashes erupted towards the sky. They appeared like bubbles of turquoise light which burst into a magnificent shower of colors as they expanded. I followed in the steps of my comrades as they took off racing towards the heart of the commotion.

Their method of war was not as I had been groomed to regard it back home. Instead, it was filled with an eerie silence, entirely absent of communication or screams. This alien tech operated with chilling finesse, performing its function without the noise and disturbing clamor of guns and cannons. We approached our forward troops as they aimed their rods, which fired rays of infrared light at adversaries in the distance I could not perceive. There, scattered among the pillars of stone, were lumps of green objects as displayed through my helmet.

The medics scampered towards these emerald beacons to apply their healing devices in an effort to help our wounded comrades. I tripped over something dark as I followed them, only to look down to see the blackened silhouette of a human form crumbled upon the ground before me. I stood there in silent horror, entirely puzzled as to why this wounded person didn't appear with a green marker. Leaning down, I touched the blackened body only to discover they weren't breathing.

There was no obvious wound as far as I could tell, though, by the position of the body, it had appeared this individual had been struck by an intense blow to have pushed them backward with such a degree of force. The other medics in my group were attending to the wounded by using the small orbs we carried, by applying them to our injured allies. With curiosity, I picked up the rod lying beside the corpse of the soldier and tried to examine how it worked. In that brief moment of curiosity, out of nowhere, a flying body hit me hard, and I was sent tumbling to the ground as streaks of shimmering light showered around the rocks where I had stood.

I shook off the concussion and tried to get to my feet, only to find I was being pinned down by one of the medics leaning over me. The person was shaking their head, but I couldn't hear a word they were saying. There seemed to be no form of person to person communications fitted within these helmets, and their smooth surface concealed the identity of the individual behind the mask. My assailant held up their hand as if to make certain symbols in sign language of which I didn't understand. With a brief pause of thought, the medic grabbed me by the shoulder and dragged me over to the edge of a stone pillar and roughly spelled out "*Renzo*" on its surface from the residual heat signature from his fingertip.

I nodded that I understood and gave the 'Okay' sign in response. Trying to speak was utterly useless, even though it was a force of habit. Apparently, Renzo had determined who I was among the group by my awkward conduct. Against the rock below the fading heat signature of his name, he wrote again in simple words, "*follow me.*"

We crawled through the broken rock and pillars of stone as the other medics went about their duties using the spheres to assist our fallen comrades. I followed Renzo as he made his way around their flank, and we effectively skirted the main skirmish altogether. I began to get worried that he was leading us in a wide circle back towards the enemy line, but he wouldn't slow down so that I could signal my concerns. He only slackened his pace when we came to a position upon a broken perch, one which peaked above a large rimmed crater behind the enemy lines. Below us, we saw a wave of honey-colored images scattered among the broken terrain.

These creatures appeared humanoid in shape, although their details were blurred by the visual mechanics of the hoods we wore. All I knew, was that their color-coding designated them as foes. Renzo had been adamant about scouting the area ahead to get a clear look at our adversaries, but I could not tell any discernable information he might be receiving from his helmet; assuming that it worked the same as my own. He signaled me to wait where I stood while he hopped off the crag and scurried down into the crater below. I looked on nervously as he began to slow down just as he approached one of the enemy combatants from behind, but to my surprise, Renzo stepped out from behind the boulder that hid him while he put down his medical orb and the rod, and placed his empty hands in the air as a sign of surrender.

There was a flash of blue light which burst into a familiar bubble that dissipated around him, and Renzo dropped like a stone. Within the visor of my helmet, the silhouette of his body immediately turned a lime green where he lay. I scrambled down from my hidden perch and rushed to his aid, to see if this odd medical sphere I possessed could somehow save him. I made little effort to hide my approach towards my fallen friend, while the creature which had originally attacked him began to slowly draw closer to his motionless body.

The shade of the being shifted from a butterscotch hue to bright lemon the closer I drew near as if the intensity in color meant to bring attention to the proximity of the danger. Not knowing what kind of risk I was taking, I reattached the medical orb to my suit and immediately armed myself with the silver rod lying near his feet. I stood there trying to look menacing as I put myself between the approaching creature and my friend lying helpless on the ground. Instinctively, I held it like a baton, as if I was going to use it like a baseball bat; entirely oblivious to which tip of the weapon was actually the dangerous end.

The being was considerably taller than I, and noticeably thinner. It stalled momentarily and took a step back. I could not tell if it was armed with a weapon, for its features were blurred with a coating of yellow light. If I could possibly figure out how this staff weapon worked and blast the creature, the result would likely only bring on a swarm of its allies down upon us.

There had been far more than a dozen yellow markers we had seen from our position above the crater, and I was clearly outnumbered. My adrenaline was kicking in as my mind raced as to what I should do next. Even if I could use this device to somehow slay the creature, my actions would likely only end in getting us both killed. In that moment of hesitation, I relaxed my arms and slowly began to put the weapon down; not knowing if it even knew this human motion for surrender. It touched its wrist as I did so, and there was a tick of white light that flashed upon my face and my vision began to suddenly fade into a blackness which seemed to swallow me. It wasn't my helmet which had malfunctioned; but that I had been knocked out cold by the stun weapon the creature had used against me.

My head ached terribly as I regained consciousness, although I was partially surprised that I was still alive to feel the pain of it. I turned my head only to see Renzo lying on a similar stone slab beside me; though despair began to creep upon me that his body no longer appeared with a greenish haze, and I feared that he had died. I was shocked back into a state of alarm when I felt two strong hands turn my head back to face upward. Standing above me was what appeared to be one of the same creatures which had attacked us.

Glancing around, I could see we were now located in some sort of domed room with smoothly sculpted walls that were littered with an array of nooks and shelves. My arms were tightly bound with a rubbery tendril on either side in such a way that I was unable to move. The strange being stood above my prone position as I lay upon the table and promptly plucked the medical orb from the skin of my suit. It then took the staff weapon I had carried and detached a power node from its center compartment, and exchanged it with the one from the sphere. The medical ball changed color from ivory to blue, and the creature returned to its position standing behind where I lay.

Fear welled up inside me as I remembered the numerous alien autopsies films I had seen, and wondering if I was now on the receiving end. A piercing hum rattled through my head and I screamed aloud as I felt a pinch at the base of my neck. In the horror of the moment I heard a splitting crack, and I imagined that they were opening my skull while I was still alive just to see what was inside. Panic coursed through my veins as it felt as if my skin was being peeled away, and my vision began to blur with a bright searing light.

Within moments, I realized I had been yelling the entire time as the helmet, which had encapsulated my head, had been split open and pried off like a shell. I quickly quieted down as it occurred to me that I was wasting my precious breath if there was a lack of oxygen in this unfiltered atmosphere. My eyes darted from side to side as I felt the clamps ease. The creature placed the ruptured helmet on a shelf and returned to a position behind Renzo.

Now able to turn my head once again, I could see with my own eyes that the mask encasing Renzo's was a glowing mass; as if his entire head was surrounded by a soft fluorescent glow, lighting it up like a bulb. Using the blue medical sphere, the being used the same procedure to remove the molded helmet from Renzo's head.   After peeling it away, the outer illumination of its surface faded and I could see that Renzo was unconscious, but still breathing.

The extraterrestrial calmly approached me and touched my shoulder as it began to speak; its words forming in a voice other than my own, quite similar to the way the hybrids communicated.

"Tranquil ...hush," it bade as its longs fingers pressed upon my arm, "we will not harm you, will not harm ally ...friend," it reiterated as it searched my mind for the right words, "ally friend, injured ...apologize we do for harming. Find peace, find forgiveness."

My pulse slowed as my anxiety waned upon hearing the creature's words. I stated that I understood, and did not mean to harm anyone; only wishing to help my friend, Renzo. The alien touched the rubbery bands which held me down, and I watched with curiosity as the tendrils separated and snaked away under the rim of the table. Cautiously, I sat up, finding it remarkable that I was able to breathe in this alien environment without the aid of the helmet gear. I scooted off the table and went to Renzo's side, but was unable to determine the cause of his condition without any obvious wound being visible to me.

"Can you help him?" I stated aloud at the strange being, its skin ashen in various shades and freckled with fine pores.

The creature approached him and paused momentarily before it gently touched me again as I granted it permission to proceed. Physical touch, it seemed, was a common way to transmit a connection for their form of communication.

"Say again, repeat desire," it spoke again in my head, though it almost seemed as if I was hearing its speech through my ears. It was a strange sensation that took some getting used to.

"How was he injured?" I pleaded again, "Can you heal him?"

The being turned suddenly and sought after something from the far edge of the chamber and produced a thin black rod the size of a pencil. The object was sharply pointed on both ends, and it turned to approach me with this dangerous-looking instrument. I stepped back upon seeing it, and the creature sensed my unease. In response, it placed the black spike on the table and turned back to touch me softly once again on my shoulder.

"This device ...helps to speak, converse, expression, tool," it bade as it raced through my mind for words to describe its intent. With hesitation, I turned to see Renzo who lay dying beside me and put my hand upon the aliens, replicating where its own hand was placed upon my shoulder.

"Okay, I understand," I expressed with hesitation as I touched its arm in return.

The being seemed surprised by my responsive touch and pulled away, then just as suddenly turned to snatch up the wickedly-sharp spike. The tool looked anything but harmless, and I began to wonder at the folly of my agreement to allow its use. I fully expected it was going to stab it somewhere in my body to activate it; but with a minor pause, the creature merely placed it upon my upper chest where it glued itself onto my suit. With a sigh of relief, I gingerly touched the surface of the device; wondering what it was.

"Transmits without the need of touch, energy, frequency, much like voice," I heard it say as it stood several feet away this time.

"Can you heal whatever injury you did to my friend?" I begged once again, as I grabbed for the blue medical sphere, wondering how it worked.

"Danger - must not touch!" The creature directed while it motioned towards the orb I was now holding. I had completely forgotten that it had exchanged the power node from the staff weapon and placed it within the device. I quickly put it back down on the counter and allowed the creature to swap out the nodes, and the orb returned to its original white hue. The being handed it back to me, only to realize I didn't have a clue how the hell it actually worked.

Testing its application, I waved it over Renzo's chest and was amazed to feel a tingle of pain in my hand as it passed over certain areas of his body. The orb pulsed slightly as it lingered over his damaged areas and the irritation in my own hand began to ease. Whatever it was doing, it appeared to work by relaying the pain to the user of the device so they could identify the proper areas of the patient which needed care. I was at a complete loss as to how it was repairing the unseen damage but remained using the same technique until the sphere ceased its throbbing.

In response, Renzo's breathing became less labored; though he still remained unresponsive. When I was done, the tall alien waved both its hands into the air above Renzo's platform and I stood back in amazement as we watched a saturated turquoise web slowly emerged from a funnel in the ceiling above and formed an enclosure around his bed. The shade of it turned a searing orange hue were it attached to the rim of the table where he lay; fully encasing his body.

The creature gently touched the webbing of light in several places, seemingly concerned as to what it read. I had no idea how any information was being passed except for the slight changes in color, but I dared not interrupt whatever process was being executed by the operation. Finally, my patience met its end and I inquired as to his status.

"Is something wrong?" I beckoned as I stared through the webbing towards Renzo's still body.

"Cells damaged, conductivity impaired, hibernation interval now necessary," the being responded while manipulating the mesh of light. Those words did not bode well for Renzo, and I began to wonder how long we had been unconscious; and more importantly, if our squad was still engaged in the conflict or if they had been evacuated back to the harvest ship. If it had, there was a reasonable chance we had been left stranded here to fend for ourselves on this hostile alien rock. If Renzo had been able to speak, he would have had some colorful words to share to that end.

"I ...I'm sorry our troops attacked you. We were taken from our planet against our will and forced to come here. We had no choice," I tried to explain to the creature.

"Not true; you did not attack, you had a choice and used choice," it retorted in its recognition in my decision not to harm them. Personally, I could not argue with its logic.

In an effort to gain a better ground in correspondence with my new host, I followed the being as it left the chamber to an outer doorway. While starting to ask where we were, my mouth fell open as the aperture opened and a dazzling scene out of some mythical fantasy filled my eyes. The glimmer of an aqua green sky scattered with thick clouds lay blanketed over high vertical peaks in the distance. Before them lay a rich valley covered in a vast rainbow of alien vegetation. Odd birds with long trailing tails soared overhead as they cried, and my gaze was drawn down upon a dozen domed buildings similar to the one we had just left; littered among the vibrant foliage surrounding us.

Among these structures were several more tall beings similar to my host, who paced among the cluster of buildings along with a handful of creatures that appeared to be of a different genetic race. I stood there in shock as my conscious mind tried to absorb it all; realizing I was standing on an alien world brimming with life like our own mother Earth. There were strange plants that bloomed into impossible shapes, while curved vines snaked across the landscape; their thick tendrils weaving a tapestry of color across a forest of stone. It all looked strangely familiar; much like the war zone we had been dropped into, although that particular location had been nearly devoid of life.

"We are Anu," the creature placed a hand to itself, "and Indu, Dorsay, and Duat," it motioned to the other alien races milling before us along our path as we walked. I lingered on that thought, trying to remember what Aaron had once told me about how the Lords of the harvest ship were just one of many such species with the technology to travel among the cosmos.

"I ...my friend and I; are Human," I replied as I placed my hand to my chest.

"We know this," was all the Anu being stated as it turned its dark eyes out towards the valley while pointing high into the star-speckled sky, "you are species known as Manu of Sol ...and are very, very far from home."

Prison Planet

Difficulties began to arise when it became clear that these extraterrestrials did not retain personal names, considering they have never had a need for them. Their minds connected to one another by link alone, and could somehow *feel* individual identities in ways I couldn't quite comprehend. It only became a barrier to me because; well, not to seem racist or anything, but more or less these aliens all looked alike to me. That tragic fault pretty much pointed out the iconic flaw which had poisoned eons of human history.

I was trying to absorb this new habit of thinking which was so far removed from the way mankind had groomed itself. With unconnected minds and a fierce sense of self-identity, we separated ourselves by class, clothing, and wealth to grant ourselves status. Now far removed from that egotistical abstraction, I could finally get a true sense of how entirely naive it was to create a society so entirely hollow as we had engineered it to be in our current day and age. If you took all the blocks from the social pyramid we had built and laid them out evenly, it would have produced a much larger foundation for our civilization to flourish upon, which would be based on a sense of equality for all. Reflecting on this, I could see how we weren't exactly the brightest race in the universe.

For posterity's sake, I applied the name 'Caesar' to the Anu being I had first met, just so I could keep my focus on who was who around here. For lack of any breasts or obvious genitalia, I had assumed it was a he; although I remember the hybrid's mention that a multitude of genders was actually commonplace among such diversified species. That was simply a topic I didn't wish to discuss at the moment with them on any grounds. Caesar, however, was gracious enough to fill me in on where I was and the status of their battle with the Overlords.

"The species you title as Overlords are known as the *Dries*;

they are an ancient race which had spread out among much of the cosmos many millions of your solar years ago," he explained, "they were once great explorers who aided newly blossoming species to rise from their cradles, and showed them ways to gain footholds towards a peaceful and prosperous civilization. However, that was in a time long past."

"What made them change," I asked, bewildered by this information, "and why do they collect humans and splice them to create hybrids from us?"

"Untold ages ago, there was a great multitude of sentient races within the known galaxy, but there came a time to pass when a handful of younger races sought to gain position above the Dries. This, of course, was impossible in the minds of the Dries, as all beings were considered equals; and thus they were blindsided when these fledgling races began mounting violence against them without instigation," Caesar explained, "over such a great span of time their civilization had become ignorant of the petty rivalries of younger species, and failed to see the dangers of what they had tailored until it was far too late. A great war washed through the cosmos as they became the hunted for their advanced technologies, until their once great race had dwindled to become but a scattered few," he confessed, and I could feel him searching my thoughts for a way to symbolize his words, "Imagine an immense pillar ground down to but a single spec of dust; and that small grain is all that is left of their once great and powerful civilization. Now they wander the universe trying to redeem the glory they once knew; but lack the ability to conceive that their time in this universe has passed."

Caesar had placed a great deal of texture into his narrative, but it still left out the reasons for human abductions and their visits to our little blue ball we called Earth. Sol, it seemed was their name of our solar system, and our young race was called the *Manu-ka*; or Mankind, as our ancestors had thus termed. Many other alien species including the Dries had been visiting Earthlings for untold millennia. They had once befriended the

Anu, because Caesar's race was known as the life Seeders, who collected and brought organisms to germinate upon new worlds.

I, of course, was baffled by this. I'm pretty sure any holy-roller TV evangelist would have had a hysterical shit-fit in denial at that claim, but it turns out that even our lowly species weren't the only beings in the universe which had created their own creators out of their blind ignorance and blatant arrogance. Evolution was a part of every living world in the universe, Caesar granted, but most of the sentient species on developed worlds utilized genetic splicing as a tool to enhance both their race and their ecology. Gene transfer was the logical step to take among such technological advances, and was actually commonplace among different species that were found to be genetically compatible.

Humans, or the *Manu-ka*, as he put it, were merely an accumulation of many stages of such enhancements since the Anu had first visited our solar system. Trying to wrap my head around the timeline which he had eluded to left me speechless, although, Caesar attempted to help me settle that distorted perspective.

"So, you're claiming that your species, among other alien races, had created mankind since the beginning of our history and helped to shape our civilization?" I stuttered to ask, hoping my words were being translated into a telepathic dialect.

"Not claiming, as you say; but stating as fact," he answered swiftly, "one must also include the countless micro-organisms which are carried on space debris you call comets and asteroids; such biology rains down on almost every world across the cosmos, perpetually," he answered.

"Still, even if we were the evolution from some sort of biological soup, you're saying the Anu were responsible for propping us up to be the dominant species on our world; is this not correct?" I suggested; trying to contemplate how any sentient species could plan so far in advance over the span of countless centuries which stretched over millions of years.

"Searching your mind, I am afraid you would not understand the mechanics of space and time the way you currently perceive it," he stated.

"Try me, I think I could," I stated with optimism.

"No, I adamantly disagree," Caesar replied with an almost human tone of skepticism, "your mind has not been primed to accept such ...complex sophistication," he paused as if to search for the right words, "however, you can try to understand the fundamental basis that, time, as you perceive it, speeds up to a quicker pace upon solar objects which possess a strong gravitational pull, and fundamentally, slows down within the null recesses of space," he answered as if to test my ability to comprehend what he was trying to say.

"So, the farther one is within the void of deep space, then time slows down dramatically for that individual compared to those who are standing upon a planets surface, correct?" I offered.

"Fundamentally," Caesar granted with what I imagined was an unheard sigh of despair, "the stronger the gravity, the faster time flows," he offered.

"I think I might have read something like that about space-time law in a book somewhere; that time flows in a river," I answered, trying to match his intellect, but failing horribly.

"No, there is no 'law' ...both the flow and course of its natural energy is always in flux. Time is not a river as you state – not water flowing downhill; instead think of it as a turbulent ocean filled with eddies and undertows, dead spots, vortexes, and ripples," Caesar elaborated.

That was where I began to lose the conversation as he proceeded to fill in his explanation with complex analogies which were far beyond the boundaries of my verbal language. His words of course, where merely being translated from the poor dictionary resting in the residual neuro-fibers of my active, if not flawed memory; so the fault wasn't fully his.

What I got out of the exchange was that our meager human perception of time was outlandishly warped compared to theirs, and the way we measured light-years from point A to point B was grossly inaccurate. Caesar did, however, clarify that even though a measure of coddling was offered to the race of Manu as they matured, human civilization had outgrown its crib by leaps and bounds during their absence. In their eyes, we were still in diapers and currently playing with matches in a nursery made of dynamite; as our species was busy creating dangerous technologies far in advance of our basic ability to use them responsibly. Personally, I couldn't disagree with him.

Instead of a path of universal enlightenment among the peoples of a unified global society, individual desires such as their lust for power, money, and greed had warped everything humanity was meant to be. They blamed that wayward course on our inability to read thoughts and our lack of telepathy to converse beyond written languages; so that we could perceive one another's intentions. It was true that the human race was pretty much famous for misreading one another, but apparently we had gained a reputation for it across the known galaxy. It was that one intrinsic flaw which had led us to the sad state we were in now.

I didn't believe the words he used when he said it the first time, so I had Caesar repeat himself.

"Your Earth, the Manu, is currently isolated under what your language would describe as an assigned quarantine ...or equivalent to a prison planet," the alien stated with conviction.

"...Why?" I choked out with self-denial, though deep down I already knew the answer.

"Humanity is a very dangerous and unpredictable species," he noted with frankness, "and must not be allowed to infect or to harm other worlds and their civilizations among the galaxy. Your minds and perceptions have been warped towards dominance, for your species are inherently violent and defined as conquerors," Caesar granted with an air of bitterness.

It was useless trying to convince him that the actions of a few within our military and government entities were not the true will of the entire human race; solely because the majority had allowed themselves to be placed under their thumb. In all respects what he said was undeniable; detailing that those few in authority who possessed the guns, and money, and missiles, fundamentally controlled the general population who were only under the illusion that they actually had a say in the direction of their lives. Ironically, the public was at the mercy of such warmongers and tyrants whom we paid and supplied with the very means to keep us on the very leashes we had woven. The unfortunate fact was, Earth was already a prison planet, and our Commanders in Chief were the wardens.

It was a situation of our own making; the human race had bound itself into slavery to a relatively few handfuls of individuals who controlled the destiny of billions of people. Looking at it from that perspective I could see how an advanced species would be afraid of us; our social structure was inherently unequal and insanely self-destructive. The fact that it was actually only a mere few power-hungry individuals in our population who were truly dangerous; apparently made no difference to the Anu or the other species of their council; because human society as a whole had failed to correct the glaring problem, making all of mankind share equally in the liability of our plight.

No matter how many times I tried to twist the story or fold the edges to persuade them into viewing our dilemma from a different perspective, I couldn't get them to understand that the many should not have to suffer for the sins of the few. However, in their dark and brooding eyes, the vast majority of our population who allowed such corruption to exist in the first place made us all birds of the same feather, so to speak. He understood very well the meaning of revolution and fighting oppression; but stated that although our species was not primarily too young to understand our failures, we were still far too naive to allow such a pronounced and undeniable stigma to continue to flourish in our society. He did, however, provide a small but positive note.

"You Tyler, as you identify yourself individually, are not one of the weak-links, if I said that correctly," Caesar stated, and I affirmed it was a proper translation.

"But what does that mean, exactly?" I blurted.

"Your mind ...your essence, is not that of a slave; if you understand my observation? You see, you know, you perceive what others do not; without effort," Caesar related with a wide gesture of his long arms to make his point.

"I fully understand that war among our kind is fruitless; but if so, why was I taken? Why was I harvested like that only to end up being used as some minion or foot soldier if I'm not personally prone to commit such violence in the first place?" I spat as I tried to decipher the meaning of it to myself.

"But you are ...you would not have been culled by the Dries if you did not possess such an *incendiary* quality of character," he countered to my surprise, "forgive my interpretation from your limited intellect, but you and the other Manu-ka which were harvested possess empathy and insight, and the ability for self-sacrifice towards a greater ...*a greater good*," he finished with a pause as he searched for the proper term, although, apparently ignorant of the insult he slathered upon me in the process.

"I, I still don't understand the purpose of being taken," I stammered while struggling to conceive of how this all tied together, "if I and the other abductees have some sort of hidden capacity or spark for such hostility and violence lying within us, why the hell would they bother? That doesn't make any sense!"

"We understand it is difficult for your mind to contemplate in such dimensions," Caesar stated to my further confusion, "so I will try to reiterate in simple terms so that you may grasp our perspective," he offered, making me feel like an immature child being scolded by a school principal, "as for what you title as hostility or internal violence, I had meant to interpret that you possess the feeling of ...*disgust*," he finally acknowledged after apparent mental effort, "this disgust, this distaste and revulsion you know and feel about the misdirection and ethical deterioration of your culture is because you recognize the *true value* of kindness, compassion, and consideration for others.

This rare and sacred quality makes you an alien among the vast majority of your own kind."

His choice of words hit me like a rock. Sure, it tapped my ego ever so slightly, but I honestly didn't feel self-absorbed with his statement. Deep down, beyond my stifling confusion, for the life of me, I couldn't understand how so many people could fail to recognize the glaring deficiencies poisoning our society the same way I had. Their willful blindness and oblivious disregard were beyond me, and perhaps that is where Caesar's point was directed. I saw the world in different colors than most, but I couldn't say if that made me a better person. I had done some pretty crappy things in my life as well, so I was having a hard time trying to weed out this sense of golden virtues and shining morality he was slapping upon me like so many layers of paint.

Then again, I failed to see things from a perspective others might have possessed; for instance, trying to hold any form of existential conversations with my choice of friends usually led to moments of awkward silence and puzzled stares. I watched in dismay as people lived unhappy lives because they put up with insults and suffer indignities in their relationships and jobs, merely for titles and pieces of paper which supposedly denoted their personal worth, merely to keep a roof over their heads and food on the table to survive. Most people on my planet lived day by day under this dark cloud, trying to pretend it wasn't there, but it would always rain once in a while to remind us that we were at the mercy of this brooding shadow hovering above our heads, and we would never truly enjoy the sunshine beyond its murky veil.

Our society revolved around finances, where money itself was the symbol of happiness. There were people who wore wealth like a badge of superiority, followed by a sense of self-entitlement. The poor were seen as leeches or worse, and our society was taught to judge success with a dollar sign. Against their common principles, the species of Manu had enslaved themselves to the idea that possessing assets and accumulation of fortunes was the core meaning of having purpose in life, and worse, that they were perfectly justified to kill one another for it. Our tiny planet, in one form or another, had been smothered in Resource Wars for centuries; and there seemed to be no end to it.

"Okay, okay ...so if all of this is true, then why not just make your presence known to all of mankind, our *Manu-ka* race as you put it, and help us stop our wars. Teach us how to feed the hungry and heal the sick, and invite us into your galactic brotherhood so we can finally elevate past all this pettiness?" I pleaded with a snort. However, what Caesar said in reply made my jaw drop at the breadth of my own ignorance.

"Your world is grossly overpopulated; you procreate by accident or for entertainment. Anything you invent you attempt to forge into a weapon so you may kill one another in the names of many baseless religions; inflicting brutality over fiction and fabrications of make-believe. Your modern societies commit such unforgivable atrocities ...and yet you have the audacity to believe humanity would actually be welcome among the stars to spread this sickness?" he seemed to question the sanity of my demand.

Caesar had a point. You wouldn't throw a slice of cheese into a basement full of rats and expect the infestation to magically correct itself. Global scientists had estimated that a human population of a half billion would be ideal to regain a sustainable balance with our ecosystem, but we had overflowed far, far beyond that ceiling; with disease and the casualties of war being the only effective counterweight to that inherent problem. Our desire to colonize space has been a blossoming dream because we are explorers and possessed a natural curiosity to search beyond the horizon. Unfortunately, once we got there, it was also human nature to plunder and acquire things which weren't ours to begin with; only to cast them aside like so much trash when we are done using it.

Caesar's perspective wasn't beyond understanding, although it still made me wish they would just abduct all the power-hungry assholes on Earth instead, and let the rest of us start afresh. The truth of the matter was; even if that were to happen, the void of power would soon be filled with more tyrants looking to make a name for themselves and the ugly cycle would continue, perpetually. At first, I was perplexed that those of us who were so-called 'empaths' or awake to the deficiencies of the human condition, were being swept up as if it were some sort of Holy Rapture; instead of letting us try and make a change by sharing our insight with the rest of the world. In all honesty, though, one tiny voice soon gets drowned out in a belligerent crowd. It almost seemed as though nobody really wanted to listen to the voice of sanity and reason.

People considered the super-rich as idols to worship and then stumble along the same dastardly path to emulate them. I had done it myself before, and it took me years to realize what a selfish jerk I had become. Gladly I had outgrown it, and came out of it concerned and upset by how easily I had been brainwashed to think that way in the first place. This focal point was the central topic which Caesar and his wise companions found so distressing about my species.

Apparently, we were all too happy to lie to ourselves while wearing a smile as our civilization poisoned itself; insuring our doom. As the population of Earth exploded there were more and more people added to the poverty list, as were the innocent victims of war; and the anguish it caused soon became impossible to ignore. Earth was a hostile planet where countless lives were destroyed for the mere benefit of the few. I was determined to assert that the human race was somehow fixable, if only given a chance ...well, 'another' chance, beyond the countless billions we had already blundered throughout recorded history. Regrettably, I didn't have a fast answer; but my alien hosts did.

"Not to shock you from the false history you have been told by your scholars, but your modern civilization is but one of many which have flourished upon your worlds of Sol," Caesar revealed, although I mistook his plural as a misinterpretation.

"You mean on Earth? I'm aware there have been ancient cultures and stone-age tribes which have died out over the past several thousand years," I admitted.

"No, you have been grossly misinformed and are wholly ignorant of such accounts, but this is not your fault," the Anu alien related with a negative tone, "it is of many millions of your Sol cycles that I speak of," Caesar related with earnest as he led me into a hollowed chamber among one of the stone huts, and touched the rim of a metal bowl that was sitting there with his fingertips. A clear liquid poured in from the bottom and filled to its brim; within this basin, several lights began to shimmer and images formed like holograms which began to float above its surface. "Manu-ka has been striving to reach its ascension for many cycles," he stated as he showed planet Earth, although the continents seemed to be oddly out of place, "many, many civilizations such as your own modern world and those farther advanced have come and gone, their societies would rise, only to fall. Each time they would start anew; only to repeat their mistakes again and again."

As he said this, the continents would shift on the model, showing a timeline spanning hundreds of thousands of years. This claim, of course, would be denied by nearly every religion in our modern world. Caesar then conjured up two more planets I did not initially recognize, though their size and placement seemed familiar.

"What are these other two planets?" I inquired with curiosity, as they were nothing I remembered from my studies in astronomy. One was half the size of Earth, like a grapefruit would be to a bowling ball, and the second mystery planet was slightly smaller than the first. I stood there in amazement as Caesar explained.

"Fourth planet from Sol..." he began,

"Mars ...'that' is Mars?" I interrupted as I peered closer to examine the turquoise world with its swirling clouds.

"Correct, as your species calls it in your era," Caesar confirmed, "Manu once lived there also, but long ago it met a great catastrophe. The other, here," he noted while showing a strangely mottled green and reddish planet with a vast polar cap, "this fifth body from Sol was called * ...it appears entirely unknown to you, as your mind has no name for it," he mentioned with exasperation after searching my thoughts.

"There is no such planet in my solar system," I responded in a whisper of silent wonder.

"Untrue, the remnants of this world still lingers, its moon is still mated within its field of debris while locked in its eternal orbit around Sol," he claimed. I recalled there was some erroneous asteroid belt in the vast field between Mars and Jupiter, and of a small dwarf planetary body that circles within the edges of its expanse.

"Are you saying that mankind also lived on these worlds?" I couldn't believe my own words as I asked him.

"Yes, true. Nurtured by the Anu and Dries long ago ...very long ago," he iterated.

"But what happened? Currently, there is no such planet beyond Mars," I professed.

"The size of the planetary body was a factor when a violent asteroid storm passed through your system eons ago, which had ruptured its mantle and weakened its core. The binding frequency of its magnetosphere became unstable, and the planet died as it shattered into the growing debris field you now see. Its moon, called Ceres, in your language, still lingers like a forgotten ghost of the world that was once its companion," Caesar affirmed.

It made me consider the timeline he spoke of, and I concluded that the asteroid storm which had passed through the core of our solar system, strangely enough, had coincided with the impact that had killed off the dinosaurs millions of years ago. By their own hand, the first tribes of Manu escaped to Mars as the first children of Men. However, only a small scrap of their civilization survived the catastrophe as they struggled for many millennia to tame the vast wilderness Mars once was; which had also seen its share of calamity during that fateful storm of rock and ice which had hammered the inner planets of our solar system.

Many civilizations rose and fell over the living world of Mars, until it too, met tragedy. At the time of the rise of Mars, Earth was a picture of shattered continents filled with wild and monstrous creatures; but it was also left uninhabitable due to the aftermath of the apocalyptic impact it had suffered. Finally, there came a time when the Manu of Mars once again rose to technological heights; but instead of using their intellect towards creating peace, they instead reconceived the brutalities of war. The types of weaponry their empires invented were beyond dreadful, and their domains were locked in turmoil which had assured their mutual destruction. In their struggle for dominion, there came a day when one dynasty finally called their enemy's bluff. What followed was a holocaust that eventually stripped the planet of its atmosphere and wiped Mars clean of all life. In reflection, it seemed that the planet Mars had been considered the God of War within the cultures of our distant past for a valid reason.

This was an epic tale I wasn't ready to fully absorb at the moment, but one I had somehow always considered as a possibility in the back of my mind. There was but a mere trifle few survivors left from the race of the Manu who had emigrated to Earth, as their third and final chance for the survival of our species. Only a handful of their ships survived their escape from the war which charred their world; with only a few humble remnants of their once-proud civilization who ended up struggling to survive like savages on the strange and alien landscape of Earth. Once again the cycle of life continued as realms both great and small rose to power, while others faded back into the dust from whence they came.

In this day and age, Mankind itself faced the same fate as its predecessors. However, our long journey migrating ever inward towards our Sun was halted by the world of hellfire that was Venus. Oddly, it now seemed our space programs were attempting to return to our past in a vain attempt to recolonize

Mars once again. In all respects, such an enterprise was a useless endeavor. Even the Anu chose not to reseed the barren planet. Its atmosphere was still bleeding out into space and was considered unsalvageable.

I imagined there would come a day when our astronauts would step foot again on the cold red planet and feel the overwhelming sadness as they mourned their lost past; shedding a long-awaited tear without knowing the true reason for their grief. The ghosts of Mars would whisper their silent warning upon deaf ears. Buried under the red surface ravaged by time, they would find the remnants of a people long forgotten, and the crew of these brave explorers would be hushed by their Commanders and would conceal all proof of its existence from the populations of Earth for generations to come, just as they had suppressed the forgotten structures left upon Earth's own moon, Luna.

It appeared that the evolution of Mankind into a new era was always held back from the very brink of its salvation by those egotistical few who were afraid of losing their grip on power. Selfish gratification was the fatal poison that thwarted us from entering a higher phase of knowledge. Humans, Mankind, the Manu-ka, by whatever name they were known; appeared to lack the ambition to be more than what they were.   That brought up the most obvious question, why bother harvesting our species if we were considered such a lost cause?

Caesar's answer was that our modern world was facing the danger of yet another Armageddon, stemming from our abuses of atomic splicing and nuclear fusion. The concern was that our society had not yet entered an age of interplanetary travel, and the ignition of a devastating war would not only wipe out the Manu entirely, but also the last of all the other living species they had seeded within this system. We were like a prize garden which had been dying off as the caretakers tried to save what was left.

"So ...in this act of harvesting; a choice few of us were being collected to be taken somewhere else?" I begged to ask.

"Possibly," Caesar answered as he disabled the holographic device, "the Dries do not communicate their intentions with us any longer, and their fear and suspicion of other races are understandable. They are the last of their kind, and we concede they may see either a certain kinship in the situation of your dying world, or perhaps a measure of responsibility for what they have sown. They may look upon you as a parent does towards a child; for you are their offspring."

"Wait, wait, I'm a little confused ...what do you mean by *dying world*, and that we are 'their children'. Is their DNA mixed with ours on some level?" I stuttered back.

"Your third planet has already entered its current cycle of magnetic shift, while your people are in the midst of great struggles and contests between power structures within your divided societies. Your race has contaminated the lands and seas to a point that your ecosystem has become irreversibly tainted and poisoned; and is currently on a rapid course towards catastrophic collapse," Caesar answered, not being shy about the barren facts, "or, it is just as likely a costly war will unravel the organic bio-systems of your environment and fracture the fragile food chain your civilization relies upon to exist. Either way you choose to see it, *things do not look good* ...as your people say."

Frankly, his words were sobering, but not surprising. I wondered what it would take for our cultures to steer ourselves in another direction; one that would be far more beneficial to the masses and promote sustainability, which would help to protect, and hopefully repair, the health of our ecosystem. As these aliens had put it, it appeared we were a lost cause. For millions of years we had been playing this game of cat and mouse with our final hour, and that train was finally pulling into the station.

"If there is such little chance for our recovery at this stage, then what purpose does it serve for the Dries to introduce hybrids into the mix?" I asked, though it took several awkward moments for Caesar to piece together exactly what I had meant.

"The hybrids of the Dries you have met were meant as a last-ditch effort to help change the tide of your race, but they're physical appearance would have drawn too much attention and they would have failed to meld or effectively integrate into your society for such a strategy to materialize," my host admitted, and I could understand that opinion, "their presence would only have caused further tensions within your people's hierarchy. Your species currently suffers from an abuse of power along all lines of authority. However, it is the failure of the whole of your combined populations, who have done nothing to correct this oversight."

I saw the viewpoint he was making, and it certainly cast us in a bad light, but what he was mentioning was rebellion on a global scale. His aim was that human societies should have elected among the majority to commit a 'mutiny' and refuse to obey this course of continued insanity we had been led to follow by the tyrannical minority who ruled us. It was at that moment that I got the impression that even Caesar, himself, and the rest of the Anu, could not contemplate our irrational method of thinking. It simply didn't compute in their minds. Why would anyone burn down their own house in the face of an approaching storm? It was a damn good question.

The first phase of hybrid clones, such as the few Marks I had met, would have certainly met with an underhanded measure of discrimination on Earth; that is why they needed to filter a more acceptable version of us that could effectively infiltrate into our current communities. The inter-species mating was not meant as a covert replacement for the human race, but as a long term plan to introduce new forms of language and communication to alter the fundamental mindset of our societies as a whole. It wasn't a scheme to end mankind, but to save it.

We already interbred species of pets to attain specific results, which people considered wholly acceptable; yet when it came to the thought of genetic manipulation on humans, themselves, most everyone had an moral shit-fit about its suggestion. The idea of biological purity had always led down the road to unhinged discrimination and genocide. The core of that reasoning was based around the self-absorbed idea that humans were 'special' and it wouldn't be until we surrender that shade of vanity that we could even begin to see the dawn. No new age would ever rise until we shed this suffocating selfishness.

"Well, truth be told, the human species would likely never accept a hive-mind mentality," I admitted to my host.

"Power is nothing if you have no-one to wield it against," he spouted like a philosopher, "yet your masses continually hand their leash to those who will exploit such positions. This is why the interbreeding of higher thinking is necessary; so those who eventually hold the reins will instead choose to remove the collars bound upon its citizens. However, if their phase of integration does not work or conform within the parameters of the project, and this strategy fails, then it is worth noting this warning I offer you; that the planet you call Earth, would be healthier without your species upon it," Caesar advised.

His threatening words were a sobering turn of face. Later that day, Caesar invited me into an assembly of the alien races who had convened into a large domed building. Within, they had converged in a half-circle around an egg-shaped sphere which lit the chamber in a dreary purple light. The room constituted of members from several extraterrestrial races. Feeling nervous upon my initial introduction, I stumbled among the group of ancient beings who carried themselves with poise and grace. Invited to sit among them, I was left speechless by the information they began to share.

Many minds echoed into mine, brewing words of caution and despair; of resolution and result. I could both hear and feel the words as if the hue of emotions behind them possessed color, scent, and taste; it was a strange sensation to experience. They revealed that the elite authorities within our militaries and governments on my planet, had colluded together in an effort to thwart the Dries attempts to infuse hybrids into our human society; for they feared not of the loss of humanity to an alien race, but instead, of losing their grasp on power from such a new era of thinking which would arise amongst the citizens of Earth. Furthermore, those same authorities took it as a brazen insult against them that the health of the planet, which our people existed on, somehow surpassed the value of the human race; and they attempted to twist that point to their own ends.

The human race was in trouble. The elder extraterrestrials cautioned that we either needed to accept a mixing of the species to save ourselves, or the rubber stamp of failure would be pressed upon Mankind and we would be removed from the ecosystem entirely. They weren't going to risk an entire garden over one specimen which had become infected. I had no idea that humanity had come so close to being placed on the cutting block. In their perspective, however, there arose a desperate need to save the tiny island we called Earth, if we should fail to save ourselves.

Seeding worlds was a great endeavor, and their resources had grown thin from the wake of intergalactic turmoil caused by many younger civilizations across the galaxy. At one time, the human race had once attained a measure of peace upon the first world we possessed, but the natural chaos of space had intervened and turned fate against us. Our stint on Mars was a prime example of what these beings wanted to avoid, and they were quite serious about the lethal outcome.

If it came to the point where mankind threatened to ignite intercontinental nuclear war, then they would take measures to mend the problem to their own resolve. There would be no invasion of space ships, or little green men shooting ray guns to conquer humanity. The cure would come in the form of a designer virus that would cause mankind to waste away, and reset the evolutionary clock. They had done it on other worlds before, and would do it again.

The Human Parasite

Their words were concise and clear about the broken principals and policies of human civilization and its addiction to betrayal. The first step into changing our crippled system of mental and economic slavery was to stop complying with it. The galaxy was filled with countless races of sentient beings which had followed in our same path, and many of them were now nothing but a fleeting memory. Very few species had ever surpassed themselves to a higher understanding and learned to let go of such petty and self-destructive insecurities.

They saw the human race as one of many children in a playground of stars. Some matured, while others took longer than most; unfortunately, we were that forty-year-old virgin still living in our mother's basement. Our race had such potential, but in the end, we always kicked our own feet out from beneath us. One day soon we would hit our head on the concrete floor and there would be no waking up from that.

In our current timeline, there were merely a few dozen living species which had advanced to a stage where they could traverse the known universe at will; and as Caesar informed me, a great many of them had been visiting my little blue planet for quite some time. The visitations of these alien species on Earth had escalated in recent decades in a desperate race to study and collect scientific samples before we entirely destroyed ourselves. Fundamentally, we were the star attraction for these interstellar tourists who wanted a glimpse of our world before our species went extinct.

The Dries had attempted to avert that end, but there was a limit to what influence they could offer; as theirs was a code of conduct not to pressure any species into servitude, which oddly went against their treatment of the abductees onboard their own Harvester ships. It did beg the question as to why they were using me and my fellow humans to attack the Anu residing upon this strange world.

"There is currently an alliance between the Dries and other domains within our *'Galactic Brotherhood'* as you so colorfully describe it, to forego assisting younger species to rise to levels where they can become a serious threat," the voices of the group answered in broken unison, "however, this accord was discovered to be in violation by the Dries themselves, since it was revealed that they had scripted an alliance with the human military complex on Earth," they granted. Personally, I was a little taken aback by that claim.

"I'm a little confused about that statement," I answered abruptly, "we have several separate nations, each with their own sovereign militaries; which one are you speaking of?"

"We search your mind and understand your disorientation," the creatures in the group answered, "the supremacy within the current age of Manu-ka rests within the hands of a very few of your people, and not of separate nations or cultures; but of the Founders, the ones who suppress your race."

Honestly, I was a little perplexed by what they had meant. I then began to wonder if these 'Founders' they spoke of were from the context of what many conspiracy theorists called the Illuminati, the Templar's, or the Freemasons; a tapestry of secluded societies so secretive as to be threaded by mere rumor. There was the claim that such entities as the Deep State and other such dark government agencies which operated beyond the sight of the general public; were pulling the strings and swaying entire societies into their desired direction. I thought it was all fanciful conjecture but apparently, there was some ounce of truth to those whimsical tales.

"Try to understand that your species, the Manu, was once at peace; but ever since the destruction of their first world all those eons ago, your people have existed in an atmosphere of discord and chaos," Caesar added to console my puzzled mind, "we cannot allow what happened upon the planet, you call Mars, to repeat itself. Thus, it is our goal to preserve your Earth and its assets. That, however, may very well come at the cost of the entire eradication of your species."

Well, that certainly was sour news. Caesar and the group of various alien races addressed my concerns to the point, and it is difficult to relate just how hard it was to hear the answers. Our biology had taken an unfortunate route where we lost our natural instincts and replaced them with a hierarchy of governing. It appears the human race had bred itself into a servant class, and unconsciously sought to replace a parent figure to give us answers we were simply too lazy to discover for ourselves. However, we were unqualified to rule ourselves to begin with; it was like children babysitting children. What we ended up with is schoolyard bullies beating up the smaller kids for their lunch money. Yep, that sounded pretty much like the entire history of mankind wrapped up into one sentence.

Mankind had wandered astray; which they saw as unfortunate because we had grown in many ways, but had sidestepped so far off the path into becoming a real threat to the world on which we lived. In all respects, it was the planet itself and the ten million other species which resided upon it which they had to consider; that in a certain perspective, made these aliens conservationists and the human race had become nothing more than a destructive parasite in their point of view. Though blunt, their analogy made perfect sense, and I found it hard to begrudge them.

The ancient race of Dries, however, had secretly colluded with the human military complex to trade a sparse amount of certain individuals for their hybrid program in exchange for a measure of their alien technology, in a logical effort that we may be able to accelerate our ability to correct our path by giving us the means to do so. Unfortunately, their benevolent intentions were whitewashed by the greed of the elitists to whom they made their deal, these so-called *Founders*, as they put it. The elites suppressed these technological advances from the masses so that their grip of power could never be challenged.

When the Anu and other sentient races discovered this ruse, a sanction was placed against Earth and its occupants. The Dries answered in kind by secretly deploying human recruits to counter the opposition to their scheme, while trying to avoid risking a breach of protocol and dissolving the alliance they held with the other domains across the cosmos. This was clearly an act of subterfuge on their part; but extraterrestrials didn't analyze a breach of law in the same light and over-complicated viewpoints as humans did. As long as the Dries didn't pull the trigger themselves, per se, they could remain within the guidelines of the standing alliance; even if they got someone else to get their hands dirty for them.

What I found the most remarkable was that they spoke of Earth as if it was a sentient creature; like a living thing far beyond the comprehension of the human mind. What we called Mother Nature was a watered-down term for the planet we lived on. As they explained it, each planet was alive in a way our primitive minds were unable to conceive. To put it frankly, mankind was at a current stage where we could kill all life and turn the Earth into a dead world. These beings didn't view planets and stars as merely spinning globes of rocks and swirling masses of gas; but as living, breathing entities in their own class.

This not only made me feel small, but I also realized that the human psyche and the boundless colorful fabrications we considered as religions, whose doctrines many swore by, would never accept such a grand perspective. We were hooked on our own little lives wrapped in its narrow context and resisted change. It was this climate of ignorance we wallowed in that made us so incredibly dangerous to the point of psychosis. The council of beings did, however, touch on a point that drew my curiosity when Caesar mentioned *other* Manu.

"You mean there are other races of Mankind spread throughout the universe?" I asked, noting that they must be seeding outlying worlds for a reason.

"But of course," Caesar answered as he spread his arms to encompass the entirety of the room around us, "...we are among you," he stated.

It took a long while for his comment to sink in. Although I felt strangely exhausted from the bombardment of the intense mental exchange during my communion with the others, I could grasp the tip of their meaning. All life, alien, human or hybrid, were all one and the same; and from such a distinct perspective, it didn't take much of a stretch to see that we were all connected. Instead of seeing each creature as separate and assigning a ranking, or class, dependent on a meaningless sense of entitlement, what they held was a profound common respect for 'all' life. They didn't discriminate based on race, gender, color, or shape, but judged solely upon their actions and principles. It was this simple recipe which had eluded mankind for untold ages.

I was still upset that so-called higher minds of the human race were being abducted and harvested only to be used as disposable servants for the Dries, but the congregation had a response to that grievance which I was not ready to hear.

"Arrangements have been made to have you returned to the Dries, per our accord that no terrestrial species from your world are allowed to be granted sanctuary," they revealed in unison.

The thought of it left me in dread, even though it made sense on one level if humans were considered an illicit species.

"I don't understand. These Dries used my kind in an act of aggression towards your world, and you're just going to return me to their care as if I was some sort of prisoner of war?" I stammered, clearly upset. This disruption of anger apparently led to a phase of distress among the congregation of aliens.

"Be aware that your emotions can cause harm, and we ask that you calm yourself," Caesar appealed as he gently touched my shoulder, "please consider that we have no means to care for your species upon this world; and though you may return to service under the Dries, in respects for what is to come of your planet, your new life among them could be considered a kindness," he related solemnly, further adding to my agitation and despair.

With a note of resisted surrender, I realized that the Dries would possess the proper genetic technology and have a far better chance of saving Renzo from his injuries. My fears lie in the fact that we would both be exposed to the Overlords and implanted to become like one of the many mindless zombies roaming the harvest ship. I imagined I could try to flee on foot and escape into this alien landscape but would face coming to a bitter end without being able to survive for very long on my own. I suddenly felt alone and forsaken, all the while wondering how an alien species from a distant galaxy might feel exiting from a crashed saucer upon our primitive Earth.

The truth was that these creatures were nothing more than explorers themselves, and merely curious biologists looking to preserve remnants of our ecology should we burn our world to a crisp. We were the dangerous predators who stalked the planet, which were to be studied or avoided entirely. Would we not act the same if mankind itself one day spread out beyond the confines of our solar system and discovered another race of beings much like our younger selves? What would we do if the native creatures we found were hostile and possessed the means to obliterate themselves, and eager to declare war against their unwelcome neighbors? Would we too try to learn as much about them and study their world, and secure samples of their organisms or capture their kind for analysis and research?

What would happen if our astronauts landed upon an alien world to greet the indigenous species, only to be captured and murdered for our technology and dissected to see what makes us tick? Would mankind react to such aggression with the use of deadly force and conquer yet another world in the name of our false definition of peace; or would we continue our vigilant observations in secrecy. Would our ambassadors also attempt to contact the leaders of their alien civilization, merely to make a backroom deal for an exchange of information and resources beyond the knowledge of their general population?

One thing I could say for sure about the human race, was that we were the kings of bigotry. We were lying and conniving beyond the scope that Caesar and his companions could comprehend; and in perspective, I could understand why they would want to be rid of their human guests as soon as possible; for we were a symbol of genetic treachery gone awry. Our very method of thinking had the ability to taint and stain their thoughts; as their method of telepathy shared emotions in the form of light, and color, and awareness. The human psyche burned and poisoned them like a virus, infecting their minds.

The Dries were only immune to this taint by limiting cerebral contact and utilizing implants as a screen to filter our mental contagion. I had mixed feelings about returning to the harvest ship, only to face being bound in the shackles of their mental control. On one hand, they were attempting to save the human species which they had fostered; but still abused us as minions to do their bidding. In truth, the real reason I felt such an overwhelming gloom of despair was that I knew deep down that the human race would never get its act together; and that we had authored our own fate. A few of us may be innocent on one level or another; but even so, we would ultimately be held united in facing the accountability for our conduct as a whole.

That was the sum of our world; blind to the universe spinning around us as we were locked in our petty dramas and squabbles when there were far more pressing matters at hand. I too had been caught up in the rat-race before my first abduction, and lived in fear from that day forward. I certainly had a sense of apprehension towards my abductors, but I feared the human authorities far more. I once wondered what I would do if the mysterious Men in Black ever came knocking at my door, with intentions to intimidate me into silence about my encounters; likely my resolve would have been to courteously invite them in and put a bullet in their heads without a moment's hesitation.

Caesar apologized for the order of his council to return me and my friend to the detention of the Dries and their harvest ship, but I knew he wasn't personally at fault for the matter. While returning to his lab across the clustered metropolis, I soaked in the wonder of this strange and magnificent world. It struck me that it was far different from the stark and barren landscape where my squadron had been dropped by our scout ship. It was upon that bleak and stormy tundra of pillared stone that the Anu scouts were busy looting the remnants of one of the fallen ships of the Dries in effort to acquire their class of ancient technology, which could seamlessly merge bio-engineering with their machines. One of their enormous interstellar ships had recently crashed upon their world and was commandeered within the protections of their mutual alliance.

In their desperation to retrieve their irreplaceable vessel, the Overlords chose to utilize their only resource on hand, the human abductees, in an effort to salvage the ship. Apparently, the third squadron deployed alongside the soldiers and our medics, were the engineers, whose assignment was to repair and recover the scuttled ship. Once it broke the atmosphere, the damaged ship was liberated from further pursuit by rules of their accord. Caesar and his compatriots regretted that there was a cost of lives on either side of the ground conflict; but they were merely defending themselves against an assault from foreign assailants, as they saw us, who had initiated the conflict with aggression.

I felt regret having to leave this fantastic world, for given time, Caesar and his people would provide many answers to the countless questions I had brewing in my head. It did feel more than a tad overwhelming, and I felt a sense of helplessness in the grand scheme of things. If I ever had the chance to return to Earth, I would attempt to make my voice heard; rather than spending my life hiding in obscurity as I had chosen to do in the past. We returned to the infirmary to find that the once vibrant webbing around Renzo's medical bed had darkened to a dull blue. Caesar attempted to manipulate the threads of the device and utilized other instruments within the lab, but finally turned to me as I stood in confusion as to what was happening.

"Your friend, your Renzo, was damaged beyond our limited ability to repair," he stated softly. I shook my head, not wishing to accept his statement.

"You ...you mean he's dead?" I whispered as I felt a lump of regret forming in my throat. I stepped over to the webbing and peered through it upon Renzo's still form as he laid there, a peaceful look set upon his glazed face.

"His consciousness is non-functional," Caesar related, "we are not bound by our accords to return a casualty of conflict. May I ask what is customary of your species to follow in this event?" he inquired.

In the grim moments that followed, we released the medical gear and I gently cleaned off the protective film from Renzo's lifeless face. Caesar was kind enough to acquire a small transport ship and piloted the vessel with me and my friend's remains to a single lone peak, placed high above a lush valley flowing with rich colors and gentle mists. Renzo's body was placed upon a wide barren rock, and I was granted a silent moment of reflection as the warm twin suns set across the vivid horizon. The clouds were filled with vibrant hues of mottled amethyst while a gentle aurora trickled like a shimmering curtain through the sky before us. When I was done, Caesar placed a small oblong egg upon the center of Renzo's cold body, and a glowing liquid seeped from its shell to envelop him within its vibrant luster. In mere moments, his entire corpse dissolved into nothingness in a shimmer of light.

The curtains of fluorescence from the bright aurora swayed within a cosmic breeze as if in honor of his passing, as the last glowing flecks of his essence dissipated into the valley beyond. The sharp twinge of emotion I felt at that moment was one of content; that my friend Renzo would finally find the peace he had long sought, resting here within the tranquility of this beautiful alien world.

The 9

When we returned to Caesar's lab he asked me to lie down on the table and offered to help me, as a form of minor condolence for losing my friend, and for suffering my unwilling return into the servitude of the Dries. He went to a shelf and pulled out a container that held a tiny teardrop-shaped stone suspended within a clear gel. He brought it over to the table by the tip of a thin blue wand, which he offered for my inspection.

"If you desire, I will install this device into your frame, which will greatly assist you while you are among the Dries," he stated.

"What does it do?" I inquired while peering carefully at the small stone, which shimmered with the colorful translucence shades of an opal within its core.

"It will counter their organic technology and block the frequencies they use to gain control over biological entities during communion," Caesar granted.

"You mean if they shove an implant in me, this thing here will keep me from becoming susceptible to their mind control?"

"In so many words, yes," he answered, "...however, there lies the chance that this deterrent may be detrimental towards any necessary manipulations of your internal chemistry, should such a need arise," Caesar warned, "and though it will impede both mental and chemical control, it may not fully counter their methods of tracking or basic communication."

"Well, that's fine," I blurted, "They didn't seem too keen on such pleasantries in the first place, so I'm not worried about it," I snapped back.

"Understand that the mental capacity of the Dries gives them the ability to overload the minds of other species, making them docile, or even rendered them unconscious," Caesar noted with caution, "in some cases, they can even cause death to a lesser mind."

Hell, I was all for getting some bio-tech counter-surveillance if it would help keep me from turning into a subservient zombie, so I agreed. The catch was that the Anu did not possess compatible medical instruments for my race, so the teal-colored energy scalpel he had would leave an entry scar; this would not be a seamless operation. With little hesitation, I conceded to accepting the implant.

Caesar tipped up my head and waved the back end of the wand in small circles at the bottom of my chin where a soft blue light danced from its tip. Twisting his grip, he made a small cut under the rim of my chin. I could feel the skin parting under the touch of the blunt wand while wondering how it worked without a blade or laser to breach the surface. After placing the small teardrop device under my jawbone, he applied a white powder to the wound, which managed to glue the skin shut.

Needless to say, it hurt, but the pain was replaced by a strange sensation of small tendrils weaving from the implant through the soft tissue surrounding it. It felt warm as it pressed against my jaw under my chin, which was a decent enough place to hide the scar.

"The blocking device has taken, and you should not feel its presence after it fuses to your tissue and skeletal structure," Caesar noted as he placed the tools away and allowed me to rise from the examination table.

There was a brief moment when I felt as if I was going to faint and found it notably difficult to swallow. After catching my balance, I thanked him for his help as he led me towards a transport sphere where we both boarded the vessel with a pair of aliens who appeared quite old. They looked fairly similar, but retained notable differences by the shade and texture of their skin, including their height and posture. I could even perceive a vague similarity to my own race, and wondered to myself for a funny moment, how strange and alien I must look to them in return.

To my amazement, the walls of the spherical ship slowly

morphed into an eight-sided diamond as it lifted up into the sky. Caesar made a gesture into the air of the cockpit, and a small cylinder fixed with a pair of dim lights, lowered from the ceiling of the chamber directly above us. Once he touched this object, a portion of the walls and floor on the outer edge became fully translucent and I could see the landscape moving beneath us. The visuals displayed upon these panels were in a strange hue as if it was a type of black & white night vision. I could still see the details of everything below us all the way out to the horizon, although it was being projected in wavelengths of light beyond my limited visual spectrum.

"We are taking you to a neutral zone so that we may transfer you to your Masters," Caesar mentioned, though I wasn't entirely fond of the caption he used to describe them.

Our ship glided forward at speeds far beyond what I had known possible, yet miraculously, I felt no inertia within the confines of the small vessel. Feeling curious about this, I asked how the vehicle worked. Caesar, noted my sense of wonder, and gladly subscribed to my inquiry.

"Do you see this?" he asked while holding out his hand, his palm was positioned upwards with his fingers cupped, while I replied that there was nothing there, "think of air and atmosphere as if it were water," while he quickly flicked his hand towards me and I felt a soft breeze of air brush across my face, "what you do not see still exists, and only when it is in motion do you notice it," Caesar defined his demonstration, "now change this context for water and replace it with gravity waves, and consider it as but a bubble traveling freely through a fluid, and you will have attained the control of a singular sphere of gravitational equilibrium."

I was impressed by his analogy, but was still in the dark as to exactly how they achieved this function by artificial means. How the fuck did the engine work? I didn't want to insult my hosts, but his two companions appeared to be quite stringent about refusing to let me see how the field generator operated.

The ship slowed down considerably after we had covered

countless stretches of terrain as we approached a storm-drenched region on the horizon. As we cleared a wide plateau, I could make out a line of three narrow pyramids made of black stone. Their shape was much taller than their bases, making them appear exaggerated in their design. Our ship drifted to a spot above the tip of the closest structure, and there we waited in silence.

My hosts were oddly calm during the interval, and didn't seem particularly interested in idle conversation; unless they were simply conversing telepathically with one another and chose to leave me out of their discussion entirely. After what felt like an hour, a series of lights began flashing within the cockpit of our ship and the transparent screen on the skin of our vessel shifted upwards for a clear view of the sky above. A saucer-shaped craft with a single cut sheered off from it, as if someone had cut a square slice from its hull, lowered out of the dark clouds looming overhead. Within moments, two bright orbs of light accompanied the Overlords scout ship while it gently glided to a position above the farthest pyramid structure.

"Farewell, one called Tyler," Caesar offered with a gentle touch to my shoulder, "we wish you peace and prosperity in your current consciousness," he noted as a blackened rift opened up in front of us where we stood within the ship. It was the oddest thing I had ever seen, for it appeared as if the fabric of the air itself had been ripped asunder, and I watched in awe as the rupture widened itself just large enough to let me enter its frame. Caesar motioned it was safe for me to step through, and before I did so, I glanced at the transparent screen where I noticed a similar dark rip in space lingering above the second pyramid poised between our two vessels.

It was like a glass pane of utter darkness with ragged edges, where vivid green particles coalesced, continually lining the outer boundary where they would merge into a rim of solid light before warping its way inwards. This strange portal was eerily silent, which only made it seem more unreal even as I resisted rubbing my eyes to dispel the illusion of it. Stepping into the blackness of the rift, these glowing pins of lime-colored bands attached themselves to the surface of my body and my adrenaline suddenly spiked as I was swept forward. The unpleasant sensation was akin to being dragged through an entire rollercoaster ride at an insanely dangerous speed.

In this limbo, I found myself in a strange room where dark shredded drapery encompassed my entire field of vision as the glowing emerald wisps continued to clasp upon my body; illuminating my surroundings for but a brief second before a similar rift with outward flowing rings of light rushed forward to consume me. Instinctively, I held up my arms in defense, only to find that I was now standing within a brightly lit chamber, on what I assumed was the opposite ship. The familiar white room pulsed and glowed upon my arrival, and I turned to watch just as the strange rift of blackness lingered there for but a second before it blinked out of existence.

I cautiously waved my hands over the area where the portal had once been, but only a mild static in the air remained. The scent of ozone was replaced by the biological stench of burning rubber. This was the ship of the Dries, and they were close by. Back within the diamond-shaped vessel of the Anu, Caesar watched as the saucer ship shot off into the clouds. He turned for but a moment, with what might be called a look of sadness welling in his eyes, for the human he once befriended had been consigned to an uncertain fate.

A thin rod of light, shaped like a florescent tube, lowered without supports from the ceiling above to where I now stood. From its surface, rays of brilliant illumination began to shed with beams that fanned throughout the room. Once a single beam struck me, the rest of them amassed upon my location like a swarm of bees to honey. The effects of the lights almost tickled as the short spurts of electricity coursed over my black jumpsuit and upward through my hair.

I watched in wonder as the light within the tube suddenly faded and the device shot up into the ceiling once again. I was left standing there like an idiot for an indefinite amount of time as I awaited the outcome of the mysterious scan. My legs began to ache, and I started to speculate if it might be safe for me to try to sit down within this room or not.

Eventually I had to test my chances of digestive discomfort, since the gravity seemed to have kicked in a lot heavier than I had felt before. Finally, the sound of a voice echoed within the room, but I knew it was in my head for the device Caesar had attached to me aided in amplifying the telepathic transmissions.

"Enter the doorway and you will stand with your back to the table; your consciousness will be disabled if you resist this command," the voice threatened.

I did, however, note that the voice of the Dries telepathy no longer sounded like my own. It contained a weak and softened voice, as though it were a single dry breath whispered from someone, or something, very, very old. A seam began to form in the wall and the outline of a doorway slid back to reveal an unremarkable chamber of brushed metal where a spotlight centered on a single plate of silvery steel awaited. Obediently, I walked forward with small steps of hesitation and turned to place my backside against the slab which appeared to hover in the air. When I did so, a sound of suction affixed my suit to the metal surface as a short burst of ivory powder bloomed from beneath me.

As I was made prone, two of the small Grey creatures I had seen before, skittered into the ring of light from the veil of shadows beyond. The harsh aroma of them entered my nostrils as they appeared to be obsessed with double-checking my bonds to make sure I was secured. Displaying an odd gesture from its four-fingered hand, one of the creatures scurried off into the darkness as the other guided my slab to a suitable position where it spun itself horizontally. Now lying below the creature's face, it looked down upon me with interest glowering in its glossy black eyes.

I watched helplessly as the dreaded mechanical arm I had seen used on the other abductees before, slowly dropped from the ceiling and into the dome of harsh light. It made a disturbing clicking sound like an angry cricket locked in a cage. One of the small Grey creatures approached the device and manipulated several thin cylinders upon the outermost ring, whereupon there sat a nasty looking spike resembling an oversized sewing needle. Just as the creature was done adjusting the mechanism, a long gray arm loomed out of the darkness and brushed the creature away like an unwanted stepchild.

A tall being stepped into the veil of illumination draped around me, standing nearly three times the height of its smaller companion. In all respects, the two beings appeared to be closely related, though the taller one possessed an exaggerated length of limbs in comparison. I had only seen a Tall Grey once before, which happened during a notably strange visitation that differed from the rest. It was back when I had made the choice to get a vasectomy in a calculated effort to thwart whatever interests these creatures had in using me for reproduction, and secondly, to avoid adding to the intrinsic problems upon our overcrowded world.

Within two days of that surgery, I had another visitation by these creatures; consisting of many small minions and one very tall being, similar to this brute now standing before me. In the previous events, I had been paralyzed while laying in bed as several of the smaller Grey's examined the results of my recent operation to prevent offspring; and I got the overwhelming feeling of displeasure and even anger when the Tall Grey arrived in my room. That particular incident was decades ago, but I now felt that same vibe emanating from its presence.

It gently touched the mechanism, and the needle followed its graceful gesture as it moved the device to linger over several soft areas of my limbs and torso, as though it was making an intentional attempt to raise my level of fear in anticipation of what it was about to do. Held prone in such circumstances would make anyone tense, regardless. This being looked distinctly aged, with wrinkled skin and creases etched upon its ancient face. There was no telling how old this creature of the

Dries actually was, nor was I able to fathom a guess. In a sudden move, it chose to finally stop playing with its prey and the needle stabbed forward into the flesh next to my groin.

The pain was intense, and I knew the infliction of it must have been intentional since the Dries were masterful at their medical knowledge of our race. Discharged from the needle, I felt a small bead the size of a tiny pea, inject under my skin and onto the surface of the muscle above my inner thigh. Once it settled there, the heat of it melted away as the needle withdrew and the wound seamlessly closed behind its passing. The towering creature peered at me intently, as if judging if I was worth the efforts it had recently paid to reclaim me.

"Move your head if you hear our voice," it spoke into mine, though not through the implant it had just placed within me as I had expected, but by the translation device provided by Caesar. I found it peculiar the Dries did not bother to remove the telepathic appliance melded to the chest of my suit. It seemed as if they had neither seen nor noticed it whatsoever. I moved my head as instructed, not wishing to antagonize my grim surgeon.

The tall being stood there for a length of time watching me intently but appeared to be discouraged by something left unspoken. The creature abruptly turned away and disappeared into the darkness just as the pair of small Grey's in the room assumed a position directly beside me during its absence. A great while later, a second elder Grey entered the chamber, this one notably different from the first tall being, due to several distinct age spots peppered across its head and shoulders.

It too gave me the third degree of stink-eye before it backed off into the soft curtain of shadow, just lingering within view. One after the other, several more beings appeared, some fairly identical in their appearance, although a few select others retained faded blotches of discoloration upon their shoulders. Counting, I noted that there were nine of them standing in a semicircle before me.

The pair of small Grey's positioned beside me scurried away

when the table I was affixed to slowly spun itself into a vertical alignment, placing me upright. I could hear them all mumbling among themselves, which I came to realize was a sort of eavesdropping on my part since their telepathy was applied with direct intention towards an individual or group. Likely it was the result of the covert jamming device Caesar had placed within my jaw, which was somehow interlacing data with the new implant they had injected into me moments ago. I got a sensation of worry drifting among these nine Overlords, who were once again my captors.

"It resists!" One voice hissed.

"Cerebral buffering felt, is it felt also?" Another seemed to ask the others.

"Pressure of subliminal frequency is near null, unable to cull neuron flow," another whispered through the haze of voices debating my apparent immunity to their mental control. I had been thankful when Caesar provided me with a means of psychic defense, but I was now beginning to think that being under the spotlight like this might put me at a much greater risk if these Elders started to consider that I might be a serious liability to them if they couldn't control my mind, and might simply chose to have me disposed of. One of the tall creatures stepped forward and reached out to place its palm against my forehead; its touch cold and clammy, yet oddly soothing. I then saw a flash of images in my mind, which I would be hard-pressed to explain.

I had never experienced anything like it before, so any description would pale to the display of lights and sounds I was witnessing; it was if my frontal lobe had been hacked. I saw an open field with bales of hay, piled up in mounds used by farmers. The image of this serene countryside was suddenly shaken with what appeared to be a nearby nuclear strike. A hot wind blew the piles of hay into a torrent of flames as they were ignited by the blast which now swept across the countryside setting fire to everything it touched. This nightmare scene of raining embers faded as a backdrop to the screams of horror and pain I suddenly felt emanating from thousands of people in anguish as their sense of despair surged through my mind.

The creature pulled its palm away for just an instant; as if to give me a momentary breath of relief, seeing that beads of sweat had formed upon my face from the psychic trauma. Without reprieve, the Elder Grey pressed its palm against my forehead once again and more images exploded into my mind. Before me was the scene of a space station set on the bleak and airless landscape of the moon, where man-made habitats were built as a base upon the lunar surface surrounded by mining equipment and machinery. The tiny ball of earth hovered in the background as several saucer-shaped craft shot into view. From these craft emitted beams of silent light which obliterated the lunar facility, and I watched as it imploded into broken shrapnel that was cast into the darkness of space.

Removing its hand once again, the creature took a moment to peer deeply into my eyes, its black orbs reflecting my sweaty and shaken face within its dark lens. The experience left me drained as I felt my legs go weak and a painful prickling shot through the nerves of my restrained arms. My head was overheating by a spike in blood pressure as I lay there gasping for air. Once again the creature laid its hand upon my head, securing the psychic connection to bombard my mind with its shocking images splashing into my consciousness.

I suddenly found myself on board an alien craft, one far different and of sleeker design from the ancient bulky cigar-shaped harvester. From a transparent interior wall, I could see that the ship was hovering in space far above a blackened Earth below us. I looked down upon the smoldering world which was once my home, feeling an ache of pity in a far lesser measure than might be expected at that moment. From our position in high orbit, I could not hear the cries of anguish from the billions of people suffering below. Our society had become infatuated with power and money, placing the will of a few petty individuals in authority who did nothing but waste their time poisoning our lives with lies and propaganda, merely to serve their own selfish goals.

It was a moment in which I realized the human race had a genetic flaw bent towards indentured servitude. It had been reflected in the history of our Kings and Emperors, our Monarchs and our Sultans, the Dictators, and Czars which had now been replaced by all-powerful Corporations that influenced entire governments and molded their personal agendas all for the sake of profit. Most of the people on Earth had been groomed to view wealth as the only vision of prosperity toward a brighter future ...even when the illusion of it enslaved them under its crushing poverty.

Now conquered, the pyramid of power had yielded to our new Overlords. As I peered over my shoulder and into those dark alien eyes of our host standing behind me, the pity I had felt a moment before was slowly replaced with a dim glowing spark of envy. These aliens could read our thoughts, and I began to wonder what Utopia humanity might have attained if we could reveal our intentions as these beings could do with such sterile transparency, and placed the value of peace and prosperity for all above the infernal sins of war. My gaze fell back upon the burning planet spinning slowly beneath us and I wondered how we could have done this to ourselves.

There was a flash of white and crimson, and I nearly blacked out as the large being withdrew its touch for a final time. Sweat poured down my cheeks as did the salty tears now welling in my red and puffy eyes. I was shaken to the core, having felt as if my emotions had been put through a wringer. The mental intrusion had left me weary and overcome with uncontrolled grief.

The being glanced away for but a moment at its colleagues, as they slowly faded back into the veil of shadows beyond the cone of light. With one swift motion, the creature touched the edge of the slate which bound me, and my suit became unstuck from the slab as I slid to the floor and onto my feet. Still feeling weak, I nearly collapsed right then and there. Only upon my release did I truly begin to feel a growing fear for my life welling from the pit of my stomach.

"Do not try to harm us, do not try to run; this will be your only warning..." it cautioned with an aged and wispy voice which fluttered through my head. Although I only nodded in agreement as a response, it seemed to understand the gesture. Several of the small gray-skinned creatures returned to the operating table and began applying a layer of fine translucent dust onto its surface and around the location where we had stood, while the tall Overlord issued a command that I was to follow him. Fighting my nausea and lingering weakness in my legs, I struggled to keep up with its pace as we wound our way through several dark corridors filled with strange and mysterious artifacts of technology I couldn't even imagine to comprehend. Finally, we arrived at a chamber, where a doorway forged itself into existence rather than by any mechanical means.

Once within, what sat in the center of the room was a riddle of theoretical energies and strange metals. The device was held together by a shifting orb of dark ebony plates which melded and rippled as if the apparatus were made of liquid. The sphere itself was embedded with silver pellets and coin-shaped slices that folded and intertwined gracefully as they shifted and restacked into new formations. The tall Grey stood before it as if mesmerized by the infinite complexity of the device.

"Hold still, do not resist," its familiar voice directed as I proceeded to stand next to the being who was transfixed before the strange apparatus.

One particular liquid plate ceased in its rotation around the orb and centered itself before me. Fine tendrils, as thin as hair, pulsed in waves as they extended from its surface towards my face; and I fought the natural reaction to brush them away as they grew closer. A dozen fine threads tipped with the glow of luminescence touched my face, and I tried not to squirm as these coils snaked across my cheeks and into the crevice of my eyes. A sudden searing pain caused me to snap them shut, though I obeyed the Overlord's charge not to resist or pull away; so I endured the discomfort a moment longer.

It felt as if a liquid was being injected into my corona, and the pain rose to a threshold I could no longer endure. Violently, I tore the fibers away, breaking their liquid strands. I turned towards the tall Grey beside me, whose stare was indifferent; though his face had now somehow changed. My gaze shot around the room, looking for an exit that didn't exist, so that I could escape this nightmare. I thought of attacking the creature looming above me, without knowing its physical strength. I then imagined disrupting the bio-mechanical orb, if by some chance that it might release me from the cage of this chamber. With overwhelming despair, I turned towards the bare wall from whence we had entered and began beating upon its surface as the pain in my head increased, while the building pressure within my eye sockets elevated, and I felt as though my head was going to burst.

Then suddenly to my shock, I found myself standing where I was before, as the strands of organic light gently caressed my face. Baffled, I turned my vision towards the tall Grey being beside me, as I struggled to understand what it was I had just experienced.

"You must let go of pain, let go of fear, let go of discord; see again..." it granted as the tendrils once again caressed my face.

It was difficult to stand there motionless as the tiny worms of black liquid tipped with light tested the surface of my skin and explored the crevices of my face, until the thin vines found their ways into the corners of my eyes once again. This time, however, I experienced no pain or pressure from within. I could still feel the movement of liquid in my retinas as my vision began to cloud.

Just as suddenly, I found myself sitting on my porch chair on my balcony back at my old cabin in the woods. It was dark outside and I had my legs kicked up on the railing as I stared up at the stars above; which I frequently found myself doing most evenings. A calming sense of peace washed over me as I found myself in familiar surroundings. The question of how this could possibly be real drifted away like the fleeting shadows from a flickering candle. I stared up at the spatter of stars washed across the expanse of the night sky, their twinkling lights offering voiceless answers to the meaning of the universe.

In a blink, I once again found myself standing aboard the ship in the same spot beside the extraterrestrial. Its posture was now more relaxed, as though he shared the place I had just visited in my mind.

"Now you see, now we can share expression, exchange of thoughts," the creature offered while the translation of its intentions searched for the closest term that I could understand.

"You ...your kind, have taken me before," I inquired, more as a statement than a question.

"Yes," it affirmed.

"But ...but why, I mean, why me?" I stuttered while reaching for justifiable answers to the questions which had been haunting me most of my life, "I don't understand why your race takes people and places them in harm's way like this, as though we were nothing more than disposable slaves..." I began to turn angry once again.

"Calm ...calm," it pressed, "no anger, no hatred, and you will have no pain," the being offered softly.

I took several deep breaths, trying to soothe my rising tension. Just as I began to relax, a large reflective plate on the orb slowly slid by me, and but for a brief moment within its reflection, I could see in my face that my eyes were now blackened orbs similar to my alien host standing before me. I gathered myself, and the creature could sense that the irritation within me had ebbed from my consciousness.

"How could we make slaves of a race which has already enslaved itself?" The creature inquired, making its point in but a few but powerful words, "your society is smothering itself in corruption, your people live in a culture where telling the truth is a crime. Your world lingers in a black shadow that chokes the intellectual. If we had not removed you, your fate would have been far more dire, uncertain, and lost. Here, we will save you, transplant the Manu-ka before the consumption," it apprised with a sense of finality.

"Why are you transplanting us, and what is this *consumption* you speak of?" I stammered.

"The decay of your age has already begun, and soon the other races will arrive to devour the energies and resources of your world," it granted, "we cannot save you all, nor would we wish too. We accept only those who can see clearly and possess the will to change."

I was astonished by its claim that the other races of extraterrestrials would commandeer the Earth and deplete our resources. Although, with a glimpse of what the Elder showed me in my mind, I had initially mistaken as to what I thought the creature had meant. It wasn't that they were after our fossil fuels, or minerals or water; it was the spark of life from the planet itself. Organic life was just a measure of recipes from the wellspring brought by the Anu. Cosmic debris had also added to the chain of life and all it produced. The Dries were the harvesters of only the choicest grapes that have not yet soured; before the plague of locusts descended upon the crop as the vine died. It was their conclusion that humanity would kill their world and take itself with it.

This harvesting was merely taking samples from the petri dish before it was sanitized. The other races were merely acting as opportunists; for they would not let the primal energy be wasted during such a shift. There was a great cataclysm approaching our world and they were the messengers of the cosmic rapture. Unfortunately, for the holy-rollers who had been preaching those words all their wishful lives, they would find themselves without a ticket to their imagined salvation. All those with weak and broken minds would be left behind to be consumed by the dark angels they had wrought from their own nightmares.

"We are, however, in a time of need; and would ask a favor of one who can see what others do not..." the Elder pleaded with

an uneasy tone as he gazed into the dark mirror of my glazed
ebony eyes.

Disclosure

Imagine a race of sentient beings which had advanced their developed skills in bio-engineering to the point they could fuse both organics and machines to serve their needs. Along their road of evolution, they had managed to obliterate racial tensions between different factions of their society by melding the DNA strings from every color and creed into one generic shade of Grey. Consider what would happen if a species chose to merge any and all diverse races in their society; then further filtered out material wealth and status from their civilization to the point where equality is balanced with social coherence to a higher cause, which theoretically, would be free to develop into a lineage of individuals who thought as one. Not a hive mind of blind obedience, but one of telepathic abilities where all members could read both truth and strategy of design without the burdens of deceit or obstruction to obscure them.

The human race itself could follow a similar path as we continue to experiment in biometric manipulation of DNA in our crops, our livestock, and ourselves. Far more whimsical ideas such as creating of a Master Race have been viewed as the carnal sin against nature itself. But if such a melding occurred and mankind learned to break the barriers of language and secured the ability to speak to one another openly; would we still strive to reach for such a colorless utopia if that impossible Eden was found to be devoid of art and music, or poetry and expression? Would we lose our appetite for such a cold and sterile existence at the cost of our individuality, in exchange for a sense of unity?

Many such races now swarmed across the universe only to seek what they had forfeited so long ago. The spark of life had lost its luster and their existence began to feel like a bitter chore. Such extended lifespans would have its drawbacks when you realize your biology has been twisted and strained down into a living form, comprised of nothing more than the practice of logic and sensibilities. Humanity would turn away from such a sacrifice, for we would never surrender our sense of self.

The Dries had been sailing through a sea of stars on a quest to bring life to its full potential, only to make countless enemies along the way. They were scorned for their meddling and detested for their arrogance as civilization after civilization reacted to the shocking disclosure of their true heritage, and they rebelled. Clouds of denial clustered into raging storms of war against their own kind; and the Dries, who were once seen as angels of truth, soon became victims to bitter accusations of being the bearers of trickery and deceit in the end.

By observation, the human race would follow the same beaten path as so many other countless civilizations which had been offered similar words of enlightenment. The powers that be who ruled our world would not relinquish it to a higher power above them. The Dries knew this, for they had seen such scenarios play out countless times on numerous worlds. They offered the truth, and were in turn, crucified for it.

"What is this favor you're asking...?" I dared to inquire.

"We have contacted the leaders of your world in the past and they brought soldiers to arbitrate in their place. They demanded our technology in exchange for what we sought, but their deceitfulness soon became apparent as they did not share our offered gifts with the populace of your world as they had pledged," the entity confessed.

The presence of the strange revolving sphere allowed it to share images of the events which had unfolded before, and what I saw did not surprise me. Nearly a century ago, our military minds had accepted alien components on an empty promise that they would help to create energy to free our world and its people from their dependence on ore and fossil fuels, and vowed they would end needless Resource Wars across the globe. We would then be able to construct transport ships for interplanetary travel, and thus, would possess the ability to relieve ourselves of the overcrowding upon our world as our population swelled out of control. In exchange, the Dries requested a small percentage of our people of their choosing, to take and teach in their ways.

Instead, in the many years that followed, the government spooks birthed military programs and secret departments which ran unbridled as they strengthened their iron grip upon the masses, and kept these vital technologies for themselves, by either suppressing or utilizing them for their own enrichment. These antagonists then turned face and declared the Dries as invaders, along with all other extraterrestrial races when they learned that these alien visitors were creating human hybrids to be introduced into the societies of our world, in an effort to enrich our lineage with a new philosophy as an attempt to help free us from ourselves and the suffocation of political control.

In response, the alien visitors began injecting their recent abductees with a critical plane of thinking, which they introduced to these victims on a subconscious level in ever greater numbers when the Dries discovered the level of treachery contrived by the military minds on Earth. These elitists, who called themselves the Founders, had shored up a system reliant on financial slavery against the masses and poached vast amounts of revenue to create a secret space program, fathered by a covert system of government, that had cast its oppressive shadow over its citizens.

This outcome was not the intent of the Dries, so they tried to repair the damage done by their intervention. Ships were sent out to scout our planet, which would raze military bases to disrupt the guidance systems of our nuclear arsenals as a show of force, in an effort to postpone the inevitable.

Time was not on our side, for if the human race did not come to terms with its own misconduct, we would obliterate ourselves before the approaching cataclysm. You see, Earth was entering another cycle of renewal, and its magnetic polar shift would not only allow greater levels of cosmic radiation to pierce our atmosphere and crash our vulnerable power grids, but would also bring intense climate changes and global disruption to our entire ecosystem. However, the living ecology of our planet would have little chance in its ability to rebalance itself, as it had done countless times before, if the war-like race of Manu destroyed themselves and poisoned the planet in a radioactive hailstorm of thermonuclear war.

Mankind itself was the catalyst to our own destruction, and the Dries were attempting to save us from ourselves. A few adjustments of enhanced genetics and its integration of brighter minds would bring forth future generations which could veer our course to a more considerate and responsible society. This idea did not sit well with the ruling class who refused to release their choking grip on power; and saw any such transitional thinking as a mortal threat. Watching the inevitable situation approach its nexus, the dying race of Dries sent out their Harvesters to gather what they could from their biological crop that resided on Earth, before the entire planet was razed. Of course, this was all news to me and I was a little dismayed by claims made by my host.

"There is a situation at hand where Human military ships have invaded a stellar cluster on the outer rift system," the Elder stated as I was still trying to contemplate how such a claim was even possible, "and their troops are currently trespassing upon a nerve center of our sub-dimensional buoys," the elder Grey asserted while my darkened eyes opened in shock.

"You lost me," I stammered, "our civilization has no such space technology for interstellar travel; and what are these 'buoys' you are talking about?"

Once again, the creature shared its knowledge through images by thought which played like a time-lapse film in my mind; displaying the combined events in mere seconds what would have taken hours to explain. On the outer edge of the galaxy there was a cluster of stars that created a gravitational well the Dries had tethered to a dimensional causeway. This allowed their ships to travel to any point within the local cosmos in relative time waves, rather than static time. These wells were tied to each and every star within the galaxy. In respect, that made our own Sun a type of harmonic gateway floating within the sea of space.

The visions displayed were far beyond my comprehension, yet they somehow still made perfect sense in execution. The space-faring technology this being had mentioned earlier, had been secretly offered to the self-proclaimed leaders of our world. Their intentions were to aid the human race into escaping from Earth in the event of such a cataclysm, since our current system was void of any additional planets or solar bodies that were habitable for our species. Instead of directing this knowledge to a better end, our corrupt military minds twisted and abused it towards their own means. I had heard many such rumors of secret space programs over the years but was entirely flabbergasted by the sheer extent of the cover-up.

The issue at hand was that their exchange of technology to any primitive civilization, such as Earth, was strictly forbidden by the council of sentient races in the galaxy. The Dries had become a dying race and had made a clumsy and desperate move by trusting the Human species in its final hour. Such a breach of protocol would lose the cooperation of all other alien races within the collective council; which was an infraction they could not afford to face. The Dries had repeatedly cautioned our governments which ran these shadow military programs, not to venture beyond our own solar system, and eventually shrank that borderline to the confines of Earth itself; but it now appears those warnings had gone unheeded.

As human minds love to tinker, our scientists had created direct energy weapons to arm their secret fleets, and used them to destroy or capture additional extraterrestrial craft in an attempt to add their technology to our own arsenal. Most people would never believe in UFO's or flying saucers and their ilk, but even fewer would accept that many of these recent sightings were actually our own ships in the skies; created by our covert militaries and shadow regimes. They operated in such deep secrecy because any disclosure would spark an international war, which would wipe out our civilization as we knew it.

It was ironic how many members in the UFO community feared that full disclosure about the existence of alien species in our galaxy might cause civil unrest; when in fact the true threat to upsetting the precarious balance within our society would be the acceptance that most every person on the planet was living on their knees in service to a mere petty handful of elites. If that unsavory assertion came to pass, the fact that aliens existed would be a revelation; but of relatively small significance of our waking up to the astronomical level of deceit and corruption which had been employed to exploit our own kind. The result of that admission would be entirely catastrophic. I now understood the argument on both sides of the coin, and why the Dries and other races of extraterrestrials were compelled to orbit around the fringe of its ragged edge. Humanity had bred itself to be its own worst enemy and we had alienated ourselves on our own little planet; one which our Martian forefathers had sequestered out of desperation.

Coming down to the meat of the subject, the elder Grey was requesting that I act as their emissary and confront this military envoy, which had trespassed upon the dimensional rift array stationed at the far reaches of the galaxy. Frankly, it was a good thing we were communicating telepathically, because I was left utterly speechless.

I didn't understand at first why they would need me to intervene at all, since I assumed they had weapons far more advance than our scientists could have patched together with bubble gum and superglue; even from reverse-engineering the tech they offered to our military goons. With another melding of minds, the Elder passed volumes of information in mere moments as to their short explanation. They wanted a savant who could see past the violent aggression; but it turned out there was an underlying reason, which was far more vital.

"The rift is a delicate structure which could cause irreparable harm to many worlds and unbalance the equilibrium of the universe if we employed any means of force," the creature related, "we would rather avoid conflict. You must face them, stop them; and turn them towards the light."

The Elder's last words rang a bell in my memory, as its poetic reflection was merely this being's attempt to articulate its intended expression, which it could only extract from the vocabulary present in my mind. At that moment, I recalled a time when I had seen a painting of a sparrow sitting on the limb of a willow tree, its back was turned towards the audience as the morning light reflected upon it from beyond. Below it was written in script, '*Turn your face towards the light, and the shadows will fall behind you.*' The Dries translation was that light was not only the embodiment of truth, but of life itself, in the way I subconsciously defined it.

Those words could be a powerful illustration when one looked out into the vastness of space and took a moment to weigh the small pins of light from distant stars, compared to all of the darkness resting in between. It didn't make me feel small or insignificant, but more of a part of something special. It was that color of thinking that the Dries desired me to infect upon the military squads and persuade them to retreat from their folly, or at least, to get them to see beyond their petty games at playing toy soldier.

It didn't take me long to consider the importance of such a mission, and I agreed to aid them in this cause. With that, the being motioned that the conference was over and I followed in its steps as we made our way out of the small chamber with its spinning black orb, and out into the upper tiers of the ship. With my newly altered vision, the hallways didn't seem quite as dark as they had before, and I gazed in wonder as strange colors flitted through the air like embers from an open fire. Smooth snake-likes structures slithered their way across the walls, hidden within the spectrum of infrared. I was astounded by the amount of visual chaos ebbing through the ship which I had been unable to see before, concealed by the limitations of my human eyes.

Whatever those tentacles had injected into my cornea, it had widened my optic sensitivity by many scales. We passed by several smaller Grey's as we made our way into a vast circular cell. This chamber was severely reduced in height, so much so, that I had to lower my head to proceed while noticing that my elder host bent its knees sharply and continued its stride; apparently unhindered by the obstruction as it moved in a crab-like manner. As we approached the midpoint, a thick pewter-colored liquid poured out from vents on either side of the room and formed into the shape of a half-shell within the center of the chamber.

The creature touched my back lightly, and bade me to enter the liquid apparatus. Just as I stepped forward upon the platform, two thin rods slowly rose from the flooring on either side, from which a pane of thin film stretched between them as I strode forward. This film enveloped me whole while the rods retracted back into the floor as quickly as they had appeared. I felt no immediate difference, but could tell my breathing had become slightly more labored. Gently stepping into the liquid shell, the pewter solvent began to form the upper half of its structure to encase me as I crouched to fit inside its cramped dome.

I quickly realized that this must be a transport vehicle designed for pilots relative to the size of the much smaller Grey's. The silver flooring around me now molded itself into odd interlaced forms I did not recognize but found myself compelled to grip the triangular-shaped handles to either side to steady myself. A series of light beams radiated from several sources within the ship, which intersected along a glassy blue pane that had risen from the fluid metal. Surprisingly, there was a small jolt, and I fumbled to secure myself as the ship was freed from its berth.

I couldn't see anything from the inside of the small vessel, but the wavering sheet of light before me displayed that my vehicle was now separated from the Harvest ship. An unpleasant high-pitched whine filled the cabin for an exhausting moment, which ended with the beat of several dull thuds. The original saucer shape of the ship shifted into the form of a three-sided flattened triangle as a black film oozed out upon its surface. All that could be seen of this stealth ship among the darkness of space were the three pale lights inserted in each corner of the vehicle, with a central blue illumination set between them.

I felt an intense hum as the vehicle slid away into the direction of the rift, accelerating ever faster. For a brief moment, I felt a strange sensation; a type of equilibrium with everything around me, as if my body was somehow connected with the ship. The awareness of it subsided as quickly as it had arrived, and the vessel came to a near halt within the atmosphere of a dark planet. This celestial body was like nothing I had ever seen before; being comprised of vast spires and arcs which encompassed a central core. Watching the three-dimensional screen before me, the ship itself compressed into a ball of light and descended onto the interior surface, where it slowed to a hover.

The ship spun me upright and folded open to set my unsteady feet upon the cold ground; the nerves in my legs still weak from the exhausting journey which had seemed to drain my muscles of their strength. As my eyes adjusted to the feeble light, I could make the outline of several exotic vehicles lining the path before me. Upon closer inspection, they were embossed with a fusion of identification numbers and military logos which I assumed were of human origin. After several minutes of searching, I noted that each of the half dozen wheeled transports had been left abandoned.

Daring to open a driver's hatch, I boarded one vehicle and rummaged through the interior. There was a slew of gear made from tech far in advance than I had ever seen before; some devices of which I could only guess at their purpose. Plopping myself into the driver's seat, I found a large green button which brought up a command console and a heads-up display. The images upon it showed the coordinates of a central structure, which was the target of the assigned squadron. There was, however, no clear indication as to why anyone would have abandoned these personnel carriers.

 After spending several moments trying to visually piece together the confusing set of console panels before me, I found what appeared to be the ignition and the transport vehicle roared to life. With a lurch, the truck shot forward as I tried to regain control of its steering with little grace. After almost smashing into the set of vehicles parked in the foreground, I managed to clear the lot and began to follow the guidance prompts of the auto-pilot. The path led into the heart of the megalithic structure where the enormous arches converged.

 The transport vehicle itself seemed like something out of a futuristic sci-fi flick; and made me wonder just how far advanced these military Special Forces were, who had been withholding this advanced technology from the public for untold decades. It also got me worried that if I thought this pumped up truck was so extraordinary, then what kind of exotic and lethal weaponry would their soldiers be carrying? I started not feeling so bright about arriving unarmed, or without a defined plan as to what my goal here might be, especially if I couldn't even interpret the objective the Dries had sent me here to accomplish.

 "Ah, what the hell am I doing here?" I muttered softly to myself in doubt as I stared out at the colossal mega-structure that enveloped the horizon before me. The massive arches wove themselves through the sky above as I pressed forward on my route towards its mysterious center.

 "Keep calm, we are with you," a familiar voice spoke into my mind, "the buoys integrate our form of communication, and will transmit our thoughts into yours," the Elder finished; although, on this occasion, there was a strange and ominous echo of many voices accompanying the creature's words, which I initially interpreted as cosmic interference.

 "What do I do once I find this military unit? I hope you realize they don't exactly have an illustrious history of listening to unarmed civilians," I rambled on.

"First, make contact with them and we will speak through you; and you will act as our voice in their presence," they acknowledged.

This didn't seem like a grand plan for an advanced species, but I had no choice but to play along. Anyone else in this position might have felt unnerved or frightened out of their wits, but there was this strange sense of serenity coursing through me which felt somehow familiar. The vehicle lurched forward with unsteady jerks and I began to fear that there was something wrong with its mechanics.

"Can you hear me?" I spoke to myself, wondering if my hosts were listening in, "The vehicle I sequestered is experiencing some sort of engine problem," I stated.

"The defect is not in the mechanism you use, but in the shifting temporal and dimensional flows which generate between these markers," the Elder added kindly, as if I was supposed to know what the fuck that actually meant.

"...I don't quite understand," I admitted with an air of mental exhaustion.

"Your species sees the flow of time as mono-directional, and at a constant pace. Such a perception is false," was all it stated as if that somehow answered my naive question.

"Okay ...uh, let's try this again," I smirked at the stupidity of trying to contemplate their explanation, "what is causing these disturbances?" I inquired, realizing I was considered the village idiot here, who needed to be held by the hand until I received a summary I could actually ingest.

"You are passing through ripples of time, now, and before, and ahead," was all the voices of the Dries said.

"Yeah ...great, that made sense," was all I could muster up as a response along with an exasperated shrug of my shoulders. Logically, I could piece together what the beings had meant, but it was one so watered down that it lacked any color to describe a true picture. I was still boggled by the vague meaning the elder Grey had deflected my questions with, until a wave of light suddenly washed over the vehicle from behind me; coursing its way towards the center of the anomaly. It had appeared like a rippled reflection that enveloped the path before me, and in an instant, the scenery around me shifted into an entirely different landscape.

The smooth stone bridges were suddenly replaced by a panorama of sandy dunes spotted with sharp rocky spires. A lilac-tinged sky melded itself into view where there had once been nothing more than a lattice of stars. I was so shocked, I almost swerved and nearly crashed the armored truck as I tried to absorb what had just happened. At first, I had thought I had been transported to another world, but I began to recall what the alien had said about time, itself, being contorted by the buoys placed in this quadrant.

A great stone spire loomed over the desert ahead of me, which appeared vaguely familiar to the structure at the central core of the twisting rings I had seen in the same location, when I had first arrived upon this strange world. The tracking device in my vehicle appeared unaffected by the visual transformation around me, which helped to confirm that my location hadn't actually changed. I was merely viewing the same area from a different period in time; though this was a change of pace I wasn't quite ready for. Dismissing the strange anomaly, I sped ahead at full throttle under the guidance of the directional screen lining the dash.

Falling into the shadow of the enormous spire towering ahead, the guidance system led me straight into its dark maw. The structure was a massive pillar of smooth rock with a gaping black portal at its base, yawning like a stone giant awakening from an eternal slumber. What I had not expected upon entering this void of darkness was that the interior seemed to extend far deeper than its outer appearance would have led me to believe. The automated lights on the vehicle popped on, wrapping the front of the truck with a fan of illumination to guide my way.

The tunnel within contained a curved ceiling several stories high, with a soft blue light that emanated from its central spine suspended high above. The channel appeared to twist without bending, if that makes any sense; as though a visual illusion was constantly shifting the light around it as the shaft snaked its way deeper into the gloom beyond. Almost screeching to a halt, I barely missed running into a similar military vehicle left haphazardly abandoned on the side of the tunnel. Slowing down to pass it by, I saw no signs of anyone within the cabin but felt it best not to stop to explore its contents while stuck within this unusual shifting corridor.

Oddly, the minutes felt like hours traveling through this strange twilight, until another time-wave suddenly rippled over my path and the slick bare walls of the shaft were replaced by floating rivers winding their way along a pale causeway littered with tall jagged crystals. The reflection from these bright shards radiated from the light of a blue sun poised high overhead. Though foreboding, yet intensely beautiful; its light filled me with a strange unease. There was no change, however, in the trajectory of the tracking system which continued to direct my path towards the central orb, which appeared to be an enormous sphere of water fed by the web of floating rivers joined upon its surface.

As I approached over the rise ahead, I discovered several military vehicles of differing configurations, moored around this watery sphere. To my stark surprise, I also saw a pair of large craft levitating high above the ground vehicles. They had identification markers splashed across their sides, marking the number "37" in roman numerals. This squadron had utilized their stolen alien technology to span the universe in order to reach this particular destination. The real question was; why were they here? One of the personnel carriers parked ahead roared to life, while its lights flashed on and spun its nose around to face my approach.

What appeared to be a gun turret, rose from the top of the canopy, and aimed its barrels towards me. If there was a similar weapon stashed in the vehicle I was driving, I had no idea how to activate it in my defense. A call came over the onboard radio ordering me to halt my advance, accompanied by a not-so-friendly warning that I would be fired upon if I failed to comply. Hitting the brakes, I brought the vehicle to a slow crawl until it stopped within a respectable distance from their approaching security team.

I heard over the radio chatter that their scans revealed there was one humanoid within, which I presumed was myself they were speaking of. Immediately thereafter, the exchange was followed by a slew of orders being barked back and forth from their acting commander.

"Exit the vehicle to your left," the voice charged over the radio, "keep your hands raised, and do not move!"

Stepping out of the high cabin, I jumped to the ground and turned towards a group of military grunts in cyber-suits, armed with a variety of exotic weapons. One man within their group switched on a laser which fanned itself over my body, and promptly disengaged.

"Human, no DNA anomalies detected, sir," he reported through his helmet to the others. At that, one soldier bearing two white stripes across his left shoulder, approached me with a tilt of his helmet, as if trying to figure out how I had managed to get out here into the far edge of the universe and was standing before him without a protective suit.

"How the hell did you get here, boy?" the man barked through his shaded helmet with an air of arrogance in his tone. Because of his helmet, I could not catch the look in his eyes when he got close enough to notice that I was not wearing any type of breathing apparatus and that the whites of my eyes were an unnatural shade of black. I could tell the moment he noticed that particular detail, for he paused and took a hasty step backward.

"I was sent here as an Emissary from a race called the Dries," I blurted in response, "apparently they're a little unhappy that you're trespassing here without an invitation."

The Captain turned his head around to look at his fellow soldiers with a chuckle as if in jest; but caught himself, and quickly reaffirmed his position of command by puffing his chest and trying to look as hard-ass as possible in front of his subordinates.

"This is our party, and we don't need an invitation, son," he barked, "I need you to tell me how you got to this quadrant, and why you're wearing that ugly spandex get-up," he chortled.

"I'm sorry, I don't recognize your authority and I don't answer to you," I replied calmly. Which was probably the wrong thing to say to a puffed-up rooster in front of his squad, but I was bargaining that they would be far more curious as to how an earthling got here and what I had to say, rather than to shoot me on the spot.

The captain strolled forward with an attitude as if he was going to plant his fancy space-boot up my ass, but just as he got within range of taking a swing, another voice came over the com radio.

"Stand down, Captain. Bring the subject on board the Orion for questioning," the man scolded; and the soldier quickly obeyed. I looked up to see that the larger of the two floating ships were maneuvering towards us, and assumed our quaint conversation had been under surveillance the entire time.

One of the armed men approached to take me by the shoulder, but the Captain snapped back in alarm, "Do not touch him!"

Waving his short rifle instead, I was prompted to follow the Captain and his soldiers over to his position, where he stood within a ring of hard light which flooded down from the flagship hovering above. The captain pulled out something from his waist belt and slapped a thin metallic band around my wrist without touching me directly.

"Enjoy the ride," he blurted in the same arrogant tone.

With that, my arm jolted upward, and I was slowly dragged up into the opening of the ship above; being glad that the cocky bastard hadn't attached the band around my neck. A circular floor cycled shut beneath me and I suddenly found myself in a payload bay with two large bulkhead doors to either side. It was an impressive ship, but far from the advanced technology of the ancient Dries, who had seamlessly integrated biomechanics into their vessels. One of the doors opened, and a man stepped through, although without all the fancy gear which the troops on the surface adorned.

"You will have to excuse the lack of hospitality from my Captain, but we really don't get many guests this far from home," he swaggered with a dry sense of humor.

"And why *exactly* are you out here?" I slammed back.

"The answer to that, young man, is classified," the older man jabbed back just as quickly, "I am, however, very curious as to how you made it out here to the fringe on your own since we didn't detect any approaching vessels..." he led on as a ploy for me to fill in the answers.

"The race called the Dries, sent me here to negotiate your withdrawal from this sector of space," I affirmed.

"Ah, those damn Grey's have always been a bug up my ass since we met them," he smirked, "I assume they didn't bother to tell you the full story as to why we came here; out to these so-called *dimensional buoys*, and what they're actually used for?"

His words caught me a little off guard, since the Elder who directed me here said nothing about their purpose, only that the Earth's elite military units had gone rogue and trespassed upon their interstellar gateway. My extended silence told him more than I could have with a simple shake of my head.

"These Dries, as you call them, and their assorted cronies intend to wipe out the human race, and we plan to stop them," he professed with a glare of conviction in his eyes.

Darkness between the Stars

Still wary about my darkened eyes and exotic attire, the crew of the Orion shuffled me into a medical bay to suffer through several tests in the midst of their ongoing interrogation. It was during this time I came to learn their motivations for flinging themselves into the far reaches of space. Earth's military elite saw themselves as protectors and propped themselves into positions of ultimate power. After all, he who has the guns makes the rules; so they say.

Like most people caught up in their own ego, they simply couldn't see past their own nose. Peace was laughed at as if it was some strange uneasy silence between wars. The human race had always bred warriors, and given the right tools, these soldiers turned from the idea of noble protectors into vicious predators. They simply couldn't contemplate the purpose of peace while they had these oh-so-awesome weapons at their disposal; which effectively dumbed-down their ideology to hammers looking for a nail.

It became all too clear that their honorable cause was to protect mankind from annihilation from an alien race ...for the sole reason that they would miss the fun of doing it themselves. Their mentality was so warped that they either couldn't or flagrantly refused to recognize that their heedless conduct was at the core of all our woes. They kept me strapped down on a gurney during our lengthy session; eventually bringing in a torture device to taunt me with, one which looked much like the shell of a cut melon.

"This little beauty here can be utilized to edit human memory, erasing anything you've recently experienced," the Sergeant advised with a threatening tone, "or it can be amplified to cause far more permanent and disabling effects."

"How does bleaching my conscious mind benefit you in any way, when my purpose here is to aid you to bring this grievance to an end?" I inquired, though with a nervous twinge glinting out of the corner of my eye. I did not savor the idea of my identity being swiped from existence or being left as a mindless vegetable.

"Actually, it benefits you enormously; if you should choose to reveal how this Rift Gate works to us ...or you can face the consequence of being coerced into compliance by use of force," he offered with a gesture towards the cupped device.

So, I was going to be subject to torture after all, and it was likely that I wouldn't even remember it. The Sergeant continued onward with his intimidation, by insinuating that his units had already used such devices to abduct countless civilians to garner information without their knowledge or consent; while left unable to remember what had transpired. If used properly, it was the perfect spying tool. The problem was that such man-made devices failed to be as efficient or refined as the neuro-link technology of the alien Grey's, from whom they stole it from. Reverse engineering had its kinks and flaws, and this particular one could leave an individual as a drooling zombie with the conscience capacity of a pea.

"Frankly, your threats are useless," I replied bluntly, "I have no clue as to how these dimensional portals operate or how the technology of the Dries works, for that matter," I granted to the man in charge of the surrounding technicians.

"Then tell us what you do know, and we'll play it by ear," the Sergeant noted as he gently edged the swiping device an inch closer with his finger as my cue to start talking.

I had been silently yelling in my head the entire time to get any form of reaction from my mental connection to the elder Grey's, but their voices had gone strangely silent. I was starting to assume there was some sort of telepathic blockage from our proximity to the dimensional buoys, and it was either that or shielding from the ship itself; having recalled how our refuge under the Cube on the harvester created the same effect.

"I know that our militaries have been secretly siphoning revenue from the citizens of earth on a global scale to fund black projects for several decades in an effort, not only to profiteer, but to keep our species in a state of economic and psychological slavery," I began to roll out.

"Holyyyy shit son, now you're even talking like one of them Grey's!" He remarked with a quirk of his mustache.

"So, you're denying the truth?" I inquired with a state of calm which threw him slightly off guard.

"Oh, every word of it is true," he granted with a cordial response, "but the masses need guidance, and there are those who lead and those who follow..." he began to yap on.

"But what *really* makes you nervous is that a better Leader showed up at our doorstep, I assume," I interrupted his train of thought, "for what becomes of a leader when they lose their followers and are left abandoned for a superior and impartial way of thinking."

At that, the Sergeant drew a scowl; and with a nod of his head towards the tone of defiance in my rebuttal, he threw a final threat in my face.

"You need to understand that those creatures you so adore have placed the entire human race on an extermination list; and we're here to protect our friends and families back home from this alien filth that is trying to control our destiny. Under their rule we would all become slaves; our entire culture would disintegrate into mindless automatons!" he began to bark.

"...You mean, in the way mankind already is at this very moment under our current militarized ...I'm sorry, I meant; our Governmental rule?" I slipped him a condescending quip.

From the look that suddenly washed over his face, I fully expected him to hit me right then and there. There was a twitch at his shoulder, but I noted that even the medical technicians in the room took care not to actually touch me without instrumentation. They were wise to the body-to-mind contact that initiated telepathic connection by their alien rivals. The fuming of his face took a moment to dissipate as the Sergeant regained his composure.

"Unfortunately, it seems those gray animals have already

poisoned your mind," he grunted in feigned pity, "but you might grasp that they sent you alone out here because they were too cowardly to do it themselves. We will use this rift to reach the other worlds they inhabit and give them a taste of their own medicine. All those alien races that trespass upon Earth are trying to take over our planet; so I say let's show them that mankind will always resist or die for our freedom."

With his patriotic speech over, the Sergeant nodded to the tech beside him and they moved the mind-wiping device below my chin while aiming its concave shape towards my face. There came a flash of blue light, but I felt nothing. A second flash was more intense and a weird sensation like my innards were melting made me feel suddenly sick. Within moments, several lights upon the monitors linked to me by wires began to malfunction, while others blinked on and off erratically for a few seconds, then abruptly powered down.

The techs were at a loss as to what was happening, for the lab and the ship itself had been designed to be shielded from such electromagnetic anomalies. What they hadn't realized was that they had just brought a physical antenna of the Alien minds into their midst; with a direct link to the 9. The Council of the Nine Elder Grey's had placed a special implant within my body, which was further amplified by the device Caesar had attached to my protective suit. Whatever energies the techs had used in their memory swiping apparatus, its feedback had penetrated the weak measure of shielding their ship had provided.

A bright pin of light formed from nothingness several feet in front of my head while the personnel in the room stared onward in shock. The spinning ball of plasma sheered out with beams of white light which struck everyone standing in the room. Within seconds, the air filled with electrified static, while the military agents stood oddly still as if they were paralyzed in mid-step. The voices of the 9 Overlords began emanating from the glowing sphere hovering before us, as one by one, the alarms it triggered in the lab faded to a dull silence.

"Your presence here is unwelcome, Sergeant," the calling of the Nine echoed through the lab for all to hear, "your leaders have deceived us into offering our knowledge to aid your race towards your collective survival in effort to establish peace upon your world; but instead, they suppressed these gifts meant for your society as a whole, and became wasted on their petty self-gain to establish positions of control and rule over your populations," the alien voices penetrated through everyone within the room, extending the mental influence of their communion to all the personnel within range of the ship, "your Lords must abandon their way of thinking or it will be your end, one wrought by your own hands."

While the reverberation of the alien voice fluttered within our heads, a stream of images began to flood through their minds, touching them with a deep sadness. It was a repeat of the impressions I had seen before of our planet's future, one where our world burned away in a view from space; the same vision they Grey's had shared in the communion chamber during my transformation. But for a brief moment, I recognized that this vision may have not have been a premonition at all, but was actually an awakened genetic memory. Throughout the entire squadron, the minds of the soldiers suddenly filled with the cries from billions of lost souls as our weapons of destruction wrought the world to a blackened char.

A dark shadow spread across the blue seas as the death of the oceans met with the poisoned husks of plant life across the globe. Felt deep within them, the horrific images were somehow familiar; like a lost and forgotten memory of a time long ago. It was the recall of a scar deeply cut into our lineage; one that would remind us of the evils we had done to our homeworld on Mars. The gut-wrenching pain of endless cycles of oppression and death we forced upon ourselves throughout history. It was ironic that we could so rarely find the courage to struggle for freedom and separate ourselves from our oppressors, only to create the same conditions we had sought to escape. Mankind was its own worst enemy, not these ancient visitors who had been our sentinels for countless millennia.

Much older sentient races feared us for our savagery; now more so since we had created weapons of catastrophic power and had proven we were foolish enough to use them. They foresaw that our intertwining paths would only lead to conflict. Humans had evolved into a prideful and ambitious race who cared nothing about whom or what they trampled beneath their feet in our never-ending pursuit of domination. Those few voices on Earth who apposed our self-destructive path were far too weak to be heard above the boisterous crowing of the ignorant and the blind.

We couldn't escape our own human nature. Our own sense of survival was replaced by self-entitlement; always taking far more than we gave or could ever need. We had become addicted to our own arrogance, convincing ourselves that we were the rulers of our world, and did not look kindly upon another species overshadowing us with their heightened measure of logic and honor which we so desperately lacked ourselves. Maybe it was the disturbing sense of unease we carried which we had constructed from our own hidden guilt, but there was this distressing feeling that lingered among the minds of men, knowing we were truly unworthy; and that sharp jabbing pity we felt had been molded into a pit of dark and brooding anger.

The sentient races understood our plight on a small scale, for our society was crippled by the fact we did not speak a common transparent language of the mind. We used this flaw to our advantage at every turn, to wield and manipulate truth and facts to our personal advantage. This reflected badly upon our reputation among a galaxy of races who sought the same goal; who strived to better themselves without treading upon the backs of others. In this respect, we had failed miserably.

After experiencing the intense visions portraying the possible aftermath of their actions, the soldiers felt stunned and weakened. For even in their kinship in arms, strapped within their high-tech gear and armor, there resided a small part of them which desired a familiar home to return to; and if that one assurance was abolished, then they were nothing more than lost souls drifting among the stars. It would be the one common perspective they shared with this ancient race called the Dries. For if they were left void of any virtuous purpose; these soldiers would struggle in their choice to decide their own destiny as either missionaries, or as mercenaries.

The Sergeant, on the other hand, saw the possibility of conquest for glory above his duties towards peace. Unlike the Grey's, Human age did not always sprout wisdom; but more often then naught, it would germinate into the consuming bitterness of envy and regret. These were the few men who lost all passion for life and cared not for the consequences they wrought without the burdens of shame. They were already dead inside, and the extraterrestrials could sense that.

That, however, was the reason I was here. I was the bane of such poisoned minds, one who could see the whole picture without cringing upon viewing the parts of our soul which were distasteful and ugly. These were flaws which had to be whitewashed from the canvas and cleansed of its venom. Feeling the power of their combined minds within me, I became a willing puppet of these ancient beings.

The restraints holding my arms suddenly buckled from their clasps and I was released from the table. Standing to my feet, I now saw that the Sergeant and the techs were frozen in a state of limbo; aware of their surroundings, but unable to react in their own defense. They themselves now faced the nightmare they had so readily played upon countless civilians, and the taste of fear for what they had done began to creep into their bones. Standing before the Sergeant, his stern face slowly turned to panic and despair within the reflection of my dark ebony eyes.

The mental power of the Dries flowed through me and I saw the crushing ugliness inside him, and it somehow made sense that sympathy and empathy had no place in his small world, and in return, he would receive none. Instinctively, I placed my hand to his chest and I felt my blood surge as he shook and rattled like a rag doll at my touch. In moments, the micro-electric static of his living cells ruptured and ceased to function; each dying a death separate and alone. The cohesive energy within his body was nullified and dispersed back into the nothingness of the cosmos from whence it came.

The techs gasped in fright as the Sergeants limp body crumbled to the floor at their feet. His corpse was intact and unmarred, but inanimate in every respect. I hadn't exactly killed him, but rather, had released him from his own painful delusions. The thought of that might have sounded unhinged; but in the mind of the Dries, the Sergeant had been returned to a state of peace that he would have never found in life. In the higher conscience of the Elders, the ending of his corrupted life was merely seen as a mercy.

The eyes of the doctors and technicians widened in dread as my dark gaze slowly turned towards them. At this moment, I could be used as a weapon to assassinate them all and end this incursion at the cost of their lives. Instead, I lowered my hands and issued my own words of warning towards the panicked personnel.

"You have not seen all that I have been shown, you do not understand the true dilemma the human race faces in this dire hour," I bade as a plea, "we cannot conquer the galaxy, for it is not ours to take. These non-terrestrial creatures you fear are not invaders; but our parents, our forefathers and mentors. The truth is, we are the aliens on our own world, and Earth will be our last home and shelter unless we learn to recognize our own immaturity."

At that, the kinetic ball of light dimmed to a small flickering orb as my anger subsided, and the ships personnel were released from their paralyzing stasis. With nervous mumbling cast between them, one of the techs stepped forward and dared to speak.

"What ...what is it that you want of us?" the man asked in a distressed tone as his terrified gaze turned from the shattered body of the Sergeant back towards me.

"Simply ask yourself a fundamental question about those who sent you here; and decide if you were invited to follow by choice ...or coerced to obey their orders?" I inquired with a raised eyebrow, "Leave this place, for no good will come of it. The alien races you so fear, fear us equally in return; and are only concerned about holding all life dear on our planet. The human race, alone, is that one spark which could ignite the end for us all; and they are merely trying to protect us from ourselves."

The ships personnel onboard the vessel and stationed on the ground were still trying to recoup from the visions which had flooded their minds of the burning planet they had seen. It was a drowning despair which wrenched their guts and made them question their loyalties to a system that would cause them to lose everything they presumed to fight for. It was the stark realization that the foolish hostilities we preoccupied ourselves with, were entirely unnecessary.

The chief technician nodded once, and with my alien eyes I could see the sincerity and conviction in the color of his mind. The telepathy I felt emanating from me was not at a caliber of the elder Grey's; but was a strange sensation nonetheless, that made me understand how the world of men was truly alone even when standing in the midst of billions of our own people.

"What will happen to them now?" I asked internally at the voices to which I played as host.

"Their minds are true, and will return to their home system of Sol. However, if they fail to convince their acting superiors of their folly, then it is quite likely they will be merely dismissed and readily replaced by others who will continue to pursue their mission of madness," the 9 replied.

I could perceive their words more clearly now, and saw that as long as the human race was at conflict with itself that we would never reach a sense of unity with the world on which we lived. The universe was a chaotic place as it was, and had no desire for mankind to spread its malady upon it. The glowing orb of light continued to proceed before me wherever I progressed within the ship so I presumed it was a type of psychic defense, mentally controlled by the Dries themselves. Once I reached the main bridge, the subordinate staff vacated to a respectable distance, having been given orders to stand down by their superiors.

On a wild thought, I turned to the lieutenant in charge and issued a stern request that he was to transfer all of their present personnel over to their sister vessel and relinquish this ship. This move was of mild surprise to the Dries, who were eavesdropping on my activities and challenged my motives.

"Before you disembark Lieutenant, I want you to transfer all authorization command of this vessel to me, understood?" I ordered as he gazed into my eerie black eyes and the alien orb of crackling light that lingered around me, which further urged his cooperation. With a nod, he stated he would have the ship's AI and tactical command transferred immediately. He and his crew knew that any failure to obey would only result in being incapacitated, and they were still suffering the effects from the unnerving visions they had endured.

"Why did you choose to sequester their vessel?" the 9 dared to ask, revealing that they were not all-knowing after all. The logic of my actions must have evaded them as they could not foretell my plan of action. It did not go unnoticed that they had failed to read my most direct inner thoughts as to what I was thinking.

"You did not want them to use the dimensional gate, for reasons of the havoc they would wreak. I, however, do not pose such a threat; although my curiosity still leads me forward," I responded to the 9. My words were followed by a series of incoherent mumbling as the elder Grey's communed among their Council.

Many years ago when I was in college, one could say that I had an eclectic taste for ancient cultures and lost civilizations. I found it a coincidence that there were 9 elders in the Dries assembly; for I had read about a similar order on an earthly scale, once known in legend as the nine unknown men of Ashoka. It was an ancient tale of nine scholars who studied natural sciences and advanced psychology. These few men, however, had sworn themselves towards the path of peace, so instead of passing their knowledge in part or in whole to the masses, they chose to shroud their studies in secrecy, in order to prevent any one person from combining these volumes of knowledge for the purpose of perpetuating the evils of war.

The first discipline was that of Propaganda, which mastered psychological warfare and was considered the most dangerous of all sciences, for its abilities to mold mass opinion and enable anyone to govern over a society through means of deceit instead of truth. The second was Physiology, and the finer details of all living organisms for their given strengths and weaknesses. The third covered the study of Microbiology, and its leaning focus on biotechnology. The fourth was Alchemy, which delved into the dynamic interactions and transmutation of metals.

The native study of Communications followed thereafter, of languages and transmission of thought; and how such talents would lead to telepathy as a higher form. The sixth scholar focused on the secrets of gravity and the lines of both chaos and order in the universe; and how it could be manipulated and controlled. The seventh was Cosmogony, which delved into astronomy and the complex woven designs and secret origins of our universe. The eighth was the study of light in all its wavelengths; including how it can be used as both a resource and a weapon. The last was Sociology, which followed the rules of evolution in societies and the means of foretelling their rise and decline.

These of course, were all open subjects of research in any modern day college worth its salt; but were seen as either divine studies or points of taboo in many ancient cultures. Wise men, Sages, and Oracles were placed with the burdens of such sacred knowledge in our ancient past, but their philosophy of use had been abused to promote the petty goals of select individuals instead of for the benefit of the masses. Think of these nine studies as colored threads which could be either woven into an enlightening tapestry to illustrate an image of fulfillment, or drawn into a distorted design of woe and despair.

I thought about this fact long and hard, and could now unravel the enigma of human nature. It seemed so utterly simple that I was unable to understand how we had confused the mixture of such elementary ingredients. I watched from the deck as the smaller military ship and the ground vehicles pulled away back towards the entrance of the rift from whence they came. With a moment's hesitation, I stepped forward and placed my hands on the control board to gain access to the ship's computer. Pressing my will upon it, a dose of mental energy fused into the mainframe; purging it with a frequency of energy which would awaken the sleeping artifacts of the biotech left buried within the core of the vessel. Without the telepathic tools to unlock them, these reverse-engineered alien ships held secrets that our military forces had no means to control.

It was a trillion-dollar vessel created by a black budget space program, and in all respects, it would have been unmanageable by a single individual. Yet through funneling the combined minds of the alien overlords, I was able to shock the sleeping technology within the ship's systems to life. Utilizing a wave of their mental energy, I redirected the manifested orb of light which the Grey's had forged for my defense and utilized it as an antenna to focus upon the colossal sphere of the rift buoy positioned in front of the ship.

"What are your intentions?" Words of worry began to seep into my mind from the Dries Council, with overshadowed whispers among themselves as they wondered how I was able to activate the dimensional gate. The answer was simple really.

"I wish to see what is beyond..." my response trailed off as if to illustrate what could be limitless possibilities. With that disclosure, defiance rose in their tone as they realized too late that by exploiting my mind to act as their host, that it could also be turned against them. The device Caesar had gifted to me allowed protection against their mental control, but had also served to keep the connection between us open by force of will. In doing so, I discovered I could also draw upon their vast mental pool and guide it as desired.

Slowly, the wall of rippling liquid that enveloped the circumference of the rift began to part, exposing a hungry light at its core. This anomaly seemed to stretch and grasp at the ambient light within its reach, consuming it. Through this breach, I edged the vessel into its maw as fingers of subatomic energy arched over the ships outer skin. The triangle-shaped craft seemed to melt into its tentacles while I heard the voices of the 9 petition and plead in their vain attempts to hinder my actions, and that I might reconsider this reckless plan.

This time, however, it was I who was leeching the telepathic link from them; for they had not foreseen that such a lower-form being was capable of mastering the complexities of the mind. They reduced themselves to begging for my return to no avail. We were both explorers, our race and theirs; and they had to recognize that this was humanities only escape from our inner demons. We would break free of our chains and run blindly into the night, merely to escape the idea of captivity locked in our own minds; no matter where it led us as we fled.

Basic control of the spacecraft made it a small effort to move the ship forward into the field of the dimensional rift. For the first time, I heard the inflection of unease in the voices of the Elders, warning me to turn back. My agenda was clear. These alien races had watched us for countless millennia and nurtured our civilizations throughout our long-forgotten history; but now I needed to learn of theirs.

As the rift gate swallowed the ship, I felt the connection with the voices of the 9 come to an abrupt halt. There was a pulling sensation at my feet; not like gravity, but more like a suction of my entire being. The monitors within the stealth craft went black as the vessel was swept through a dimensional river into the endless darkness between the stars. I felt an anticipation wash over me, unlike seeing something mysterious and new;

but more akin to the feeling of reuniting with an old friend. In a disquieting way, this moment felt somehow familiar.

Maybe I was expecting some sort of illuminated tunnel winding through the depths of time and space from watching too many movies, but instead, the ship merely moved to another place without delay. The monitors on the ship went haywire for a minute as they attempted to verify telemetry in an effort to calculate our new location. Bypassing the monitors entirely, I activated the sensory skin on the hull of the ship to become semi-transparent. Standing upon the bridge, the field of view opened up to a swash of planets before me; each held within a prism of light ornately decorated by a shower of stars.

The sheer beauty of it caught my breath for a moment as I stood there in silent awe. Dimensional shifting through space can be described best by imagining a light bulb being turned on in a room of mirrors. The light travels from the source, yet back again at the same time; illuminating countless angles from which to originate and ricochet from a central point. That analogy might sound absurd at first, but one must be positioned within the room's center to fully appreciate its perspective.

In but a mere blink, I had traveled across the galaxy into another spectrum of space. The worlds floating around me were entwined with vibrant clouds that danced and swirled into complex designs. An odd feeling washed over me just then; and though it was difficult to describe, it seemed as though I could actually *feel* that life existed here. It wasn't just on the nearest planets surface and oceans; but was also present in the space around me, everywhere.

With a touch of the panel, I directed the ship towards this strange new world that beckoned, to see what it held beyond its misty veil. The triangular stealth ship swooped down at impossible speeds until it came to a gentle glide high above the surface. Energy capsules from each of its corners leveled the ship as it came to rest in a gentle glide. Looking below, I saw ribbons of light reflecting back; revealing the signs of a sizable civilization upon its surface.

The thrill of the unknown struck me, making me wonder how it must have felt to visitors who trespassed upon our own alien world. The underlying truth was that Earth itself was a new host to our species, and we had barely explored the depths of our own oceans which comprised well over two-thirds of our tiny blue planet. Even so, somehow we found it necessary to fling ourselves into the darkness of space.

Drifting closer, I wondered if I would find some primitive civilization struggling day by day or an advanced society which excelled in education and learning. Would I need to encounter the indigenous people, or evade them to avoid influencing their culture while studying their species? First and foremost, was to engage in reconnaissance to ascertain their level of hostility. At the end of that line of thinking, I had to step back and ascertain my own intentions. Were my actions being drawn by my own selfish curiosity, or was there a better way to make first contact to satisfy the information I desired?

Alien species had made it a habit to exercise stealth to explore my world, while abducting helpless people in the dark of the night. In all regards, they were emotionally blind to the trauma that they caused to their victims; as their logic for pursuing a means to an end simply had no room for the luxuries of empathy. Could I envision a better way to approach this same scenario? There was certainly room for improvement which could involve pure transparency and trust; but only if the indigenous population was able to accept such an idea, which might very well depend on their state of technology and philosophical advancement.

It was clear to me now that mankind, in our current childish and egocentric state of mind, could not handle nor accept communion with an advanced race. We had a habit to shoot first and ask questions later, and irrationally feared what we did not understand. Consideration of these facts placed any alien emissary in harm's way. Like an explorer arriving on an island of primitive cannibals; you might envision greeting friendly natives, but it wouldn't be too surprising to find one's head on a pike by the end of the day. The risks came with the territory.

A technologically advanced race would likely have an entirely different reaction: one either benevolent and welcoming, or instantaneously deadly. I could now sympathize with the challenges the many extraterrestrial species had with the human race. Mankind had been tagged as dangerous and unpredictable; and unfortunately, we possessed the ability to be a real threat to ourselves and others.

My approach was likely reckless, but I chose to disable all stealth protocols running within the ship's defenses, and broadcasted my approach to anyone who might be listening. Down through the sky, I glided towards the nearest aurora of lights emanating from the encroaching shadows of dusk which had fallen across the dark horizon. I had expected the source of the illumination to be the glittering skyline of a vast metropolis, but was both amazed and baffled by what I saw.

There was little to be seen in the way of a thriving society bustling below me upon the surface, as I might have expected; instead, what I found were chains of light emanating from vast structures of fluid design. These prisms glimmered through tubular causeways and tall cones which unfolded like the petals of a flower. This was something far more strange and alien than I could have ever imagined, and frankly, I was astonished by the sheer simplicity of the architecture.

There were no moving vehicles or beings to be seen below; nor was there any response to the ship's hails. Manning the controls, I led the vessel to the nearest open port that could accompany the size of my ship, and brought it to anchor as it hovered within the mooring. Once assured that the command modules would follow my instructions, I left the bridge and made my way to the transport bay where a gravity beam touched the surface. Stepping into the field, I gently drifted to the ground directly below the floating ship.

Subconsciously, I had expected troops of armed guards and crowds of strange beings to come flooding to this location upon the arrival of my alien craft, but there was no one to be seen and I was only met with an eerie silence. The landing led to an interior walkway awash with a pleasant orange hue, one set with gentle curves and slopes which added to the graceful flow of its design. These wide corridors were illuminated by a soft glow that appeared to have no direct source, and I was left baffled by the technology. I made my way through to the floor of a service lift which brought me down several levels into the presence of a white caldera. Within these bleached walls was contained a wide shallow pool filled with a cold blue light that trickled with dancing reflections throughout the room.

It was a bizarre and lonely experience to wander these strange organic buildings while knowing nothing of their function. Drawn to the blue pool, I basked in its calming light as I gazed in wonder. Needless to say, I was startled by the sound of a voice which addressed me; and a human voice at that.

"Visitor to our world, you are invited among the Keepers. All beings are welcome here," it spoke in a soft female voice. However, looking around the room, I could not see the source of the sound, though its voice could be heard audibly and mentally in unison. I merely assumed the translation must have been made by the alien biotech I adorned.

"As your humble guest, I appreciate your gracious reception," I replied, "and I would very much like to meet the people of this new world; for I have come a long way to see them."

There was a queer silence that followed, and I mistakenly assumed the speaker was arranging for someone, or something, to come greet me in person. That, however, was not the direction the conversation flowed.

"You misunderstand, visitor, for there are no individual beings present here," it revealed, "we the Keepers, are everything that you see before you," the female voice acknowledged as the room pulsated gently with light. To my astonishment, it was during that still moment I came to realize that I was standing within a living entity.

Full Circle

The collective entity known as the Keepers, were the end result of a biological technology infused with its own artificial intelligence. The voice of my cordial host helped explained in terms I could understand, regarding the history of this world and many others like it while I returned to the upper floors. Outside, great spires of colored lights wove through the horizon of the setting sun while the veil of night fell across the sky. Strange constellations beckoned back at me from above, accompanied by a mild peace overcoming my thoughts from knowing that I could now touch each and every one of them.

"There have been many diverse species who have visited our distant world," the voice of the Keeper spoke, "even of your own genetic line."

"Mankind has been to this place before?" I nearly choked on my own words in response.

"Why yes; we have also seen the Manu-ti, the Manu-sa, among several others who had excelled in their societies to be able to visit these lands. However, it grieves us that there were also countless others who were never able to reach our shores," she finished with a hint of sadness.

"Do you mean people from my solar system?" I asked, wondering if it was possible that all the stories the Dries spoke of were true; and that Mankind has been wandering the galaxy for countless generations. I stood there alone, looking out into the night sky to wish and wonder.

"Not of the Sol system, but of numerous others within the vast sea, far beyond the stars you see before you," she answered, "and of extraterrestrial races, as you call them, whom you are all but different shades and breeds of the same family."

Her words were shocking, though I could piece together the logic of her meaning; stating that all the alien races I've met thus far could be derived from the same genetic root. The truth was, black or white, yellow or brown, or even gray; we were all aliens in a certain way. I chuckled to myself at the thought of it; no matter what country our people came from, we were all extraterrestrials on Earth. We had simply forgotten where we had originated after squatting there for so long. Humanity had been riddled by vicious racism throughout our known history, and there was not one ounce of reason for it. Mankind was such an angry little child that we made enemies of ourselves out of spite.

With their advanced technology, these enlightened beings rose through several progressive ages of invention and came to excel in biological science. Once they had merged it with artificial intelligence, they discovered that there truly was no such thing as being *artificial*. They saw evolution as a fundamental truth that life would continue to seek life. And thus, after they created the ultimate utopia where their societies could flourish without want or need; they instead, chose to abandon it.

This world and its exotic flora would be considered a paradise to anyone in the human race, but to the species of the Dries, it represented a goal of life without substance. In this reflection, they took again to the stars in ancient ships to seek out new worlds to explore and analyze the struggle of life in an effort to learn what they had lost in their pursuit for perfection. Now the Keepers stood as a lonely oasis as did other such self-aware worlds, who found a final peace in their solitude. They were the flower that took countless millennia to bloom, and we were but the seeds cast into the wind among a valley of stars.

I suddenly felt an overwhelming sadness befall me as I gazed upon the perfection of this sentient utopia. I could imagine how many people it could house and nourish, and bring relief to the people of Earth who struggled day by day to put food on the table and a roof over their heads. It would end the senseless deaths caused by the petty wars busy pushing borders and consuming resources. The truth was; Earth itself was already an Eden; we had merely failed to recognize it as we were too busy bickering among ourselves while we crushed this fragile garden under our restless feet.

In our struggles, we left our homes and families behind in search for a better life where we could learn and grow. In this respect; that small alien gene pushed us forward. I had to ask myself; if mankind one day ended all their quarrels and created a utopia such as this, would they too become bored with their creation and cast themselves into the cosmos to share their message? There was only one answer.

I gathered my composure and turned back towards my private stealth ship where it had been docked. Approaching the deck where it was left anchored, the Keepers made a final request before my abrupt departure.

"If you would excuse us for inquiring, but we have accessed the records on your vessel and it has come to our attention that the social order of your current homeworld has not reached the approved status for interstellar travel, nor permissions to access the dimensional gates through the rift," she announced, "may we ask what are your intentions, now that you know of us and what lies beyond the boundaries of your closed world?" the Keeper asked.

It was a simple question with a difficult answer. What good could one lone traveler do among an endless ocean of stars? The consumable supplies aboard the military vessel I had sequestered might last me a while, but my time on board would be limited. The best I could hope for would be to find a world with a society of friendly beings where I could live out the rest of my days; given they would be so accommodating, even if their atmosphere was compatible with my biological needs. I struggled for a moment only to conclude that the right thing to do was to return to Earth and let the general population know what I had seen; and at the very least, make an attempt to stop the madness we so frantically stowed upon ourselves. In bitter reflection, once this truth was revealed, it was very likely that society would dissolve and governments would fall in the aftermath that would follow.

An alien race disclosing the truth about the universe and the conspiracies embedded deep within our government would likely be received with suspicion. However, if a fellow human spoke those words to the masses; then the outcome might lean towards a more positive response. I stood there for a moment weighing what I should do. Should I travel the universe and leave my broken world behind, or make a stand and compose a way to end the chaos mankind had wrought? There were countless souls on Earth who wanted to expose the great lie we lived in; who ached to hear the words spoken which they already knew to be true. In light of that burden, I realized I had an obligation.

"It is my wish to return to my own world and share the knowledge I have gained here, in order to assist my species towards attaining a better direction." I acknowledged, "Is there anything you can offer to aid me in that endeavor?

Once again there was a long silence as lights hummed and throbbed along the entire biological structure known as the Keepers. Their answer was one I had anticipated.

"We have accessed your ship, and as such revealed through the logs of your vessel and the knowledge in your own mind, that your species is warlike and in a state of great peril," the Keeper announced, "it is improbable that your social order is currently settled in a balanced state to hear the truth you propose to offer; and is one they are inclined to either not believe, or more likely, will refuse to hear," she granted.

I could not argue with that logic, but felt as though it was my responsibility to try. It would be a heavy burden to bear if I disrupted the presumed peace and tilted the nations of Earth into global warfare; only to manifest the very outcome I so desperately sought to avoid. I felt an ache in my heart; for following such actions could lead towards the meaningless deaths of countless billions and usher in a state of suppression if those few who held the tether of power felt threatened by the knife which had cut at their leash. We were a species who feared change and the idea of true freedom; for it was our only unreachable delusion that kept us struggling day by day, looking ever upward so we wouldn't have to see the chains around our feet.

If those restraints were cut, would we even have the strength to walk those few awkward steps towards a better future?

"I understand and appreciate your concerns," I offered humbly, "and admit that I am ill-educated to fully perceive what could be the consequence of such a reckless venture. Perhaps you could offer a second opinion; for I would greatly value your insight."

Lights rippled along the intertwining structures out beyond the distant horizon in a cascading dance of colors. I waited patiently as the Keepers evaluated the collective knowledge it held from a thousand worlds. Finally, the entity made a simple gesture to resolve my dilemma.

"Our analysis of your desired venture concludes that your society is too young and naive to perceive the knowledge you have to offer; and would fall the way of many other worlds before it who have faced a similar crisis," the Keepers advised, "but if you are truly determined in your goal, we will offer to aid you in the only way we can; by giving you the tools and guidance to act as a curator, if you will ...and to stand as a steward of your troubled world," the voice offered.

With a burst of mental data, the Keepers sent me the full meaning of their intent. They would infuse the energies of the dimensional rift into the stealth vessel; so that I may use the flux of space to manipulate the flow of time. Entering the flux would slow time dramatically while I awaited signals from their gravitational beacons they would transmit to my world. I was advised they would send signs which the computers on my ship would be able to interpret, although I was astounded by what they had proposed.

For centuries, there have been reports of phenomena such as fairy rings found in remote grasslands and fields, which soon grew to tales of 'mowing devils' shortly after the age of agriculture was introduced for cultivating crops. This was the bio-energy they used to speak from one world entity to another over great distances; which formed complex designs embedded with multi-dimensional structures set within their intricate patterns. In short, creating what was widely known in our modern era as crop circles.

Entities from other worlds had also sent such communications embedded with a biological attunement to certain types of plant life that flourished within the specific frequency of its living energy. Such a method of biological data transference only operated in large volumes of the same genetic material, which could be restructured by a single note; much like a tuning fork that held a single tone and resonated with other biological forms that existed within the same wavelength. Unseen to the naked eye, these images in the fields contained complex dimensional architecture which held vast amounts of encrypted information. Being ignorant of such bio-technology, we humans only saw flattened wheat; and were unable to perceive the boundless framework of data it contained.

These circles had always been a mystery to mankind, and those few scientists who attempted to provide similar theories were considered nothing more than delusional quacks. However, those oppositions in the know, quickly made short work of these inter-dimensional signs and flooded the media with fabricated hoaxes and misinformation in its wake. The practice of such deception helped quell the public from asking too many questions if it became widely rumored that these signposts were created by intentional trickery and deceit. The elitists knew far too well, that the truth was far easier to hide than it was to explain.

"So you would have me act as warden to my own planet, to what end?" I asked with rising curiosity.

"Unlike the other military vessels your race has engineered with stolen technology, your ship will be able to shift between dimensions, so that time will affect you on a far lesser scale than those who cannot, and thus, will extend your lifespan several-fold than what is normal for your species," the gentle voice of the Keeper advised, "we will strive to deliver these data signals to the biological portions of your ship, which you will be able to interpret and choose to act upon."

"I'm still confused how that will address the dangerous state of affairs on my world and deliver my message," I struggled to ask while juggling the logic of their proposition.

"You alone, would be able to intercept and negate escalations between your warring factions upon your planet with a defensive ordinance that will not harm, but may effectively disarm their destructive weaponry. Furthermore, you will have the means to keep a vigilant eye upon your societies until a time they are ready to receive the message you desire to deliver," the entity advised.

In a way, I too, would become a Keeper. A protector of the human race until a time humanity had matured to understand and absorb the idea that there was a better way to live. I faced an internal conflict over this council, since I wanted to make a difference here and now. But with a measure of contemplation, I began to recognize the tactical wisdom in their offered solution. I would not endeavor to force a change, but to wait for the opportunity when the few who are able to see, became the many. However, I would require a measure of patience until such an opportunity might present itself.

With unspoken words, I agreed to their terms and the Keepers sensed my approval of their plan. They imbued my ship with their biological energy which coursed through the ships frame, effectively releasing the full capacity of the bio-ware from the alien technology locked within the ships systems.

Unfortunately, to do so, the Keepers noted that there was one more guideline which I would have to agree to. Once I was attuned with the ship's functions, I could never leave its confines; for I would be mentally linked with the ship itself. The human mind was far too weak to break such a bond, even for a short time, and I agonized over the thought that I may never again feel the sand of the beach or the grass between my toes. I was to forever surrender the caress of an evening breeze as I sat upon the deck of my cabin while lazily staring up upon the evening stars.

I would substitute the warm glow of my cabin's fireplace for the throbbing fusion chamber of the stealth ship. I would have to trade the fresh smell of rain upon the wind for the sterile ozone of the vessel's bridge. My reach upon the world would become much longer than any human before me; yet I would not be able to grasp it. With a final nod of surrender, I agreed to their conditions. Once aboard the warship, I transferred to the bridge in order to address the Keepers of this lonely world.

"Your vessel has been saturated with as much living knowledge as it is able to absorb, and provided coordinates to return you to the part of the galaxy within your own solar system," the female voice related, "once you place your hands upon the control console, the energy of the ship will become attuned to your genetic code and a biological link will be woven between your mind and that of its operating systems," she noted.

"Well, this should be fun..." I stammered half-joking as I slowly placed my palms into the control board on either side.

"No ...be assured it will not," was all the Keeper responded before a surge of electricity jolted through my body, lighting up the entire bridge with arcs of raw energy.

They were certainly right; for the wave of energy was a level of pain I had never experienced before. It felt as if tendrils laced with hot razors were climbing through my brain. I wanted to let go of the control board, losing myself to the primal instinct to end the torture, but found I was unable. My body wouldn't obey as I was locked within a prison of light.

I felt as if I was going to pass out and collapse a dozen times over, but the energies in the ship forced me to remain conscious throughout the ordeal; until mercifully, everything around me went dark. There was only the sound of my panting left echoing through the corridors of the vessel; I was now one with the spacecraft and its enhanced systems. Looking around as I gathered my strength, I nearly lost my balance from the ship's extended perception as its sensory data permeated my conscious thought.

"Congratulations, you have survived the transfer," the Keepers announced as though I had won a prize at a county fair.

"What the ...you mean, you didn't expect me to?" I choked.

"Truthfully, there was a high chance you would have suffered organ failure and ceased to be," she noted nonchalantly, "but it was a reasonable risk considering your apparent devotion to your cause," the entity replied, "take care to understand and control all aspects of the vessel you now possess; for your very life is tied to it. Are you now ready to depart?"

My mind flooded with images and sensations of everything the ship could see and feel in degrees far beyond the simplicities of the human body. Though mentally, it felt like a knight wearing encumbering armor, I had also felt a subtle yet unshakeable sense of freedom, beyond anything I had ever experienced. There were no words to describe the sudden release I felt from the confines of my own frail body. After a brief pause, I gave my confirmation.

The ship released itself from its moors to the deck above the complex, and sailed off into the morning sky. The warm glow of dawn pierced through the command bridge the moment the ship breached the atmosphere. Like the crack of a whip, a ray of light shot out from the ship's core directly into the rift, and the vessel began to accelerate as it scaled through the spectrum of light; accelerating ever faster along this tether.

The human body wasn't designed for such trauma as traveling through space and time, and I nearly blacked out from the mental effort to absorb the overwhelming information flooding into my mind. There was no vortex of light as I had been groomed to expect; there was just a simple blink, as though someone had simply switched off a light. The ship had been awakened and was a biological entity in its own right, and I was attached to it as its host. As I emerged from the corona of the sun, I could feel the needles of empty space pricking upon me as the ship neared the little blue planet called Earth, and what I saw there astounded me.

There were alien ships everywhere, countless hundreds of them of every size and shape, from lumbering monstrosities to tiny orbs of faint light zipping about within our planetary orbit reaching as far as our moon. I was viewing this spectacle through the sensors of the ship which could interpret the sub-dimensional spectrum far into the infrared. Here was evidence beyond any shadow of a doubt that alien life inhabited our galaxy, yet it was just outside man's ability to detect it. The Earth itself was a hot-spot of activity for observation and research for multiple species throughout the universe as it had been for countless eons.

Speeding through the solar system, the ship wove through the alien vessels peppered around the planet and quickly became a center of attention for numerous craft the moment we came into range. A dreary voice echoed through the hull and into my conscious; one I had never heard before.

"What are you called?" it demanded, "this planet is under communal quarantine and any encroaching species must abide by the treaties dictated by the Council!"

"I am of Manu-ka, and your foreign rules and treaties to not apply to a native of this world," I answered smugly, though not really able to help myself, "My purpose here is to end the deception to which you are all equally party to, as much as the race of Men."

Continuing to evade the alien vessels, I guided my ship to skim the upper atmosphere. An influx of mental chatter filtered into my head, so much so, I had to smother the lines of consciousness being driven into my mind like pointed spears. Several alien ships broke off from their former trajectories and took pursuit of my stolen stealth craft; gliding in and out of the upper stratosphere, hot upon my tail.

"Surrender yourself to our care, it is strictly forbidden that those indigenous of this species may not possess bio-technical craft," a baritone voice ordered, "You must comply, or face destruction!"

With that threat in mind, I concentrated on defensive tactics and felt a cold twinge as the ship phased into sub-dimensional space. The scouts chasing me came to a slow halt, seeing that I had disappeared into nothingness. However, their craft did not possess the power of the Keepers who had upgraded my stealth ship to a degree rarely seen in the galaxy. Although I had made short work of them, with a worried glance outside my ship, I could tell I may have inadvertently jumped from the frying pan and into the fire.

A violent stream of dimensional waves coursed over the skin of the ship, knocking it from its trajectory and sending me into a spin. The core of the ship operated by producing its own gravitational field and used that self-sustaining bubble to resist gravity streams which any mundane ship would have fallen victim to. Having slipped the stealth craft into another dimension to evade the pursuit of my alien antagonists, I could observe this world between worlds; and found it terrifying.

Living creatures swarmed through empty space around me, which had now taken on a reddish hue. The Earth, itself, had turned a vivid green with turbulent oceans swirling with colors of honey and lavender. With curiosity overtaking my better judgment, I guided my ship towards the surface while noting that even the interior of the stealth ship took on a different tint of light. Soaring over the expanse of a continent, I dropped within several hundred feet of the terrain below.

I could see the shapes of familiar trees, but it was if they were being viewed through infrared light; bleached white while swaying in subtle shades as they quivered in continuous motion. I looked for signs of human life in this strange new world which masked our own; only to find odd and unsettling dark shadows pacing through the vegetation. It was like something out of a nightmare; and I almost resisted accessing the ship's data banks to decipher what I was witnessing. Coming up blank for an explanation, it was the familiar voice of the Keepers who answered my curious solicitation.

"If one looks closely, they would find an abundance of life in but a single drop of seawater, yet its presence goes unnoticed if left unseen. Your world is a living being bound together in many realms of space. Just as there are frequencies of light your unaided eyes cannot perceive; yet these wavelengths still exist nonetheless," the voice conceded, "there exists an exotic flora and fauna in the electromagnetic range tied to your planet and many other such living worlds. This is why the species of so many distant races fear the actions of Mankind; for if you poison your planet, you also destroy theirs," the calming voice of the Keeper related as the ship's sensors shifted through multiple dimensional scales; each more strange and unique than the last.

The human race had a history of acting selfish and naive; so much so, that they had gained a reputation for 'taking-the-cake' per se, compared to similar civilizations across the galaxy. Men would cut down a tree to build a fire for a single night without considering the shade it provided, or fruit it bore, or the numerous creatures which lived within its branches and roots; we solely took what we wanted for the here and now. We saw ourselves at the top of the food chain, and our acting authorities wanted to keep the masses thinking that way. Under their rule, we were kept blind by intentional design.

We already knew that we shared Earth with ten million other species of life on our little blue planet; but how would our population react if we knew the actual number was a thousand-fold? Without the ability to communicate honestly with one another through telepathic means, Mankind instead, turned to social fabrications such as governments and regimes to burden the responsibilities of providing peace and unity to the people. However, it was a feeble and inefficient substitute for a civilization that could see mind to mind and communicate heart to heart. We were speaking to the deaf and using sign language to talk to the blind; by definition, our social system was doomed to fail. There was only one answer to save ourselves; we had to open our psyche to a new way of thinking.

Our Earth, this living being known as 'Gaia' in many doctrines throughout ancient history, was home to many sentient forms of life other than our own which were far older than we could ever imagine. Earth was but one of the many sacred trinities recorded in our theologies; a world who mourned as she watched her sisters die, one by one, over the great sea of time. The parasite known as Man had infected her with its sickness; a malady other beings from distant worlds had sought to cure. From forgotten text and superstition, the tale of these three sisters endured by frayed strings throughout our long and tattered past until it became considered nothing more than an imagined legend or whimsical fairytale. The mythos of the triple deity Goddess derives from every corner of the Earth, each a twisted tale in its telling referring to our people's ancient and forgotten past of the worlds which bore our young. I had spent many years researching ancient and forgotten civilizations, and recalled the countless references to such a triad which had been replicated and retold throughout time among many cultures.

Having evaded my pursuers, I phased the ship back into normal space and suddenly found myself above the outskirts of a major city. I hovered there contemplating what I had learned as I placed the pieces of such a grand puzzle together in my weary head. Much to my surprise, military chatter began to filter in as the ship absorbed radio communications from all restricted bandwidths, at the same time, the proximity alarms in the vessel warned of a pair of incoming jet fighters set on an intercept course to my bearing.

"Bogey one at twelve hundred, we have a visual. Push to blue, confirm, over," the stern voices echoed over the transmission, "Squawk, zero, zero, one, zero, confirmed, over," the responding pilot announced, "TR-3B Alpha 10, personnel aboard, you are in possession of a stolen military craft," the harsh male voice cut into the chatter, "you are ordered to stand down and follow the escorts approaching your proximity, or you will be fired upon! Respond, over."

With a shrug of my shoulders, I almost found the threat as an overstatement of confidence on their part. Scanning the complex functions of my ship, I concluded my vessel could outmaneuver and outpace these jets, or simply phase-shift as a last resort. It would even evade any ships our secret military might have of this same model. This vessel was beyond unique and far too powerful to be allowed back into the hands of the military; let alone the fact that my mind would likely be broken if I was ever forced to part from my link with the ship.

"This is Alpha Ten, listen well, for this will be my one and only response you will receive," I called back through the military channel, while mentally deactivating the previously unnoticed transponder embedded within my ship, "Humanity has been quarantined on this planet by a thousand other worlds because they fear us; not for our might, but for the sickness in our minds from which this affliction sprouts. I have taken this ship and pass along the message from these sentient beings, that mankind is to dissolve its military space programs and relinquish the technology we have been gifted back into the hands of our people, so that it may benefit all. I plead with you to put aside war, and concentrate on peace," and with a final pause I thought it appropriate to add one last morsel to my message, "Advise your generals that Earth has a new guardian ...and I will be watching," I warned with a calm but forceful tone, and promptly cut the transmission.

The military jets arrived moments later and executed a flyby maneuver, though my ships' advanced sensors noted no weaponry had yet been activated on their part. My stealth craft had been armed with a concentrated electromagnetic pulse targeting system, which had been enhanced several fold, thanks to the energy upgrade by the Keepers. After a brief moment, the military personnel attempted to respond with additional threats and ultimatums, but their protests were thwarted by the feedback reflected across the frequency that garbled the hails of all transmissions in the area. One of the jets armed a lock onto my craft, and though I could have disabled his ship with a single beam of energy, I chose to phase back into sub-space.

The pilots of the jets were just as confused as the personnel manning the military radar at the nearby base; for my triangular ship seemed to have disappeared from existence. Dimensional space wasn't without its risks, but it appeared time itself was altered and wildly manipulated when my craft slipped into its envelope. Bringing my vessel back into high orbit, I phased again into normal space to face the wrath of the aliens monitoring my homeworld; while wondering how long we would have to play this game of cat and mouse.

"We heard your words," a voice called into my head while my ship tracked several exotic alien craft flitting above the Earth, "You are the one who sees. You will be left to your own objectives and may continue your mission unhindered, but only as long as you do not interfere with ours; and the Council only requires that you are not allowed to leave this solar system," the alien warden conceded, "We welcome your vision."

After the communication the formation of alien ships slowly edged away from my proximity, and I turned my attention to the sea of stars beyond, accented by the soft glow of the moon and the vast swash of the Milky Way splashed upon the darkness of space. These alien races had welcomed me into their folds with but a single condition; that I remain within their scope of surveillance. The energy granted by the Keepers would keep the gravitation fusion core of my ship powered for centuries and I could pass through dimensions unhindered as time itself left my physical body nearly untouched while I became ever more fused with the biotechnology of the ship.

Tapping into satellite transmissions, I learned to filter out the billions of voices and streams of data to listen in on secured military channels. In all honesty, I got a certain thrill making unannounced visits to nuclear bases on a whim and disarming their missiles as a show of force whenever my ship was challenged by armed aggressors. Aided by the knowledge of the Keepers embedded within my vessel, I was able to predict military encounters between nations; and take measures to thwart them before the point of escalation.

After much time, I eventually found myself missing human contact, like an ache that couldn't be cured, though knowing I could never return to the life I once knew. In my weakness, I couldn't help the temptation to cruise along the outer edges of cities in the dark of night and search for a lone cabin in the countryside; merely to eavesdrop on strangers, just to hear a human voice and dream of the quiet life I had left behind. On rare occasions, I would regret my decision to play Sentry over this unruly playground called Earth, and the clouds of data embedded in the ship's systems did little to relieve the feeling of loss and crushing loneliness which frequently haunted my mind; although, the weight of my quest and responsibility to a greater good was a heavy a burden to bear.

I was more than human now, but missed being what I had once been; though realizing the weakness I had felt was an insightful tool towards solving the dilemma which faced all of humanity. It made me wonder if mankind secretly feared what we may find beyond the horizon, and stumble upon a future that might one day cause us to turn and face the ugly mirror of what we once were, and eventually, what we had become. We were explorers, but the irony of it was that we still had yet to discover ourselves.

There were times, on an especially quiet night, when I would dare to reach out and contact a lone individual, mind to mind, in an attempt to share my message; always acting under the radar and beyond the reach of the watchful alien brood and their harvest ships. To this day, I continue to travel the globe to touch those special few who reside beyond the masses and separate themselves from the pack, in hopes to plant a seed in their minds and offer them a glimpse of the reality which they have been groomed to deny. Whether they chose to believe my message or not, the sobering truth was that mankind has never been alone in the universe, and we are about to open our eyes to see a world beyond ourselves.

ଞେଓଓ

The following is the true account of
the Authors abduction experience

৪৩

The Real Story

This sci-fi novel was comprised from hundreds of actual contactee testimonies and thousands of photographs, videos, and reports related to the UFO phenomena I've researched over the decades. There is undeniable proof that alien visitations have been recorded throughout human history in every form, yet this fact is generally suppressed from the common knowledge of the public by the powers that be. The reason for this is clear; because those in control, cannot imagine a world where they themselves, hold none, nor could they bear to be seen as mere equals among others. Not only do they fear the repercussions that would dissolve our society into chaos, which would most certainly erupt from exposing the reckless and widespread deceit they have bred, but that with an abundance of technologies which would grant a greater equality among men; then greed and the despairing entrapment we live in might be cast along the wayside and this perpetual era of global slavery may see its final sunset.

Most everyone from any walk of life can recognize that it is a common desire to improve ourselves and make the world a better place. Yet there exists this taint excreted by those few who will always demand to possess far more than they could possibly ever need; there are those of sick and twisted minds who will take every measure to attain a choking grip upon their fellow man. This very flaw is why mankind will always fail to evolve beyond such pettiness; because we are our own worst enemy. Earth itself, is but a tiny island among a vast sea of stars, and at every dawn the tide encroaches ever higher upon our shores.

The following text in this novel is my story, as the Author, of my own experienced abductions which I am sharing here with the public for the first time. I attest that the following content from this page through the rest of this book is of true events I have personally witnessed as an abductee and my close encounters of the fifth kind. Only minor omissions were made to protect the identities of those involved.

Online images:

The original sketches related to this story are available online under this book title at: www.GreyForest.com.

(1) The alien, as seen in my home.

(2) The UFO craft seen during my first encounter as a child.

(3) The portal door which appeared within my bedroom.

(4) A device that they used that was much like a key where each of the hooked tips could be manipulated to open panels, it could fit into any triangle shape and adhered like a magnet. They could manipulate the appendages protruding from either side of it for different functions 'much like a skeleton key' to turn in either direction, to open or activate a device, or utilized to push or pull like a handle.

(5) This device was shaped like a thin cooler consisting of a chromed handle with ribbed sides; measuring about 2 ft. in length. In a beam of light from a hovering ship, one simply needed to hold onto it, or touch this device, to ascend or descend safely within the shaft of the gravitational cone. I had only done so once, and recall the tingling sensation from its contact. Frankly, I was tempted to let go of it during my experience, just to see what would happen but was warned not to do so as the beings read my intentions, and with little debate, I eventually thought it best not to act upon my curiosity and risk the fall.

The Visitors

"I ...I need to tell you about something that happened to us during our road trip," my mother commented nervously while preparing a meal in our small kitchen, though she was noticeably distracted by something on her mind, "we were on our way back after dark on the highway just outside of Benson when we saw a bright light appear in the sky and it began to follow us," Diana mentioned, referring to my stepfather Ray, who had been working as a prison guard at a penitentiary near Safford while they had left my adolescent ass back in Tucson in the care of our babysitter for the past several days, "and something strange happened..." she trailed off, clearly disturbed by something in her recollection of that eventful night.

My family and I had just moved to a house near the outermost edge of the city where the streets were still gravel roads at the time. It was located on the outskirts of town, but new houses were being developed in our area. Our little quarter acre home was placed on the street corner where my school was conveniently situated at the end of our block. It was mid-summer of 1975, and I was only eight years old at the time. My mother had it hard for years being a single parent, and for some reason, she found satisfactory companionship by getting married to a tall redhead psychotic prick named Ray, who as it turned out, only put on the charm to get into her pants before showing his true colors.

His personality fit to a tee what you would expect of your average Federal Prison guard; abusive, mentally unbalanced, and prone towards bouts of uncontrolled aggression. He also had a degree as a certified draftsman and was frequently assigned government projects to redesign circuit board layouts for missile guidance systems and the like, which he secured through ties to my mother's job as a secretary at a missile plant for Hughes Aircraft. Following the side street next to our house would take you directly south to the Davis-Monthan Air Force Base. I have no idea where they had met. Prior to their marriage, my mother had frequently worked two full time jobs and it was all too common to wake up in the morning to find a note on the kitchen counter for breakfast beside my lunchbox, only to get back home from a day at school, only to find another note tacked on the fridge describing what was sealed in the Tupperware as my dinner, and I would usually be in bed and asleep before she got home after her night shift past midnight.

There were times I would barely see my mother for five minutes during the weekdays as she tried to pay the mortgage and raise a child on her own. So, in a way, I could understand she needed help; be it an associate, a lover, or a partner in crime so to speak; that any measure of companionship would have been a relief, even if it was to a bull-headed maniac. Well, I'm sure there are plenty of women out there who have done worse; but approaching nine years of age, I couldn't claim to be a matchmaker.

As summer met its peak, Diana and Ray took a three day weekend to visit a nudist camp called 'Healing Waters' located near Safford, Arizona. When my mother told her fantastic story about their strange experience during their drive there, I began to scrunch my face in suspicious disbelief, as I had still felt the raw emotional scars from recently being told that Santa Claus was not actually *real* in the months that followed the preceding holidays. Lying to an innocent child like that and crushing their dreams was the mark of parenthood at its cruelest.

"What do you mean by a light in the sky?" I asked, still interested in hearing her out, and could tell she wasn't quite herself. She seemed phased about the entire incident, as she lingered with a distressed look in her tired eyes.

"Oddly enough, there was no one else on the highway going in either direction. I was driving the car while we were out in the middle of a desert stretch when Ray and I saw this huge bright light appear in the sky near the road and it began to follow us; then it came directly over our car!" her voice got excited when she remembered that specific detail as she stared off above towards the kitchen ceiling, as though she was reliving the moment then and there.

"You mean like a shooting star that got real close?" I blurted out, reaching for conclusions as most kids my age did.

"No, not like that, I think it was something else..." she trailed off with a distraught tone in her voice, "both Ray and I woke up at the same time in the car with the seatbelts off, finding that we were now parked on the side of the road," she revealed with an expression washing across her face which slowly turned sour, "we didn't remember pulling over or going to sleep, and when we checked the clock there were several hours of missing time," she confessed with a gasp.

Although she seemed quite unsettled, I called it all hogwash. I gave a frown of disbelief, wondering if she was putting on an act just to pull my leg. Was there some secret book that all parents used to groom their children into believing their audacious stories, just because they're parents said they were true? I mean, after all, I had swallowed the rubbish that there was a grotesquely obese man from the north pole who ran a child labor camp for deformed kids with pointy ears; who made toys which were all miraculously delivered across the world over the course of a single night. He landed on rooftops and snuck in through windows and down chimneys like some midnight creeper, and payment for his gifts were made by steering this old goat towards diabetes by leaving him plates of cookies. Year after year without fail, as evidence of his presence, the old fart would take one damn bite of the cookie and one sip of milk, and I would assume they must have either tasted bad, or were not up to his high quality of standards because he just left them to rot there like a rude bastard who didn't appreciate proper hospitality.

So here I was, being expected to believe in aliens and flying saucers and all this bull-crap she started letting on about, and honestly, I was a bit miffed at the thought of being subjected to this ridicule. However, my mother wasn't exactly prone to telling wild tales, as I had known her my entire life after all. Whatever had happened to them, it was something that disturbed her deeply. When I asked what Ray had remembered about the event, his response seemed angry and he refused to talk about it. He most usually gave me crap and bullied me whenever my mother wasn't around, but oddly enough, he was evasive and kept to himself for the next several weeks thereafter; which was strangely out of character for him.

* * *

Little did I know that only three months after their encounter on that lonely stretch of road, that 100 miles directly north of that lone highway where my parents had their encounter, there would be one of the most famous abductions ever told, of a man named Travis Walton, resulting in a movie based on his experience released 18 years later.

Both my mother and stepfather acted strangely the following weeks after their incidental weekend road trip. Their bedroom was across from mine in the house, and my stepfather fell into becoming far crueler with his words, which quickly escalated into physical abuse. It was like something unspoken had broken him inside. Many nights, I could hear them yell at one another and her crying through the doors from across the hallway. In his disdain, I was shocked to discover one day that he had flipped the door handle to my bedroom, locking me inside. Trapped as I was, I couldn't even leave to use the bathroom and after banging and crying at my bedroom door to be let out; I was eventually forced to piss in my own dirty laundry basket to soak up the urine. Life at home had turned strangely ugly and surreal since their fateful trip on that desert highway.

Being in the middle of summer, there was no school in session and I began to realize my life had suddenly fallen into a rut where I would attend our family dinners while the three of us sat in uncomfortable silence; as if there was a black cloud hovering above darkening the mood. I was looking forward to my next birthday and talked about presents and cool toys I desired to amass, like any child with a healthy appetite to devour their parent's money on such trinkets, but my dreams were quickly squashed by Ray as if he was fulfilling the role of some evil stepfather directly out of a dark fairy tale. The days were filled with facets of crying, suffocating silence, physical beatings and locked doors, pissing into my closet late at night and getting yelled at for it the next day ...it all turned into a cycle of torment. Truth be told, I had no clue what a real fucking nightmare was until the night the Visitors arrived.

I woke up in the middle of the night during a new moon, not knowing if my parents were home at the time; but my bedroom door was still securely locked. I don't recall what it was that woke me, but I saw a slowly flashing light entering through my paned window, so I crawled up upon my thick wooden desk sitting below it so that I could reach high enough to peer outside. Almost out of view at the corner of our house was a large round object emitting a harsh pulsating light. Now I thought this strange at first because we were located at the edge of a neighborhood that surrounded us, and was wondering why the neighbors weren't outside looking at this thing, which would have certainly gotten everyone's attention.

Suddenly and inexplicably, I found myself standing outside on the road in my pajamas, engulfed in a blanket of darkness as I looked directly at this unusual craft. It was certainly saucer shape; the color of brushed pewter, nearly as wide as the two-lane street where it hovered barely a foot above the ground. It had a distinctive enormous stubby antenna located at the top centermost part of the ship. There was a lit ramp on its edge facing me ...but, suddenly again, time flashes forward and I'm sitting naked on the floor of a white-lit room. When I say white, I mean it was entirely bleached of color, with curiously curved edges on the floor and ceiling so that they joined without breaks or corners. It almost seemed as if the very walls and floor were lit from within. The design of the room warped my sense of perspective for lack of visual clues to determine distance or space. I sat there for what seemed like an eternity after banging on the walls and calling out for someone, anyone, to help me get out. Then she came.

Well, truth was, I couldn't tell from a hill of beans if the strange creature that retrieved me was either male or female, but at least my pajamas were returned to me, so I put them on and was promptly led through a very small doorway into an adjacent chamber. I imagine that the minds of children are less shocked by strangeness, as they are curious and eager to learn the new and fascinating oddities of life. The creature that released me didn't look at all like the generic 'alien' little green men or colorless midgets with large heads and huge almond eyes as I had seen in television shows and comic books. The being didn't move its lips when it spoke, but communicated through words inside my mind; which was comparable to listening through earphones and you hear their voice in the center of your head. As it turns out, the tone sounded similar to your own voice, as though speaking to yourself.

"Come, don't be afraid," it urged gently.

I wasn't scared, but I could admit I was pretty stunned. I had never bought into the whole UFO and aliens or flying saucers lunacy, and thought it was just a bunch of malarkey merely for movies and entertainment. In comparison, I had certainly seen this dude the adults called 'Santa Claus' at the local mall, which had helped to dupe me and countless other naive children who put far too much trust in the word of their parents and society at large. If I had been actually taken to the North Pole in a flying sleigh; that would have certainly convinced me beyond all measure that the fat guy was legit. Little did I realize, that was a pretty direct analogy to what was going to happen next.

The chamber we stepped into was curved, and I assumed we were on the outer hull of the same ship I had seen before. The walls were also the same whitewashed ivory texture as in the holding room where I had been left waiting; though here the level of illumination was noticeably lower. There were three of these creatures present; a pair of them were operating consoles while my host held my hand to guide me around. They wore no coverings that I could notice, and were clearly gaunt compared to a normal human frame; with far less of a normal coloration of flesh rather than what I would describe as a bland skin tone. They were entirely hairless head to toe, with sparse mottled patches of darker skin peppered across their heads and shoulders. As they all appeared alike to me, these age spots were the only attributes that aided in distinguishing them apart.

They had larger irises, but the eyes shapes weren't terribly accentuated as was so widely portrayed. They walked and stood with their knees bent strangely; making it apparent they would be much taller if they stood fully upright with their legs straightened. They possessed only four fingers and toes on each appendage, though the heels of their feet were pronounced and angled off the ground, giving them an almost cat-like appearance. They possessed no external sexual organs that I could see, (the alien models in the 1993 'Fire in the Sky' film which came out nearly two decades later, wasn't entirely accurate, but scarily close to what they actually looked like).

I would dare to say that my initial meeting with them was a fairly pleasant experience, as I was curious to discover what my chaperone seemed all too eager to share with me. My host showed me a console upon one nook in the wall, where there was a moving display of worlds they had visited - one I recall in detail composed of a snow-white landscape with cracked crevices and oddly formed tubes with tall protruding globes scattered across the terrain. It was explained these structures were hollow and the native terrestrials could climb up inside them to serve as safe habitats during times when the planet's oceans rose hundreds of feet during the gravitational pull from a nearby colossal planet, comparable to an enormous high tide. The tube-like formations would trap breathable atmosphere within its air-tight bulb. I was shown several other images, of planets, stars systems, and distant galaxies; but not being into astronomy at that age, I didn't find the rest of the displays exceptionally interesting.

However, I did get the chance to ask if the ship was able to fly since I had only seen it hover inches off the ground before being taken aboard. The interior walls were linear and smooth; control panels and consoles seemed to form out of the walls themselves, as did a seat which actively molded itself from the wall when one of the creatures made a motion to sit. The small stool molded outward from the side wall as though it was comprised of hot wax, supported by the wall itself. The console set before the other two beings lacked any buttons or levers I could observe, though they busied themselves by manipulating glowing lights and small objects which lay upon a type of transparent sheet before them. If the ship had been cut into a four-section pie, we only occupied a small quarter of the outer shell. My chaperone touched a device that slowly lowered from the ceiling, and suddenly the bottom portion of the floor and wall before us were we stood, turned transparent. Through this odd window, I could see that we were currently hovering around a hundred feet or so above a neighborhood resembling my own. The image appeared as what we would consider night vision, but the view was entirely black and white. I distinctly remember saying to myself "*How silly this was, because if we were flying so low above a city suburb, then everyone down there would easily be able to see this ship!*"

After inquiring to see the rest of the ship to satisfy my curiosity, I was strictly informed that my request was not acceptable. When I thought about peeking through another doorway past them, I was immediately informed with a louder voice in my mind that such conduct would **not be allowed**, as the warning was hammered into my head. Apparently, they could read a person's thoughts and intentions as clear as a bell, which was merely a natural form of telepathic communication between their own species.

There was no real way to deceive or misdirect them, since they always had the initiative of reading your thoughts. That in itself was a form of intrusion which would be a source of great alarm in our current society; and viewed as a violation of privacy. Then again, our species was prone to being shrewd and crafty, always striving to get an upper hand through leverage or deceit. That frame of mind had been bred into the human psyche for countless generations. Apparently, the very idea of a society of "*haves and have nots,*" and living out an existence based on how cunning one could be; simply did not compute from the elevated perspective of these creatures.

After a brief conversation with these beings, next thing I knew, I found myself waking up in bed the next morning; although, I was keenly aware of what had transpired. It was now early morning, just after sunrise. My door was still locked but I cried out that I needed to use the bathroom. With a few grumbles and groans from across the hall, my stepfather finally got up and unlocked my bedroom door. Both of my parents continued to look tired and despondent as that morning progressed, and I mulled over the tale she had told me about the missing time on their trip the week prior, when I didn't believe her story at the time or in the silliness of aliens and flying saucers, but I sure as hell did now! Ray, himself, seemed to remain detached as if he was in a state of denial, and would always leave the room if a conversation on the subject of their abduction began from my mother. I knew I had to tell her what I had just experienced myself, so I approached her as she was folding clothes in her bedroom. As it turned out, that was when things went from strange to downright weird.

I didn't know where to begin, and like most kids my age who seem to spout out everything on their minds without stopping to take a breath; I attempted to do just that. I wanted to start with the space ship I had been taken into, on the chance that she might have also had a similar experience as my own.

"...?" I tried to say something as I stood there like a dolt with my mouth open, but the words wouldn't form. My presence didn't go unnoticed, and Diana asked what it was I wanted.

"There's cereal in the cupboard if you're hungry," she blurted like a parental automaton without giving me a glance as I stood there with a glazed look in my eyes, wondering what the fuck was going on and why my mouth quit working. After an awkward moment, she finished folding her clothes and turned to see me with my eyes rolling and my mouth still agape, "What are you doing, silly? Are you alright? You're looking a little flush," she inquired as I stood there nearly paralyzed.

"I, uh..." I lingered in my speech, tongue-tied for a confusing moment. She just gave me a quizzical look as I stretched my jaw around and appearing like a complete imbecile. I had everything I wanted to say to her at the tip of my tongue but was unable to form the words vocally. At that point, I started to get scared as to why my speech was paralyzed, and I rushed back to my bedroom in a panic. I imagine she probably just thought that kids were being their own weird selves as adolescence rewired our bodies and brains; at that point in time, 'Attention Deficit Disorder' wasn't quite 'a thing' yet for the medical community to profiteer from.

I stood there alone in my bedroom across the hall, scared as hell as I was facing the wall. I suddenly found that whenever I tried to talk aloud about the abduction experience, that I began suffering from a severe stutter that completely blocked any ability to communicate. My train of thought was clear, but I was unable to express what I was trying to say. It was in that troubled moment that I could hear a voice in my head that wasn't my own, which made an explicit and startling demand that said; "*Tell no one!*"

Now I was officially freaked out. The voice wasn't like the communication with the beings which had been a live feed; but more comparable to a subliminal command. I had never encountered anything like it in my short life, so I was a bit shaken by what I was experiencing in the current moment.

'Tell no one?' – Well, I wasn't going to have any of that nonsense, I had just met some freaking aliens and I was going to tell everyone in earshot! I paced back and forth in my tiny bedroom while trying to get my voice to work again; hoping that whatever had just happened to me wasn't permanent. After several minutes of conscious effort, I was able to speak somewhat clearly out loud again and rushed back to find my mother, who I found in the kitchen getting breakfast together for the family.

"Who were you talking too back there?" She queried to my embarrassment; not realizing I had been overheard mumbling to myself. I had only been trying to get my voice to work again since it seemed to be rusted stuck the first time I tried to speak with her.

"Uh, no one," I responded; unintentionally repeating the very words I had heard in my mind moments ago.

"Well, Ray and I have to head out here shortly, so let's grab you some cereal. Faye isn't available to come over today," she mentioned my usual babysitter who lived a few houses down from us, "so we are trusting that you're big enough now to be left by yourself?"

I could see through the reverse psychology used against a child and the cunning use of applying words of confidence to sway an adolescent, so that they could be left unsupervised without the expense of a babysitter. Of course, any kid would jump at the chance to go untethered like that, even if it was within the confines of their own home. Like any child who sees such an opportunity presented to them will pounce on it, while putting on an obvious act to appear 'adult' enough.

"Sure, it's no big deal," I managed to blurt while stifling a grin. Ever since they had their experience of missing time on their road trip, and Ray started locking me in my bedroom at night, I was desperate for some personal space. To a kid in my age-range, boredom ticks away in minutes, if not seconds, in the mind of an idle child.

"Here, go eat," she ordered while handing me a box of cereal from the high cupboard above the stove; while finding the bowl and silverware were already set upon the table.

"Um, Mom, first I wanted to tell you something about what happened to me last night..." I began with a serious tone, having already lost my appetite for breakfast that morning from the excitement of my evening's adventures aboard the presumed spacecraft. That elation soon surged into a wave of trauma when I realized I was standing there with my mouth agape yet again, not able to sound out the words in my head that I was desperately trying to say. My mother just looked at me like I was a nut-ball, and probably dismissed it as an early onset of puberty or something of the sort, setting me off on its cruel chemical imbalance that would last through my teens.

"What happened...?" she led on with a prompt, which was more like a casual response of polite conversation rather than of honest interest. Being known as a child of a thousand questions, I had a reputation of being a tad more inquisitive than your average bear. Likely that routine had worn her down a bit, as most kids do to their parents withered patience.

"Last night I ...I saw, uh..." and it happened again; I experienced a complete verbal lock. A mental block kept me from voicing the story I wanted to tell her, and I started to become visually angered and disturbed when I discovered I couldn't talk about the aliens I had seen the night before, or describe their flying saucer or the things they had said to me. Then that weird haunting voice came back into my head, echoing its command *'Tell no one, only observe.'*

Observe? Observe what? Me looking like a complete idiot to everyone? Some sort of subconscious block had been placed in my head to keep me from speaking about the encounter in any manner and left my voice literally paralyzed. It was the most aggravating thing I could imagine; having something important to say, but unable to express it. I just sat there despondent with the blur of tears welling in my eyes as I sniffled in desperate silence; wondering what it was the visitors had done to me.

The Message

It was a dry feeling of despair trying to make sense of things you have never been educated on. I did enjoy science fiction and stayed up late at night to watch countless old black & white films about Martian invasions and bizarre alien monsters from distant galaxies. The premise of such movies was fairly typical, if not downright predictable. Monster crash lands encased in a meteor; escapes its shell and eats several people along the way, or alien saucers come down and bug-eyed creatures turn people into zombies or harvest them to eat their brains, etc, etc. I had seen purportedly so-called authentic reports in newspapers, but it seems they were always ridiculed to a defined measure as they approached the last paragraph of the story. Clearly there was a certain stigma attached by society whenever such witnesses allowed themselves to look like a fool in the eyes of the many.

When it came to aliens and UFO's, previously I had always passed it all off as a hoax, stating "*I'll believe it when I see it with my own eyes,*" I would giggle to myself. Well, as they say; watch what you wish for. Though there was the burning question as to why there was such sparse information on the subject outside of fringe reports; which were extremely rare to say the least. It also appeared to be a subject of taboo among major papers and news stations. There was nothing I wanted more than to ask my parents as to why they never told me these creatures were real, however, I was unable to do so, due to the subconscious block constantly pressing me into silence.

The days and weeks that followed made no difference in my inability to alleviate my verbal handicap on the subject of the alien visitation. I would make drawings or try to ask my mother face to face about the visitors, only to have my voice stripped from me when I tried to speak about it or compelled to hide the sketches from my parents and my friends.

"*Tell no one,*" became a repetitive mantra which haunted me daily until I began to wish the whole event had never happened. Even my mother soon ceased speaking about her episode of missing time. This made me wonder if she had also received a subliminal suggestion to keep quiet, or perhaps had faced ridicule from her own peers as well.

The encounter played over and over again within my head as I tried to remember every detail; especially the message they had given me just before returning me to my bedroom that fateful night. After creating the transparent window within the ship's skin to reveal that we were airborne, I had asked the one question most anyone would in such a situation.

"Why are you here and what do you want?"

Which I believed was a logical inquiry after being shown the places they had visited and their extensive star system charts, I, of course, wanted to have them come into the house and meet my parents. I mean, what kid wouldn't? While showing me the images of various other worlds at the console within their ship, my host answered question while displaying particular planets with dead civilizations; explaining they had been devastated by cataclysmic war. My chaperone also noted that they had similar concerns about my own species.

First and foremost, they were troubled about our rising overpopulation problem, and how this only bred conflict and despair among our people. The battle between capitalism and communism had certainly been building up across the globe at the time and I had seen several atomic bomb attack drills; the kind where you see children jumping under school desks – only to learn decades later that such folly wouldn't do dick to protect you from a nuclear blast. There were also the televised TV evangelists who perpetually sought money meant to buy food and bibles for all those impoverished women and children in Africa, or other far flung countries. Apparently these poor souls were trapped within their remote villages where they had no farms or even water to drink, but found enough time to hump each other like crazed weasels to pop out more children;

which only added to their hardship. So I had to agree on whatever under-educated level I was at for my age, and conceded that the industrial age had prompted a concerning spike in the reproduction of our species in every culture across the globe.

Secondly, these beings were troubled that the human race was developing technologies far, far in advance of our ability to use them responsibly. Being only eight years old at the time, I trusted that all grownups pretty much knew what the fuck they were doing. As long as there was food in the cupboards and electricity for lights, there was no real reason to be worried as far as I was concerned while living in the tiny bubble of my prepubescent world. Nuclear power was being promoted as the greatest thing since sliced bread. The gazillion bombs we had were all to protect us ...somehow. Each country trying to puff their chests and swagger to show that they had a larger dick or a bigger stick to swing around; for human history was built upon such flamboyant pissing contests. So when my alien host tried to convey the true scope of technological abuse, I was completely lost.

Third, was the warning that "they" (meaning a consensus of several different species of aliens) did not want mankind running amuck exploring the universe. I thought that was a pretty snarky attitude to take, considering how curious the human race was. We were born explorers, pioneers, and adventurers; you couldn't tell us just to sit on our own thumbs after recently landing on the Moon. So of course, I had to ask "Why?"

The explanation that ensued in their response were difficult to follow, and likely a measure of it was lost in the translation. In short, the more people there are on planet Earth, the larger the pool of minds there were to draw from in effort to advance our technologies. This analogy was perfectly logical; however, mankind tends to adopt or transform anything it creates into a weapon. To clarify, the extraterrestrials would simply rather keep us landlocked and quarantined here on Earth in an effort to keep the rest of the cosmos safe.

The whole idea of that was silly to me. Astronauts were the poster child for our vision of the fantastic future awaiting us. Exploring the far reaches of space and discovering new life and new civilizations, per se, was our dream! What they disclosed was pretty much the worst news any kid could hear who had a love for fiction. When I asked why we were being confined, the words my host chose to answer that question, hit me like a rock in the head.

"Because mankind is a dangerous and unpredictable species," the being declared bluntly.

"But ...can't you just teach us not to be?" I replied in all innocence while reaching for the most rational resolution, all the while noting their obviously advanced technology and their calmness in the way they carried themselves. Certainly they could act as mentors to educate an inferior race such as Man. Its answer was a simple and anguished "*No.*" Of course, I had to ask for an explanation once again.

"...Because you kill one another over make-believe," was all the alien said with a bitter tone mixed with sadness and pity.

Those were its last words conveyed to me before I was returned to my bedroom that eve. Apparently, they had a way of erasing memories to a degree; but I had retained a select few moments, (or) they had allowed me to keep them by choice. Honestly, that flat answer the being offered had left me righteously stumped, because at face value it didn't make a lick of sense. It took me several agonizing decades to figure out what the alien actually meant by '*make-believe*' being our bane.

I had seen the film "The Day the Earth Stood Still" some years later which pretty sums up the human response to such outside threats. We fear the unknown. Imagine a scenario where one day an alien armada arrives in our solar system and locked themselves in orbit around Earth, they would interrupt all television and radio broadcasts worldwide to give the message that they were here to greet us. Doing so on such a global scale would thwart any attempt at a government cover-up, and they could pick any date, and time, and location to land with added instructions akin to: 'Be there or be square!'

In reality, the resulting encounter would pretty much go like this: Emissary Space Ship arrives and countless thousands of people are at the location to greet them, all armed to the teeth of course – with cocked guns held behind their backs, while waving an olive branch with the other. The door of the flying Saucer door opens, alien steps out and we all gawk for a silent moment and our global Dignitaries would say something akin to: "Welcome to Earth, we look forward to sharing our cultures and knowledge. We do not claim to be perfect, but we hope that in a mutual friendship you could help us cure diseases, show us how to efficiently feed the hungry and end wars between our nations; and welcome us into your Galactic Brotherhood where we can explore the cosmos together."

Which all in all sounds like a pretty much human thing to say, and was certainly colored with the undeniable hint of selfish expectation. After all, if a so-called advanced species arrived on our tiny planet, what the hell would they possibly want in exchange from a bunch of loony primitives? Perhaps our authorities thought they might want a few shelled necklaces and shiny rocks as a souvenir to take back to their own galaxy.

"Well actually, we had just the opposite in mind," would be the likely response from the Alien Emissaries as they gazed into our beady little eyes, "We are already aware of your tarnished culture and its lack of values. We have no intention of sharing our technology, because you would only misuse it. There is no need to cure your sick or to feed your people, or to help end your pointless wars for that matter, since you have a notable, if not pronounced, overpopulation problem. Oh, and just to set things straight for the record, this isn't a fraternity and we don't want you out exploring the stars where you are most certainly **NOT** welcome!"

I can just imagine the dumbfounded looks on the faces of every world leader of Earth as the aliens turn heel and board their ships and whisked away into the blue yonder.

Psychologically, mankind is obsessed with the entitlement of freedom to do as we please. If an alien species showed up and spouted off like that; Humanity would outright rebel, because "*We do what we want!*"

Of course, there would be a small percentage of the human race that would truly understand the alien's rationale and adopt a new philosophy to comply with their cosmic enlightenment; if not by outright common sense. We have gotten too big for our britches and there needs to be a serious thinning of the herd on our little blue planet. Our concept of Utopia might entertain an idea akin to a Garden of Eden, but are instead, illustrated as nothing more than condensed cement hives we call 'cities' in a world where the air, soil, and water has been polluted beyond repair. We were killing this planet without the maturity to admit so, and they knew it.

During that conversation I had aboard their ship, they stated that mankind should not build a base on our Moon or they would be forced to destroy it. My dumbfounded reaction to that declaration was just to shrug my shoulders as if to say; 'Duh, I'm just a kid, you're really barking up the wrong tree, dude, because I have *absolutely* no control over that!' I was baffled why they would include that mention, but it did fit along the lines of keeping our sorry butts within the atmosphere of our own planet. I distinctly remember watching the live stream of the first astronauts walking on the lunar surface when I was a wee tyke; and it saddened me that such a noble ambition would never come full circle.

It wouldn't be until many years later, that the entire context of their message would begin to fit into the empty pieces of this puzzle they presented. You can't fit the square pegs in the round holes, even if you go to insane efforts to file them down ...you have to make a new board entirely that accommodates your aspirations. It takes an open mind to realize that our ideology and method of reasoning are entirely askew; even irrational. Little did I know that my first abduction was the only positive experience that I would ever have with these strange beings.

It wasn't long after that encounter I noticed I had a red mottled triangle consisting of tiny red polka dots on my right hand, that were just barely visible, which eventually took several decades to fully fade away. Later that week after my initial visitation, I kept feeling a strange lump on my inner leg which I would constantly itch, to the point I finally took the opportunity to take a good look with a flashlight and a mirror. What I discovered was a bizarre little skin tube that had not been there before, and without any sense of pain, I squeezed out a tiny white cube from the incision. There was neither blood nor pus, just an odd quartz cube which ejected itself. I had to use a magnifying glass to see it clearly, but it appeared to be made of some sort of white stone about the size of a blunt pencil tip with several gold veins running through it. As much as I wanted to tell someone about it; somehow I couldn't bring myself to do it. Like a broken record, the same command entered my mind upon revealing this foreign object which had been placed within my body; "*Tell no one, keep it safe.*"

I had a small plastic box with a magnifying lens on its lid that was used for inspecting bugs, and crystals, and other miniature things, which is where I kept the object sealed and secured on my dresser; until one day, the implant simply vanished. In retrospect, anyone finding such an alien object implanted in them would have had it photographed and x-rayed, tested and cataloged. It was a strange ordeal to be beaten down with the power of suggestion. From my research after all these years, this is where abductees begin to wonder if their minds are broken or become burdened and overwhelmed with self-doubt. Regardless, who would have believed such a wild tale from the mouth of a child?

In the months that followed their desert highway abduction, my stepfather started to become a different person altogether and was increasingly verbally violent and physically abusive as he seemed to drift into a dark place within his state of denial. That diseased and poisoned garden in his mind began to flower into an abusive relationship that was filled with isolated assaults and threats by my stepfather which dragged on for years; until one day my mother could no longer ignore the bruises I had suffered and became a victim of the battery herself. What followed was an abrupt divorce. I could only speculate if the paranormal event they experienced had any true connection to that failure in their marriage. Though honestly, I would bet money that it had.

If things hadn't gotten bad enough while my family dissolved around me, it so happened that I would continue to receive visitations in set periods every two years; and they always came between the months of June or July. In all honesty, I can't fathom any reason why the visitations were limited to those months mid-summer, or that the time frames where placed at two year stretches. Of course, it wasn't until the second and third consecutive visits that I began to notice the pattern of these arrivals and became increasingly agitated because of the aggression displayed during such visitations, which became ever more disturbing as time progressed. I would learn decades later that these were classified as close encounters of the 4th & 5th kind.

As the years passed, the city boundaries expanded farther east so that our house was now settled into the middle of a growing suburb, and it still didn't make any sense to me why concerned neighbors never came frantically knocking at my door after my encounters. Nor did I hear of any reports of UFO sightings on the local news during those episodes. As an open possibility, there was the chance that others in my area had also experienced similar visits and suffered the same subconscious affliction to never speak of it. Their arrivals always seemed to transpire after midnight when it was darkest, and the beings could apparently enter a locked building without restraint.

The first introduction to their species was friendly enough, even though there were clearly spots of missing time I couldn't quite recall. However, the visitations that followed were anything but cordial. Every two years I would stare at the calendar with dread, for these once polite hosts evolved into unwelcome intruders. Thereafter, there were no gracious conversations or displays of kindness, for now whenever these visitors exercised their will, they were silent and cruel.

I had learned to become a light sleeper over the years, and it was an unpleasant experience to open your eyes in the middle of the night and enter a state of panic when you realize your body was entirely paralyzed as these creatures poked and prodded. It wouldn't be until years later into my adulthood that I would discover this was the typical cookie-cutter encounter. I was, however, left shaken and confused as to why I was completely unable to communicate about it to anyone.

The visitations became more and more distressing as any mutual consent I had once known, had entirely dissolved. They simply arrived to conduct their exam every two years, without any cordial communication which was initially displayed on our first introduction. I was treated as if I was merely an object to be studied. Oddly enough, even though my mother exercised an extremely healthy diet and never smoked nor drank alcohol; it was eventually revealed a few years later that my mother had contracted an excessively aggressive form of cancer, which eventually resulted in her obtaining a double mastectomy. The doctors swore up and down that they had gotten all of the malignancy after removing her breasts; but less than a year later, follow-ups showed her cancer had progressed and spread to her brain and lungs.

I had graduated from high school two years ahead of my class, being jumped up through my academic grades since my test scores were frequently higher than average. To my own surprise, my IQ tests upon exiting 8th grade were marked at 148. I didn't 'feel' that smart, as they claimed; I just saw myself as any average kid whenever I looked in the mirror. I was downright embarrassingly horrible at talking to girls, hated homework, and wanted to explore life just like any normal kid; though it slowly became clear to me that I saw the world in different colors than most.

I ended up getting hired by IBM as my first job at the age of sixteen, and was still living at home taking care of my mother as her condition worsened to the point of being placed on oxygen. From the effects of her sickness, I would hear her vomiting in the bathroom almost every night, especially after intense sessions of chemotherapy. There is truly nothing worse than seeing someone you cared about in pain and feeling completely helpless as you watch them dying before your eyes. I was by her side when she literally suffocated to death as her lungs eventually shut down, and she crumbled on the floor of the waiting room of her radiology appointment. She was only 36 yrs of age. I had just turned 17 when my mother had passed away, and I suddenly found myself on my own.

Still living in the same house, I redecorated the master bedroom that my mother had used and made it my own. It was a three-bedroom home and all the rooms were adjacent to one another at the end of the short hallway, which spanned from the dining room and kitchen. Over the time that followed, every two years during mid-summer I made a regiment of securing and locking all the doors and windows, even going so far as to remove the latch handles; but the alien guests still arrived, and I was always left wondering how they had gotten in.

It was a common problem among abductees and those visited, who feared the stigma and ridicule that is associated with this type of phenomena; especially so when it is experienced alone and you don't have any photos, co-witnesses, or any physical evidence to support your claim but your word alone on a very wild and outlandish story. So I delved headfirst into research on the subject wherever I could find it. I collected books and magazines, and attended UFO seminars within reach. Still, I never told a soul as to my own experiences.

Every other summer, I was left dreading the impending visitations, and even tried to assemble booby-traps throughout the house in a paltry effort to give me some sort of warning; spending two months with sleepless nights got a little weary on the nerves. Fishing wire made great trip lines, I tied bells to doors, placed kitchen knives balanced in the top door jambs so that they would fall on anyone creeping in, and even pseudo-jungle traps to make it impossible to venture through the house without making a veritable racket. It was quite an elaborate routine to go through every night before bed just for a little peace of mind. Regardless, not a god-damn thing worked.

One evening, I was startled in the middle of the night to see what appeared to be a dark figure looming over me beside my bed. At first, I was a little astonished that I wasn't physically paralyzed, but was able to move without constraint. This dark object was jet black without any perception of depth. I cautiously leaned up from my pillow to note several irregular rings of green light energy warping in waves inwards upon itself within this opaque object. Almost hypnotized, I stared at it in a mix of horror and fascination for but a moment when it suddenly 'blinked out' of existence. Warily, I stretched out my arm to see what had been there, but whatever it had been was now gone; with nothing left but a slight lingering static within the room. It was the first I had ever seen that type of phenomena, and was so upset that I reduced myself into calling an ex-girlfriend out of fear and desperation in the middle of the night – only to be left lingering on the phone, not knowing what to say.

It wasn't until countless hours of research over the passing decades that I began to conclude that the dark energy object I had seen was a form of doorway or portal, as outlandish as that assumption might seem. The analogy I had pieced together began to make sense, considering all the professed claims by numerous abductees stating they had been levitated or beamed through solid walls, and that these alien culprits had repeatedly entered through untouched locked doors without hindrance. Movies like to dramatize this kind of forced entry by beaming bright lights and rattling doors; but in truth, the method of their access is far less cinematic.

This all leaned me towards believing these home invasions were conducted by utilizing an advanced form of sympathetic resonance technology. Imagine if the atoms of a solid object were vibrated to the point they can be separated without losing cohesion. Then pass a solid object with a specific electrical frequency through that plane of the excited atoms; so you're basically nudging the atoms of one object through another. In our era, there is a long history of science fiction becoming science fact; so I'll leave it at that.

At the ripe old age of 22, I had a girlfriend move in with me and allotted her the small bedroom across from mine for her own use since I had rooms to spare, and we slept there frequently as my own bed in the master bedroom was merely a small twin size mattress; and at over six feet tall, I could barely fit into it myself. My method of thinking was that if I had someone else there, then these secret abductions might cease if they found a stranger present. Or, on a darker note, I would at least have a witness to the event. Though in that regard, it didn't enter my mind that my reckless scheme had also put my girlfriend in danger of becoming a victim of the same type of abduction assault; which in retrospect, kind of made me look like a real bastard after the fact, especially since I had never told her about these paranormal events.

Having been groomed to be such a light sleeper over the years, one evening in early July, I suddenly woke up in the middle of the night and sat up in bed with my girlfriend still fast-asleep beside me as we slept in her room. From the edge of her bed, you can see directly through the open door and across the short hall into my bedroom. There, I saw what I presumed was one of the original aliens I had met during that first encounter when I was a child. It was standing within the master bedroom peeking around the doorway only a dozen feet away. From what I've researched, this was one of the rare occasions where these aliens demonstrated an almost human-like expression. While it looked directly at me, its dark eyes widened, and its tiny mouth dropped open as if it was surprised to find me fully awake and staring back at it.

Now, my first reaction was purely a product of pent-up

frustration and grief which I had suffered over these many years, and in that moment, all I could think to myself was: ***"I'm going to catch this fucker, and end this!"*** And then I would finally possess the living proof to show what had been happening to me was real. Well ...it never got that far. I made a hearty attempt to leap off the bed, intent on rushing into the hall and tackling this thing; but then I suddenly, and quite abruptly, went out like a light. I had blacked-out completely as though I had been hit by a ton of bricks.

I woke up much later at dawn, fully aware of what had happened and jumped up to search my master bedroom. Once there, I found the curtains had been moved even though the window was still firmly latched shut. The crank handle itself wasn't there, since I had removed it entirely to keep it from being cycled open. Searching further, I also noticed the contents of my closet by the window had been clearly disturbed. This was on the same joining wall where I had first spotted the alien craft twelve years prior, just outside of my adjacent childhood bedroom. In all respects, I felt upset and shaken, but didn't tell my girlfriend what she had slept through, nor did I wish to scare her.

I was still on the defensive, but having a live-in lover at the time I certainly didn't have any wish for her to think I was a kook by placing out all my booby-traps about the house, as I had done many times before; even as ineffective as they were. It took me a while to realize that the alien being I had confronted probably sensed that I was quite angry, having the ability to read my thoughts and responded by hitting me with a double-dose of their form of mental tranquilizers to keep me docile. I had no idea how they did it, but it seemed they had the ability to manipulate the chemical and electrical impulses of the human mind and could turn it off like a light switch.

When such disturbing events happen to you without someone else to attest as a witness, one tends to intentionally suppress the experience to keep from mentally dissolving into a state of paranoia or irrational panic. It is very easy to dismiss them to the point of telling yourself: 'You just had a dream ...a very vivid dream' or some other excuse to make sense of it all in a desperate effort to keep a grip on your sanity. I did not believe my mother's story either when I had first heard it from her, which made me feel like a real lout over the years that followed. Needless to say, that shaky relationship with my live-in partner didn't last long after that event.

Two summers later I had a full-time night shift job at a local movie theater just a mile from where I lived. One morning at daybreak, I awoke to find myself fully clothed lying on my living room floor right inside the front door. The door itself was still locked and closed but my body was pointed inward towards the living room face down with my feet nearly touching the closed door, as if someone carried me in and just laid me there. One must also keep in mind there is no way to open or shut the door with a body left in that position where I lay, because the door swung inward and simply would have been blocked by my legs.

Honestly, I thought it was odd to wake up like that lying in the living room floor with my clothes all in a jumble as if someone else had put them on for me, but all I could repeat to myself in my current dazed state was *"go to bed,"* which I immediately did as I lumbered into my bedroom and slept for the next 12 hours straight.

Now, before jumping to conclusions, my friends have known that I simply didn't drink alcohol nor have I ever done drugs of any kind in my life, and I was always appointed the designated driver when I was out with my associates. No fun, I know; but there was no chance of being incapacitated by booze, medications, or drugs in this matter. After having slept through the entire day and into the early evening, I got up to eat dinner and was barely off in time to catch my night shift at work ...and this was where the story got truly bizarre.

I showed up to work as usual and greeted everyone, but then they started making odd comments such as "Hey, where were you yesterday?" My reaction to their remarks was obviously dumbfounded, as I asked several members of the staff as to what they had meant? My manager wasn't really angry, since I was such a reliable employee, but stated that they tried to call me several times the night before, but that I didn't answer and repeated that I hadn't come into work last night.

Well, I know that was false, and my reaction was literally word for word: "Hah, real funny, but I really don't see how that's a joke?" I answered in my confused response, thinking everyone was either playing a private prank on me or just being idiots because I have never missed a day of work in any job, ever. With a furrowed brow, I assumed they were just fooling around and playing some sort of stunt on "Mr. Reliable" as I was known. Storming up to the Employee Staff Room, I thought they were all just jerking me around, that is, until I got to the card room to punch in.

I took my time-card and punch the clock, only to glance down to see there was an entire day missing on it. I fell back upon the wall in shock, entirely confused; then stumbled back to the lobby in a daze, utterly bewildered as I asked everyone what day it was, only to realize that they hadn't been lying after all.

...I had experienced an entire day of missing time!

Living alone as I had at the time, nobody knew where I had gone. From whatever stint I had experienced, I had woken up on the floor at my front door to find an enormous black and blue bruise on the front of my left thigh, appearing as if I had been hit by a truck. The wound looked like it should hurt like hell, but strangely enough; I felt no pain from it. Just as curious, the bruise entirely healed and disappeared in less than 48 hrs, as if it had never been there. I tried to rationalize what had happened at the time, remembering ...yes, I did come into work last night, and specifically recalled going through the motions at my workplace in my head; however, I didn't actually recall talking directly to anyone at my job as they seemed to be nothing more than wispy shadows in my memory. The more I thought about it, the more chilling it became. All I could remember from the night before was moving shadows of figures, nothing more.

I can only assume now that they were implanted memories as if I had been hypnotized by suggestion to recall them as such. This was in the late 1980s, at a time long before cell phones, household internet or digital cameras were readily available, and most people used wall calendars to track the date. I, of course, was left bewildered as the next several days passed in a misty haze while I beat myself mentally while trying to remember what had actually happened to me. At one point in the evening between sunset and sunrise, I had lost my entire memory of what had transpired or where I had been.

It wasn't a week later that I began to recall where I was that missing night as the haze upon my blurred memory began to fade; realizing I had been taken yet again. The evening I had gone mysteriously missing, I recalled having gotten into my car and was compelled by some subconscious urge I had never felt before, to drive out at night upon the same lone highway South East of the city to the area where my parents had reported their initial abduction and missing time. At one point along the two-way desert road, the battery in my car had inexplicably puttered out. Admittedly, I had problems with the electrical connections before, so I didn't think it as exceptionally abnormal. I pulled over off the road as my car coasted to the shoulder.

It was a full moon and the sky was mostly clear under a blanket of stars, but unfortunately, it was still not enough light to see the engine connections as I had failed to stash a flashlight in the vehicle. The battery appeared quite dead, without even a click of power from the ignition switch. In all sincerity, I was annoyed about my own stupidity for having driven out in the middle of nowhere for no logical reason in the middle of the night, only to have my car die on me. I waited quite a while standing outside by the side of the road to flag down someone and hitchhike back into town to get a tow, but it seemed a little strange that after waiting nearly half an hour, that no cars had driven by.

Nearly straight across the road from where my vehicle had broken down, I had noticed a lighted fence post at a gated entry to a section of private property. Losing patience waiting out in the dark by the empty road, I finally decided to see if I could contact the residence; even though I didn't want to be so rude as to wake someone, or worse, being seen as a trespasser creeping up onto someone's property in the dark of the night out in the middle of the boonies. I crossed the street to the gate just to see if I could possibly borrow a phone to call a tow truck or get some help to jump the battery. Once at the gate, I found it extremely unusual that the gate entry itself hadn't been lit by an actual electric light, but instead, was illuminated by an old fashioned railroad oil lantern hanging upon a hook beside it. Noting that curious point, I figured someone must have lit it earlier that evening.

I found the wire fence gate had been left unlocked, even though there were an array of obvious signs lashed to the gate with wire, warning; GUARD ON DUTY - NO TRESPASSING - BEWARE OF DOGS, plastered on the front of it in large bold letters. With due hesitation, I tried calling past the gate; hoping someone might answer, and turned my gaze back towards the empty highway in exasperation. With nowhere to go, I warily unlatched the gate and wandered inside while keeping note of my steps in case I might need to jump back and close the gate if some nasty guard dogs came barreling after me. There was a dirt road beyond and a short walk merely a hundred feet past the entry, where I came across a small white trailer along with a handful of stucco adobe buildings lining the dusty drive which was littered with bulldozers and piles of gravel typical of any construction site. However, there were no lights on anywhere.

I strolled over and knocked on the trailer door, hoping to find an understanding security guard, but there was no answer. Still wary of rousing any vicious dogs lurking in the shadows; I went to the nearest adobe building and ended up having to climb over the stucco wall as the front gate to its enclosure was locked from the other side. I tried to ring the doorbell, which I couldn't hear beyond the door so I assumed that wasn't working either, so I knocked repeatedly, but still to no avail. It was just then that I noticed how peculiar it was that this oddly shaped house had absolutely no windows whatsoever, anywhere upon the ground floor.

It was a two-story building and there was a balcony to a sliding glass door immediately above, so I ended up carefully mounting the enclosing wall and hopped over to it as the railing was within easy reach. I attempted to see if there was anyone or anything inside but was disappointed to find the walls were still bare and pristine as if newly painted, and I had to consider that this site was apparently still in its phase of development and that nobody actually lived here. Exasperated, I sighed as I stood there in the cool desert air while I looked out across the construction site from the balcony, wondering what I should do, and quietly contemplated if I should just go back to the car and wait ...but what happened next, nearly made me jump out of my skin.

From inside the balcony window, a lone figure appeared wearing what appeared to be a one-piece jumpsuit. It was of average human size, but with a softly glowing hairless head. Its facial features were entirely indiscernible and I had never seen anything like it before in my life. It leaned in towards the window as if to look at me with its terrible hollow eyes, and I remember whispering to myself "*What the fuck*..." in a trembling voice, and almost broke my neck jumping down off that balcony and scrambling over the wall in panic.

As I was now standing back in the center of the dirt road, I turned and saw the being standing fully within the frame of the sliding window looking down at me with its blank face and empty eyes. I quickly began to saunter back towards my car just to get the hell out of there as my adrenaline began pumping, filling me with fear; but in a twilight-zone moment, two additional beings, similar to the one in the window, stepped out from the trailer behind me to block my exit. As I turned, even more of these entities began to appear from behind the buildings as their numbers increased to over half a dozen.

For those not familiar with the Arizona landscape, the one thing you absolutely do not want to do is run through the open desert; especially at night when you can't see crap. Sharp rocks, rattlesnakes, scorpions, and all the goddamn prickly pear cactus growing wild out there can bring anyone to a sudden and painful halt. The only direction I could retreat to was down the razed dirt road in the opposite direction away from these things, with only the moonlight to keep me from stumbling and falling on my face in the dark. Within a few dozen yards, I had approached a large mass of sandy dirt which had been dumped into an elongated pile.

Fortunately, the glowing beings weren't chasing after me in hot pursuit, but slowly following my path, step by step, which I found even more terrifying. The pile of sand was set next to a large mesquite tree and sported a fairly deep trench dug around its base. The whole pile was a good twelve-plus feet high and three times as long, and I could hide behind it from direct sight of the slowly approaching group of entities. Looking down, I noticed that there had been a wooden plank set across one point of the trench which led to a pocket set deep within the sand. With no other choice at the given moment where to take cover, I made a hasty decision to hide there.

Upon crawling into the sandy crevice, I discover that it opened up into a small tunnel hidden within. It was then I noted that this large pile of dirt had been hiding something beneath it. The walls of the three-foot wide shaft were semi-translucent and began to glow with a white pulsating light, looking as if it were shining through a layer of thin fiberglass. At the far end of the tunnel, I could see a brightly lit room beyond, and from my point of view, the twenty or so feet length didn't seem like it would take but a few seconds to reach. So I tried to crawl my way through towards it, only to note that the circumference of the shaft quickly became more constricted the deeper I proceeded.

When I got within arm's length of the lit room, the shaft walls began to compress around my body and I couldn't move a muscle, and suddenly found it hard to breathe and I eventually passed out. When I awoke, I found myself lying naked in a large and unusual chamber of about 3000 square feet, along with a half dozen or more unclothed people (both male and female who appeared human) within an enclosure that had a small water channel pumping through it on one end and several strange trees which had unusual shaped fruit growing from their branches. Oddest of all, was the sharp jagged white crystals that blanketed the edges of this unusual courtyard.

Not a single person was talking to another, though I approached one woman who was sitting on the ground beside an elderly man who was next to her. They just stared blankly forward with a dazed look in their eyes as if they weren't mentally present. I saw one man stumble over to the edge of the ground barrier while answering the call of nature, and he proceeded to urinate at the edge of this thicket of minerals. When he was done relieving himself, the shroud of crystals immediately began to grow over where he had just went, as if either to feed off of it, or was merely designed to seal away the liquid waste.

There was also this curious silvery creature present, which was lanky and clearly taller than an average man; that possessed a notably sharp-pointed nose above its equally sharpened chin. This creature vaulted around the room at incredible speed whenever I tried to look directly at it. I kept asking aloud what this place was to the other people in the room, but not a single one of the other abductees seemed to be in their own presence of mind. I became discouraged to find none of them would talk, or they were simply unable to speak to me. I picked up a handful of the sand lining floor and sifted the dirt between my fingers to make sure this was all real. I even dared to approach the barrier of jagged minerals and tried to break off a crystal so that I could somehow take it with me as a souvenir after the abduction to keep as hard evidence, but was unable to snap one off. There was no way to tread over them without sustaining injury while barefoot as I currently was, so that I could properly examine the outer wall.

I longed to obtain a response from someone just to get their name or where they were from, which would have helped immensely to provide some information, but the other abductees merely loitered there in an unshakable stupor as if they had been drugged. That was the first and last time I would ever see that curious place ...at least as far as I'm able to remember. My opinion was that it appeared to be a long-term holding cell which provided the bare minimum of food and water for the contained subjects, and the strange crystalline growths acted as an efficient form of waste disposal, which clearly doubled as an effective deterrent to keep their captured patients from exploring the outer areas that were covered by these jagged shards.

I couldn't say exactly how long I had been held in that strange enclosure with the others, for I don't recall anything past that point until I woke up on the floor inside the doorway to my home the following day. Somehow, my car had been returned to my driveway, but I don't remember how I actually got back from where my vehicle had broken down nearly 50 miles away down that desolate highway.

Earth as a Reservation

Since the visitations had begun I've experienced countless reoccurring dreams of UFO's flying overhead, rings of fire-like lights darting through the sky while standing upon the roof of my house, and even ships landing in the outskirts of the city chased by police vehicles. Even more peculiar, I would always find myself compelled to race towards these grounded saucers to get inside, as if it was somehow a place of sanctuary. The logic of it all was entirely contradictory to any sensible thought, which left me perplexed as to what kind of mind-fuck I had been exposed to.

The overwhelming compulsion to enter these extraterrestrial vehicles was an impulse I can't explain even to this day; and even found myself designing homes that fit a similar genre. It wasn't until many decades later when I discovered common instances of these types of neurological control in my research of similar ET events. These beings had the ability to speak to people directly into their minds as an advanced and effective form of translation, bypassing the need to learn a language or dialect by using words the subject already knows. Several researchers and abductees have related the same effects; that these creatures have the ability to render a human unconscious, by either will of mind or by device, and drop them like a stone or merely put them in a catatonic state of suggestion and control to meet their given agenda at the time.

Literally out of the blue, it wasn't until well over two decades later I had my first flashback of a pair of Grey beings removing me from my bed in the middle of the night when I was a child. Recall is a tricky thing, being that the mysterious human brain can reconnect severed synapses between cells without notice. Anyone reviewing such wild and fanciful testimony which lingers on such fringe science must take a step back and weigh the statements and evidence, or lack thereof, and conclude what is fact or fiction; as any researcher would be expected to.

Believe me when I say that such events weigh heavily on every abductees conscience as they grasp onto they're own sanity while trying to make sense of it all. I would also presume that same analogy might also apply to say; any wild Bear who sees a strangely lit vehicle of unknown origin infringe upon the territory of their known world upon the frozen tundra, and stares on as odd-looking beings step out from their craft and points a silver rod at it. The next thing it knows it feels a slight sting and knocked unconscious, only to be groped for blood, hair, and skin samples, along with stool and DNA swabs by these weird looking creatures. These poor animals wake up hours later psychologically traumatized, while a little worse for wear, and stumbles back home wondering; *"What the fuck was that all about?"* Well, that would be quite a wild tale for the cubs back in the den, who would likely think their sibling had lost their furry minds.

Wildlife scientists engage in such biological studies every hour of the day on helpless animals across the globe by land, air, and sea; yet the regular skeptic somehow can't connect the dots. So my defense to the truth of these experiences would be to consider that even if I had been completely delusional and these were all simply fabrications of the mind; then how would one account, that even decades later, that the original message from these beings remains the same:

(1) Humanity has a severe and escalating overpopulation problem, which is causing a great deal of conflict and strife on our planet, that is fueling a secondary concern;

(2) That we are creating advanced technologies far, far beyond our ability to use responsibly.

(3) Time and again, mankind has proven itself to be a dangerous and unpredictable species and they would rather keep us quarantined here on Earth, and not running loose among the stars where we are not welcome.

Nobody can disagree that even without fangs or claws, that humans are the most dangerous animals on the planet. We excel at killing things, anything, even just for shits 'n giggles, and call it 'sport.' Fundamentally, it's colored our history and defined our legacy upon this planet; as the belligerent unruly children that we are. I was brought up in several different religions, which at a later age, prompted me into studying world doctrines and ancient cultures in all their forms of worship, in an effort to better understand this constant and perpetual tug between morality and superstitious beliefs that have always plagued our societies. Mankind has either killed, or enslaved, and suppressed others solely because;

(1 - Discrimination) they have a different pigment of skin or automatically segregate and judge someone solely because that person was born in a different part of the world,

(2 - Greed) because they merely possess something you want (but not necessarily need),

(3 - Complacency) they might choose not to follow another's doctrine or parrot their mindless chants and prayers to some mythical being. Of course, the last one on this list is the most atrocious and unhinged based on this single fact alone: That *Mankind is the only species who creates their own creators.*

This was the crux of their message about humanity killing one another over what they considered "make-believe." The poison of both ancient and our modern major religions have absolutely nothing to do with biology, our resources, or daily survival, but are merely a self-granted delusion that one person is superior to another based solely on an entirely non-existent and purely fabricated phantom, and following their set of rules. There is no rest for the wicked, and humanity seems to be anxious to no end making up ways to prove how one man is superior to another. Unfortunately, one must remember that within our caustic human societies that "*superiority*" is faithfully married to another unpleasant word we call "*entitlement*."

Imagine for a moment what our world would be like today if everyone had such telepathic insight and knew each other's true intentions. If we were unable to lie to each other and had never gone to war over such absurd and senseless reasons thus mentioned; but had instead, strived to enrich our lives with creativity and compassion for one another and for the planet on which we live, what utopia could we have evolved to? It's a compelling thought, but far from realistic from what we have to admit are the faults of this malignant state that we suffer called **"The Human Condition."** The real question isn't ' if ' aliens are real or not, but if we, as a race of self-conscious sentient beings, are able to steer ourselves towards a different path?

Greek philosophers from antiquity claimed that ancient records they had studied regarding our true human history on this planet extends far beyond our comprehension; and that this world we call Earth, periodically experiences a great upheaval where Mankind must begin again as children. Some have attached the mysterious planet Nibiru (Planet X), or deadly gamma rays lashing out across our planet from a distant dying star, or even a magnetic pole reversal, which could easily act as such a viable culprit towards that end. Whether natural, cosmic or otherwise; for all considerations it appears that history tends to repeat itself here on our dismal little world, and that we as a species seem to continually gravitate towards the same beaten path of despair, regardless of the era we live in.

Few can disagree that we need to evolve and reorientate ourselves to face a new, more positive direction. In all sincerity, mankind has a unique talent to be selfish, conniving, and backstabbing for the sake of greed and control of others; and I must concur that we frequently apply these shameful traits under the guise of religious beliefs and doctrines. We are all victims of self-serving manipulation in one form or another; and that is what dooms us from becoming something more than what we are. This isn't a rainbow-gushing hippy mindset spouting fairy glitter and crystal-energy gibberish ...but if you step back for a moment, that certainly falls within the manner of thinking our civilizations might need to pursue one day. How is anyone going to convince those selfish few who are addicted to money and power that such concepts have no true value in our future as a whole?

One must consider that there is a great deal of media manipulation and disinformation currently conducted by both Militaries and Governments across the globe. Even in the self-reflection of my personal abduction experience ...you might find it shocking that, though grudgingly, I must concur with our Authorities' decisions to suppress the factual evidence and censor such paranormal encounters. Now this is a turn of face most people won't understand at first, and tilts past the ideology that an abductee would want the truth of this matter exposed, and that we must pursue transparency and disclosure. Unfortunately, that is where I waver and tend towards the dressed suppression and measured release of such facts.

Now, why would I say that? Mainly for reasons that hinge on the message I was given during that very first encounter. Yes, even as an abductee, I support non-disclosure at this stage; which might seem like a kick in the face, but one must realize that mankind itself, as a whole, has a generic mentality towards being subservient. Our cultures appear to always end up being based around a pyramid of obedience where the masses blindly follow the guidance of the few.

Now let's say for the sake of argument, that one day all governments worldwide stepped up and admitted, yes, there are alien species with advanced and superior technologies to our own; and furthermore, if these alien creatures appeared to the entire populations of Earth, and verified to all the skeptics that they are indeed real. There, it's done. What do you really think would be the aftermath of that knowledge and the residual effects on our societies worldwide? It's a serious question.

Fundamentally, it would guarantee the fall of our civilization. All forms of government in any format across the globe would have to resign their illusion of authority to the uprising civil unrest and pressure of both public domains and private citizens, who would no longer recognize a 'lesser' authority (either municipal or religious) and society would dissolve into utter chaos as the people reevaluate whom they should follow – their untrustworthy governments – or an alien visitor who would be seen as their savior and a source of higher enlightenment?

Who knows, maybe it wasn't some natural or cosmic source from which the ominous cycles of cataclysm that humanity has experienced throughout our ancient past, which had brought each era of mankind to its knees; but maybe it was our neighbors from other worlds who innocently dropped by to say "Hello" in full transparency, and our superstitious ancestors promptly shit themselves and we brought our species to the brink of extinction in the ensuing aftermath. A self-induced apocalypse as the result of being mentally unable to accept a new reality; is not so entirely unbelievable.

In some ways, it's a human trademark that defines our standard reaction. God forbid that we aren't the center of the universe and the tippy-top of the food chain. It's a very medieval way of thinking. Don't question authority; just listen to the common sense of your clergy, and don't bother to sail beyond the horizon ...because you'll only fall off the edge.

If indeed otherworldly entities exposed themselves in force, they would be seen as "Gods" and those newly appointed deities would abandon us to our own means, and in turn, our species would be at each other's throats all over again, to choke one another and bleed out in the wake of their disillusionment. If an alien race revealed their existence to the world in full disclosure, the human race as a whole wouldn't be able to handle the reality of it, and we certainly wouldn't like their answers to our exhausting questions.

We have not earned a place among the stars because we act like rabid animals. Despite all of our art, and culture, and technologies we've created to bring our world together, we have spent far more time and resources devising the ability to burn the world down and blow ourselves apart into bloody little chunks. Basically, it would be like a parent telling a child they're grounded; and no, you can't go out to play in the universe until you take a bath and clean your room. The way we have polluted this planet and abused its resources, leaves us a lot of toys we have to pick up to impress our alien babysitter.

So to all the Ufologists and believers, ask yourself what scenarios do you think would be the least harmful (or least disastrous) plan to expose alien life to the average citizen? Maybe the hard-core fans might take it in stride, but there are countless others that would freak-the-fuck-out, and do so in a very unhinged and destructive way. All it would take is one religious nut to try to kill an alien while screaming they were demons in disguise, and they zap him in self-defense; which of course, starts the cascade of hostilities that follows the familiar script of pretty much every alien movie, ever. Humans; good! Aliens; bad! Earth; ours!

Some day our species might wake up and realize that we are only borrowing this planet and stop attempting to outwit Mother Nature by trying to control her; and learn to share this world with all the other living creatures that exists upon it, and beyond. I simply don't believe we're at that point yet. Try to consider that a measured level of disclosure would be less shocking to the masses; but the argument heard (and it's a valid one) is that disclosure simply isn't happening at the pace that's considered acceptable to most in this field. Many believers just want an in-your-face alien landing to get the weight off our shoulders, which will confirm we aren't all nutcases after all; which on its surface would be a huge relief ...but watch what you wish for. Would you want full disclosure of UFO's and Alien races if it came at the cost of devastating our social structure and beliefs and turning our world on its head?

On one hand, I would say; sure, go for it. The human psyche could use a good kick in the nuts, and it might even put our ideology on the right track. On the other hand; that might just be wishful thinking and we might grossly underestimate how bonkers the rest of the world is, and we suddenly find ourselves in the middle of a thermonuclear war! I would like to believe we are better than that ...the key phrase there was "*would like to*" but I'm not that foolish to expect the worst might never happen. The sheer stupidity of creating nuclear devices for nefarious purposes, let alone manufacturing hundreds of thousands of them out of paranoia, is simply beyond my comprehension of sanity. I imagine Alien races who visit our world think us quite insane ...scratch that, they already view us as unhinged and schizophrenic; which is probably why we mostly see the saucers fly by and rarely land. Visiting earth must be like a tour through a dangerous barrio on the seedy side of town while telling the driver, "Holy shit, roll up the windows and keep driving!" As they peer out the portholes. If they stop, we would steal their hubcaps and try to jack their ride; which is exactly what the military does whenever they are given the chance. Tell me I'm wrong.

I've been interviewed on the subject after several decades of remaining silent, and was asked: *"Why do I think I was 'chosen' and what was it all for, and what do the aliens want with us?"*

Well, for one ...I don't think I was chosen, I imagine I was merely a side-note that got attention after my mother and stepfather were abducted on that lonely desert highway; and these beings likely installed similar implants to track them back to our home on the outskirts of Tucson, and continued their observations even after my stepfather moved away and my mother had perished.

From my initial view of being a stern non-believer in Alien beings as a child, I have since studied countless reports of extraterrestrial encounters and their companion UFO files. I've weighed abductees' testimonies and examined thousands of videos and photographs, and connected with other victims of this phenomenon who appear to have suffered the same level of trauma. The general public must keep in mind that there is a high level of misinformation and fallacy to sift through, which has been intentionally added within all available documentation in an effort to water down the truth. False reports, testimonies, doctored photos, all the way up to bold-face pranks. Although, rarely among the vast sea of misinformation, you can find those few accounts which can't be so lightly dismissed.

In all my years growing up, I had never told my best friends or even my mentor who is a much older founder and CEO of a major corporation (Who by chance had a similar UFO sighting with another company executive along that same desert road where my parents had experienced their missing time; and reconfirmed his testimony shortly before he died in 2017). Alien encounters and their agenda are something I take quite seriously and do not brag nor joke about in the slightest.

In all my life, I've only told two people up to this moment. The first one was entirely incidental who only found out by sheer circumstance after I moved into his house, and he himself encountered that same being who had apparently followed me there one evening. After that disturbing event, I moved several states away and have never had another encounter since. The second time I told a girlfriend whom I lived with; and ho-boy, that did not turn out well at all. Keep in mind, that among all the visitations I had experienced prior to moving from my home, that no one else co-witnessed these events, even the one time when my partner was asleep in the same bed.

After I left my childhood home, I moved in with a long time friend I had known since I was very young who lived about 10 miles away. The first few days after I had moved in, my new roommate confronted me one morning, and with a raised brow, he straightforwardly asked me what most people would find to be a very bizarre question.

"Are aliens following you?" He asked with an air of seriousness, and keep in mind, that up to that time, I had never once told anyone about my encounters over the previous years since they began. At face value, it was a very odd question to ask a new roommate in the tone of an accusation; except in this case. After granting a shy stutter towards the bluntness of his inquiry, I gave a meek and guilty response saying, "Yes..." and felt as though an enormous weight had dropped from my shoulders. In return, I had to inquire as to why he would ask such a specific question out of the blue like that.

Although I hadn't experienced a recent visitation, he claimed the previous evening after I had retired to my bedroom, that he had fallen asleep upon the couch and woke up in the middle of the night to see what appeared like an alien-type creature leaning over him; which he described to a tee, as the beings I had seen as a child and the one I tried to chase down within my house. He said the creature was standing over him as he lay on the couch, looking down at him as he awoke with what he described as an uncanny sense of peace. He stated that seemed 'female' and spoke to him in his head without moving its lips, attempting to communicate while questioning him about me as I slept in the next room, and inquired to ask; **"if I was okay?"**

"Sure ...I guess so," was all he managed to reply to the mysterious being until he said everything faded to black after gave his answer. The next the morning, he awoke with full memory of the event. Well honestly, I didn't know what to make of that, so I just nodded and told him I really didn't wish to talk about it further. At the very least, it was the first time anyone had ever corroborated my story.

I remained lingering in a state of shock for several days afterwards, wallowing in a fair measure of despair, because I had thought I had escaped that scenario by moving away from the place where all those traumatic experiences had occurred, and had no idea how those creatures had been able to track me. Logic says there may very well be another implant placed within me somewhere, or they have some other means to keep tabs on people they find of interest. Before the end of that very week, after my roommate left for work, I packed up all my belongings and fled in fear. I drove several days and nights without rest until I found myself several states away. Since then, I have never had another visitation to this day.

Reflection

All these decades later, I have come to terms and even feel a sense of guilt that I had tried to attack and capture the alien during that one incident in the middle of the night at my home, and for my pent up anger which I had felt after years of what I perceived as a violation into my life. The initial visitation was of a friendly nature, and perhaps I had even given them my consent to such future studies, but it had been wiped from my memory. Honestly, I was never truly harmed as far as I can tell, or maybe they were trying to correct something they had done by accident which had caused my mothers ruthless and aggressive cancer, and they were seeing to it that I would not face the same fate.

Such paranormal experiences are highly disturbing and difficult to process and you do run it over and over in your mind, wanting to believe it never happened. The only solace I had left is in knowing that the events took place, which was proven for the first time during my confrontation with my roommate over the visitation he had also witnessed, confirming that what I had seen was real. Of note, the beings which had been observing me during that period in my life, for whatever purpose, had shown a level of concern for my well being in the end – enough so as to expose itself to another witness, for I understand now they had never meant for me to feel afraid.

As for the little warning about not building a base on our Lunar surface, an 8 yr old child has little sway in the events of the world at the time; but decades later my voice can be heard cautioning the powers that be. So, at the risk of appearing like a loon, I've merely told that section of my tale to NASA and several Space Exploration labs throughout the industry; and honestly, I think it was information they already had known but didn't wish to make public. From what I have read after compiling many years of research in silence, I imagined I was just beating a dead horse on the matter anyways. As greater technologies become available to private citizens, the airbrushed photos of our Moon and Mars are being exposed for what they are and the numerous unaccounted anomalies among their records are beginning to stick out like a sore thumb.

I try to imagine how my own tale of events along with so many other abductee stories might be able to make a positive difference in the way we shape our societies, but it seems like not enough of us are listening. There will continue to be a policy to keep the subject obscured and the public blinded under a blanket of suppression. As I noted earlier, this is for good reason. Although it's not a reason that I fundamentally agree with, but a lot of innocent lives would be put at risk if the truth was ever unceremoniously dropped at our feet.

Many such testimonies include the insertion of hybrids and alien-human mixes, wherein we are used for interbreeding and gene editing, or outright experimentation. In all respects, this is something our own biologists are doing by hacking our genome. Frankly, the practice of cross-breeding is nothing new among our own species, so altering a biological life form to better accommodate a different world or environment makes perfect sense. It's merely acclimatizing on a grander scale than we are used to thinking.

From my several decades of study, the reported alien agendas vary greatly. As one might expect, there are several different races, ranging from benevolent to what we would describe as outright hostile; though a great majority remain neutral. In all respects, we have a unique planet containing a vast diversity of life; and we need to learn to appreciate what we have and become better curators to protect this Eden we seem to take for granted. There are countless sci-fi novels and movies that depict Earth in the far future as the razed shit-hole we turned it into, where nobody wants to live; and thus bolstering reasons to explore off-world in an effort to establish new colonies across the galaxy.

From that point of view, I would try to stimulate another

vision of our future in which we should do everything we can to keep that forecast from manifesting such a dark fate. What it all comes down to is asking the hard questions. Is the human race so desperate for an answer to fix this dysfunctional society we've created, that we look towards the stars for an answer to our woes in sullen desperation to save us from ourselves? The human race shouldn't come first, it should be this planet we call our home that should be the center of our attention; because it is the only one we will ever have for the foreseeable future.

As an author, whether I'm writing science fiction or fantasy, I try to embed this philosophy into the core of my novels as I weave its ideology into the storyline. It's simple really; be kind and take care of yourself and others, and this home we call Earth. Respect life, and no matter what path or career you follow; step back and take a hard look, and ask yourself if what you do encompasses an act of creating – or if it primarily fosters destruction. These are the two sides of the coin. Don't live your life flipping that coin only to sway from one side to another, but press it into the sand right side up.

Either you are helping or harming, so choose the field in which we can all grow together. Our world doesn't need to breed such hostility, but to care about one another for the benefit of all; not merely for the privileged few. The words from sages and philosophers over countless millennia say *"There has got to be a better way for us to live."* Instead of nodding in agreement in the moment, only to turn our backs and continuing to whittle away at the failing ethics and broken morals of our various cultures; we need to do something radical to change our path. Unfortunately, we can't turn to the cosmos for the answers to our own self-inflicted plight; because not enough of us are listening.

From the testimonies of countless abductee reports I've seen, the message these beings have repeated was simple advice; that we need to change our ways. We already know that practicing peace will save us and war will not; yet we still continue to push and shove at one another across fabricated borders. Few know that we already possess advanced technologies which would benefit the masses; but these inventions are controlled and suppressed by the minority for the sake of profiteering and nothing more. It is this mentality of greed which steers our societies, and everyone reading this knows it will be the cause of our eventual downfall; but yet, our world stays fixed on this dark and dreary course. Personally, I think the human race is screwed; but I'm just one person telling my tale:

"I was taken, and this was their warning."

I do have a few words of advice for anyone who might face the same situation and what they can do in such an encounter; and that is to not struggle nor fight them within the mindset of fear. The human mind isn't adapted to such encounters, and the first reaction tends to be one of shock; which is understandable. Resistance is the natural reaction, but it can only create mental scarring which makes things far worse in the end.

In the vast majority of the cases I've researched, these beings aren't out to cause intentional harm. We are just a subject of interest and study. Once you're captured, the best thing you can do is to try to stay calm and attempt to communicate. Remember that they possess the ability to both read minds and intentions (at least within close proximity) with the ability to disconnect your conscience like a switch. With great effort, it is possible to resist such mental control, but it's not always successful.

I had several such experiences as this, when I found myself physically paralyzed during one particular visitation, where I couldn't move my limbs - but your eyelids can open and you are able to see and hear what is going on around you. It's similar to the effects of sleep-paralysis which is all too frequently misdiagnosed as the medical excuse given by doctors who are skeptical about such paranormal reports. I could see the beings around me (on one visit there were several smaller ones and one very tall one), and you can strain to move; however, it is excruciatingly painful to do so (I would describe it as feeling as if the blood in all your veins had turned to brittle glass which snaps into tiny painful shards whenever you attempt to move).

Again, these creatures appear to become alarmed when someone is able to fight their mental restraints. I would imagine it would make as much sense to a wildlife biologist in the middle of a live study if that wild bear they had sedated started to squirm and awaken while they were occupied collecting research samples. They would have to quickly hit the animal with another tranquilizer for their own safety; taking the risk that too much might be fatal for the observed patient. Unfortunately, there have also been records of fatalities to such human encounters with alien abductions. So again, stay calm and try to open a dialog; your efforts might go ignored, but a peaceful frame of mind will elicit a better outcome. Frankly, I would warn against making them feel endangered, for they can pick up the mood of their subjects.

Sadly, our society has groomed most people to fear the unknown, and human beings tend to overreact violently in such situations. In reality, you have to be at peace with yourself to survive these encounters without coming away mentally scarred. Ask them questions, learn as much as you can, and hope that you're able to retain the details of the encounter. Try to understand their perspective and make an effort to relate your concerns to them. Their ethics and morals are far removed from the human condition; so don't assume you'll both share the same point of view.

The species I met didn't appear to understand the purposes or function of our music, sense of humor, or even art. I asked one of them its name, but they called themselves whatever their assignment was at the given time; much the way we would offer generic titles to any given duty. It was quite possible they were akin to clones themselves or were beyond such individuality when their culture works like a collective mind. Of course, everyone who follows the UFO phenomena wants to know "What do they want?" Well, I bet a lot of lab monkeys and countless other animals we've studied and hold in captivity in laboratories and zoos across this wide planet are asking the same goddamn question. Most likely, even if they told us, we wouldn't fully understand their answer.

Then again, there are many different races of beings, so they each have their own aims and goals. If we knew what they were, we likely wouldn't agree with it, regardless. Humanity has lost its way and the institutions we invented to provide us with a sense of security are just delusions. We are forced to live in a polarized culture of war, competition, and separation every hour of the day for the sake of personal profit rather than to the prosperity of all.

If an alien species wanted to take over our planet there are many different ways they could accomplish that end. There would be no flashy air battles or giant tripods roaming the landscape, for the end of our species would likely be obtained by the introduction of a designer virus to our environment. It may not be quick or clean, but it would provide surgical results without the vast waste of energy and resources to rid them of the pesky humans who infest this world and teeter daily on burning the planet to a crisp many times over due to our own petty insecurities. Personally, I think the other ten million species who we share this world with would breathe a sigh of relief if mankind suddenly kicked the bucket.

Experiencing an alien encounter of the 5th kind can either rattle your life to the point of paranoia or it can change your perspective entirely, and you can see the world in a different light. Honestly, from what I learned from these experiences took a great while to actually sink in; and that I could find peace if I turned a new leaf and actually took the effort to shy away from what it was to be 'human' and withdrew from the mold we have been coached and coerced to fit into every day of our lives.

As of the date of this publication, I live in the countryside at the edge of the forest, and most every clear evening you can find me sitting on the open deck under a curtain of glimmering stars; gazing up into the heavens and wondering at the magic and mystery of it all, which led to the unorthodox title of this book. From a certain perspective, monsters, witches, faeries, angels, demons, and sightings of other curious beings could very well be linked to extraterrestrial visitations that would explain many strange accounts referenced throughout history, that fell into a category so bizarre that they were excused as nothing but myth and lore with ties to the paranormal. As of this hour, I see the human race as spiraling towards a very shallow existence with a bleak and sour future waiting for the generations that follow in our footsteps. The only way to change that dark destiny is to start seeing the world in different colors than we were taught and to break this cycle of self-destruction, and realize we have to save ourselves before there is nothing left to salvage.

Afterword:

No one can deny that we have entered into an age of constant surveillance and unprecedented censorship, which is designed to veil our personal perspectives and social views from subjects which linger on the outer fringe of our scripted lives. As a example of this, in mid 2016, within 48 hrs of publishing my recent novel: 'Broken Mirror,' about the approaching Apophis asteroid due in early 2029, my site was data-mined by a US Defense Contractor of Homeland Security; and in the following weeks thereafter, additional scrutiny from the FBI, CIA, along with the DHS and the NSA offices in the heart of Washington DC; all of which data was recorded by my server as evidence.

That particular novel touched upon underground government bases, biowarfare labs, and secret space programs within its storyline of an upcoming Apocalypse. Just as interesting, my very first shipment of books were intercepted en route and confiscated by the Postal Marshal for over a month without any provided explanation. Any person might question why our illustrious Authorities would turn so paranoid over an eccentric sci-fi novel; or perhaps it was the chronicled contents therein which rubbed someone within our military complex the wrong way, as it might be considered that the very core of the storyline may very well be ***entirely true***. You be the judge.

Whether writing sci-fi or fantasy, in one form or another, I strive within the content of my novels to reveal the essence of humanities connection to the Earth on which we live, and to plant a seed of conscious thought to share with the reader about our obligation to this fragile world we call home. Publications of such extraterrestrial accounts such as this always seem to ruffle our federal officials and their affiliated institutions. Just as surprisingly, I once again fell under tight scrutiny by the US Department of Defense less than 12 hours after placing this very novel online in the summer of 2017. So, if by chance anyone might notice that I went mysteriously missing one day; it was likely that I was quietly *made* to disappear.

In all honesty, witnesses, experiencers and abductees who step into the limelight have a valid reason to fear for their health and safety while existing within the caustic political confines of our toxic world, where those few who stand up and pronounce themselves unswayed by our current system of oppression and share their message, are ever so frequently, sanitized from existence. If I should ever fall victim to such a consequence, I would leave it to my audience to figure out what fate I may have befallen; and by all means, feel free to exercise your wildest imagination.

...for as they say, truth is stranger than fiction.

Michel Savage

About the Author

Michel Savage has been devoted to writing throughout his career. If one reads between the lines, they will find his novels revolve around the reminder that we are only borrowing our small place on this planet but for a brief period of time, and to take responsibility for the environment, for one another, and all other living creatures with which we share this world. And in doing so, hopefully planting a seed in our conscience of the importance to preserve what is left of the wilds, our untainted woodlands, and ever-dwindling rain forests.

He has had the blessing of sharing his stories and artwork around the globe, which is a gift in itself, and would encourage others not to waste too much of their lives chasing someone else's dreams but to follow their own.

One of the most valuable lessons he has learned in his years is that there are far more important things in life than power and money, such as kindness, compassion, and consideration towards others.

...share that thought if you will.

Enter the Grey Forest
www.**GreyForest**.com

Also by
Michel Savage

Outlaws of Europa

The 2nd moon of Jupiter has been turned into a prison planet. Where for several generations, robot drone ships have been dumping the scum of the universe and are patrolled by a ring of advanced security satellites that would destroy any vessel attempting to land. After a century of research, old core samples from the ice reveal that the frozen oceans of Europa hold the base element of an immortality drug that can extend the human lifespan several-fold. Now greedy military corporations raced for the new fountain of youth, only to discover they couldn't disable the orbiting sentry which was programmed to protect itself at all costs.

It appears the Confederation has a problem. How do they get past a self-evolving AI that has appointed itself as Warden, and furthermore, retake a planet roaming with Earth's worst criminals who might well be immortal themselves...

Hellbot – Battle Planet

Tranquility was one of those out of the way planets in a system far out of reach from the normal space lanes. Loners, dreamers ...whoever they were, chose to colonize this world. Thirty cycles ago something went terribly wrong. It was rumored their terraformer reactor went critical, and few escaped the chain reaction that clouded the atmosphere with a planet-wide sand storm. A decade of hard labor evaporated overnight. What wasn't buried under the ocean of sand was left to fry under the twin suns. Human explorers began to wander back into the forgotten zone. No one knew of the machines that had evolved, or the war that raged beyond the edge of the universe ...where mankind did not belong.

Broken Mirror
Apophis 2029

Hurtling through space was an enormous tumbling rock known as MN4 our astronomers affectionately named after an ancient Egyptian god of destruction. Asteroid Apophis was the talk of the year that every scientific community on Earth was aware of, though its flyby in April 2029 was to be nothing more than a spectacular celestial event; but as warring nations were locked in global conflict, our civilization was unprepared for the devastation that followed in its wake.

Several years after governments fell and society dissolved a ragged pack of survivors stumble upon the buried truth, revealing what circumstances had led to the aftermath that ensued; leaving them to question their struggle to salvage what few splintered shards were left of our world that would forever define our bitter legacy.

Forgotten Future

At the edge of the world an impossible relic from the fables of antiquity has risen from the frozen wastelands of Antarctica. Professor Logan and his exploration team rush to investigate this historic find, but this unique discovery puts their lives in peril when they unearth the remnants of a long forgotten civilization left buried beneath the ice.

Within the twisting labyrinths below the melting glaciers they uncover an ancient culture which had perished from a mysterious cataclysm. They soon realize it was a polar shift which had caused their destruction, and our world was presently facing the same fate.

Project EVE

In the late 1940s after the 2nd World War, a classified government program was created in order to explore the military use of psychics to gain an advantage for their soldiers during armed conflict. At a remote laboratory in the mountains, a secret compound comprised of several hundred test subjects were trained to enhance their abilities with the goal of achieving the skills of telepathy and mind control.

Assigned to investigate this covert project, Walter Grant found himself entangled in a web of conspiracy and deceit when he discovered that the residents of the colony were being held captive by the scientists who had hidden the ugly truth behind their dangerous experiments.

At the heart of the project was a girl named Eve, whose extraordinary mind held the key, a child who would prove to them why humanity could not handle such power.

7 (Seven) - The Fall

A strange and unexplained phenomenon led to the fall of civilization. It began on an evening like any other. The Sun had set on another day, but by the next morning, humanity realized that there were no more stars in the sky. Somehow, overnight, mankind had become alone in the universe and only an AI program knew why.